IN FLAMES

THE PETE PETERSON TAPES PART II

Des Tong

APS Books
Yorkshire

APS Books,
The Stables Field Lane,
Aberford,
West Yorkshire,
LS25 3AE

APS Books is a subsidiary of the APS Publications imprint

www.andrewsparke.com

Copyright ©2023 Des Tong
All rights reserved.

Des Tong has asserted his right to be identified as the author of this work in accordance with the Copyright Designs and Patents Act 1988

First published worldwide by APS Books in 2023

This is a work of fiction. Names, characters, places and incidents either are products of the author's imagination or are used fictitiously. Any resemblance to actual events or locales or persons, living or dead, is entirely coincidental.

No part of this publication may be reproduced, stored in or introduced into a retrieval system, or transmitted, in any form, or by any means (electronic, mechanical, photocopying, recording or otherwise) without the written permission of the publisher except that brief selections may be quoted or copied without permission, provided that full credit is given.

A catalogue record for this book is available from the British Library

IN FLAMES

CHAPTER ONE

Gerry Fortuna's funeral had been a major event, taking place on a bleak winter's day in Birmingham Cathedral. It was made all the more poignant as it was there he and Janine had married only four years earlier. The magnificent setting was filled with mourners, along with hundreds more outside braving the bitterly cold weather, just to pay their respects to a man who had single-handedly changed the music scene in the city.

Janine had wanted it to be a private affair, but public opinion had been so strong that she had reluctantly agreed to their wishes. On the day, she was tastefully dressed all in black - a tailored Dior suit, a stylish fedora and a huge pair of sunglasses, perfectly portraying the grieving widow. Sitting in the funeral limousine alongside Janine, DCI Ray Law felt underdressed in his black work suit, white button-down collar shirt and black tie. He couldn't help thinking about what she'd told him the day after Gerry's death; and how he had begrudgingly agreed to hold back on any action until the funeral and all the memorial ceremonies had finished.

Gerry's secretary Judy Watson had attended with her boyfriend, the singer Pete Peterson both also dressed in black. Pete wore a full-length military-style leather coat complete with epaulettes, bought especially from a stall in the trendy Oasis market, and tight black jeans. Judy at his side, was in an elegant ankle-length cashmere overcoat with a black fur collar. They had accepted Janine's invitation to ride in the funeral car alongside her and Ray. Sitting in silence as the cortege set off on its journey from outside The Hideout, they too shared the knowledge of what Janine had told Ray about the conversation she overheard between Gerry and his best man Bobby McGregor, but had agreed to leave what happened next up to him.

The congregation had comprised friends and associates of Gerry, including members of the Barton family who Gerry had worked for when he first started in the business. Even the retired owner of the Coliseum, Harry Castle was there. Chief Constable George Williams had who attended in his full dress uniform was sitting with members of The

Flames, Pete Peterson's band and many other local musicians who had played at Gerry's clubs. The Cathedral was bursting at the seams with councillors, politicians, and and sportsmen, while sitting unnoticed in a pew at the back, the footballer George Best, who Gerry had named his bar Georgie's after, had turned up to pay his respects.

It had been an emotional service, punctuated by various speeches, some funny, some sad. Followed ironically by a recording of a piece of music played by Alex Mitchell, finished off with a eulogy read out by Bobby McGregor.

It had been difficult for Ray to stand next to Bobby McGregor in the cathedral watching as he shed tears, when he knew the truth of what had happened the previous week. The trouble was he only had Janine's account of the conversation, which she overheard take place between her husband and McGregor in the FAM office when they discussed the planned murder of Alex Mitchell. He didn't think it would be strong enough to stand up in court; especially as he'd already interviewed Gerry alongside his solicitor Julia Davies, who he knew would offer a formidable defence if it was decided to pursue it any further.

The uplifting sound of the choir had accompanied the congregation as they sang the final hymn, *Onward Christian Soldiers*, one of Gerry's favourites. Then it was all over. Gerry's coffin was taken for private burial alongside his parents, and finally Janine had arrived home to the empty mansion she'd shared with her husband in the Warwickshire countryside.

After showering and wrapping herself in a luxurious, towelling dressing gown, feeling lost and alone, she went downstairs and in the huge kitchen she'd designed herself opened a bottle of Bollinger; something Gerry had introduced her to the first time they met. Pouring herself a glass she looked around and came to the conclusion she didn't want to be there anymore. She decided tomorrow would be the first day of a new life. The time to do something fresh and exciting, and drinking the glass back in one, she knew who she wanted to share it with.

DCI Ray Law was in his office at police headquarters, when George Williams, the Chief Constable and his mentor called, asking him to come up to his office. He ran up the two flights of stairs and knocked on the door.

"Ah Ray, come in; come in," George called out. He was already brewing a pot of his legendary coffee and poured out two steaming mugs, handing one to Ray.

"As I didn't get the chance to talk to you yesterday at the funeral I thought I'd have a chat with you personally before the news leaks out." He motioned for Ray to sit in one of the two leather armchairs in the corner. "I'm retiring, Ray. I've had enough and feel it's about time the wife and I did something for ourselves. I'll be frank, I don't like the way things are going in the force, and I've decided to get out now."

Ray started to speak but George carried on.

"I know it might seem sudden, but I've thought long and hard about it, and I've made up my mind."

"I'll be sorry to see you go, George," Ray said trying to hide his disappointment. "Any idea who will replace you?"

"As far as I'm aware no decision has been made yet, although I think they'll be starting interviewing candidates pretty soon." George gave a sigh. "I'm sorry Ray but what with the bombing and then the shooting, I think it's time I handed over to a younger man." He paused taking a drink of his coffee. "While you're here though, is there any news on the Gerry Fortuna case?"

"Not a thing. The assailant just disappeared into thin air. There were plenty of potential witnesses at the scene as you know, but nobody could finger him."

"What about Janine? Didn't she think she heard the man say something to Gerry?."

"She thought she heard someone say *Bocan* and possibly the name *Mulligan*, but it all happened so fast she can't be sure. And there were so many people milling around them, she couldn't identify anyone. The guy was clever. I'd say it was a professional hit."

George sat back warming his hands on his coffee mug.

"What about Alex Mitchell? Any more on that?"

Ray had decided not to report what Janine had told him, and now that

George was leaving it seemed pointless to say anything to him. He shook his head. "I've spoken with Ginger Thompson in forensics. He said the body being in the water destroyed any evidence. We constantly seem to be going down blind alleys. It's really frustrating that there were two major murders in the city within days of each other, and we don't have a single strong lead on either."

"Well keep me in the loop. I'm not going just yet and if you need any help, let me know."

Ray's phone was ringing as he walked back in his office, and he picked up the receiver.

"Hey DCI Law, how are you?" It was Janine Fortuna.

"I'm fine, Mrs. Fortuna. What can I do for you?" he replied trying to sound professional.

"I was wondering if you'd like to come out to the house for dinner tonight? I have something I'd like to run past you. Oh, and I'm cooking ham, cabbage, and spuds, an old Irish recipe."

He'd never been there before. Their nights of clandestine lovemaking had only ever been at his tiny apartment in Barlowe, so he was intrigued by her request and the prospect of seeing the amazing Georgian residence.

"I'd love to," he said writing down the directions she gave him.

"Grand. Be here at seven-thirty." She rang off.

It was a fine sunny evening as he drove out of the city in the new white Ford Escort he'd bought to replace the one he'd written off in the incident with the Irish bomber, Frank Kelly. The 1300cc GT Sport wasn't a patch on his old 1.6 Lotus, and he thought to himself he'd love to be winding his way through the Warwickshire countryside in it.

He turned into Janine's gravel drive, parking at the side of Gerry's gleaming Rolls Royce. He was standing looking at the wonderful old mansion and its surroundings when Janine came running out of the huge front door and threw her arms around him. She kissed him passionately, dragging him by the hand into the oak-panelled hallway with its suit of armour standing erect at the bottom of the winding staircase. He thought it wasn't the only thing that was erect as she led him up the stairs and into the bedroom, with its imposing four-poster bed.

Ray lay soaked in sweat after they had finished, watching as she climbed out of bed and walked naked across the room, which was now bathed in winter sunshine. She opened a bottle of champagne and filled two cut-glass flutes. They clinked glasses in a toast as she sat down on the edge of the bed.

She was thoughtful for a moment sipping her champagne, then she finally spoke. "As a result of recent events I'm now a very rich lady, and I've decided I want a new challenge with some excitement in my life." She paused and looked at Ray. "And I want you to share it with me!"

Ray almost choked on his champagne. "Wow, but yeah, of course. I mean why not. We already do don't we?" he spluttered surprised by her statement.

"I've made a decision. I'm going to sell the mansion and move to Los Angeles and I want you to come with me!"

Ray was taking in what she had just said but before he had chance to speak she carried on.

"I've also decided I'm going to manage Pete Peterson full time. He's got a great deal in the States and although he's a pain in the arse sometimes, I want to be there to make him the biggest star in the world. Gerry saw something special in him, and I'm going to carry his work on. He's leaving for LA in the next few weeks, so I've decided I'm going with him and I need you by my side. I love you Ray. Say you'll come with me."

Ray was speechless. He just stared at her and started to laugh.

"What are you laughing about?" She sounded annoyed. "Come on, what's so funny? I'm being serious."

"I can't believe what you've just said. I've been considering my future with the police, especially since George Williams has announced he's retiring. I was wondering what the hell I was going to do, and now you've just made up my mind."

She put down her glass and held his hands looking him in the eyes. "So what's your answer?"

"Try and stop me!" he said pulling her to him and kissing her. "I love you too."

They finished the bottle of champagne, and she started stroking him seductively before suddenly jumped up. "Oh my God, can you smell burning? Jeesus, our dinner!" She ran down the stairs pulling on her dressing gown.

The following couple of weeks saw Janine, Ray and Pete faced with huge life-changing challenges, which they all handled in their own ways. Christmas was approaching, and Janine was anxious to get everything sorted before the holidays were upon them.

She had systematically arranged each of her meetings, allowing herself plenty of time to make sure everything was completed. Her first job was to get the Georgian mansion on the market. She was pleased that the original estate agent had agreed to handle the sale. He'd explained he felt an affinity with the property, and true to his word within days had arranged viewings. Janine was confident it would fetch her million-pound asking price and left him to it.

Her next task had been a pleasurable one, officially appointing Judy Watson as a director of Fortuna Artist Management in the UK a position which brought with it a generous shareholding. Janine had already spoken to Judy about her own plans, and when she had asked her if she would be interested in taking over running the business, she had excitedly agreed without any hesitation. It was a huge responsibility, but Janine had been impressed by how she'd handled everything that had been thrown at her up to now, and was confident she would easily cope. Judy also had some interesting suggestions of new bands she would like to sign to the company, and for someone so young she already had a lot of respect in the business.

An approached had come from a local brewery chain with an offer to buy the original Hideout along with its suite of offices. This meant Judy would have to move elsewhere, but as Janine had decided to keep The Lexxicon it seemed an ideal choice for her to set up the new offices within the club. At the same time Judy would be taking over its day to day running.

Janine had also been in touch with Manny Oberstein at Westoria

Records, outlining her plan of managing Pete Peterson and moving over to LA. She was pleasantly surprised he sounded genuinely pleased; offering his advice on anything she needed in the way of visas, work permits and, most importantly, accommodation. She'd gladly accepted and was looking forward to moving into the beachfront property he'd recommended. He'd also arranged for the label to rent a small apartment for Pete in Venice Beach, a vibrant area just along the coast from Santa Monica. He thought Pete would love the scene there, with lots of music always happening in the area.

She had met with the local brewery representatives at The Hideout to finalise the sale. She found herself standing in the empty offices upstairs, thinking back to how it had all begun. It was sad in a way to see it go, as there were so many memories in that building especially Georgie's, like the first night she met Gerry and how she was so brazen as to go up to him and introduce herself. She could still taste that first sip of Bollinger he'd poured for her. And her first night as a topless barmaid. The times they had there were unforgettable both good and bad. She remembered the night when Gerry had gone down on one knee and proposed to her. she instinctively felt for her engagement ring and turned it on her finger discreetly wiping away a tear. But she was a realist, and the deal she was about to sign would guarantee her future financially whatever she decided to do, and despite everything that had happened, she knew Gerry would be proud of her.

She had a lump in her throat when she shook hands with the managing director of the brewery. Then, taking one last look around, she walked down the stairs and out of the door. Climbing into Gerry's Rollie she drove away without looking back.

She'd actually offered Rollie to Judy, but being so small she'd declined the offer, saying she was happy with her mini, and actually wouldn't be able to see over the steering wheel! And so Janine had asked the estate agent selling the mansion if he would include it in the sale, which he thought was a fantastic idea. He felt sure anyone buying such a property would love to have a car like that to go with it.

Her one regret was not being able to say goodbye to her parents. After the mysterious conclusion to the enquiry into the explosion at Rudi's, her father had gone into hiding along with two other Irishmen who he used to meet at St Mary's. Although Janine had tried to find him, he and her mother had disappeared, it was rumoured back to Ireland. She'd asked Ray if he could help, but George Williams had told him the information was not available for him to see. He hinted it was something to do with the Home Office and suggested she let it go for the time being.

CHAPTER TWO

Judy had noticed a change in Pete since the opening night at The Lexxicon, and the chaotic fight in the dressing room after the gig. They had been seeing a lot of each other since she had stayed with him while he recovered in the clinic after his dramatic collapse on the last night of his tour, but recently he had seemed distant and moody. His whole persona had changed, almost as if he believed he was a superstar already. It was alright to put on a front to people he didn't know, but not to her. They were more than just friends.

Then one night lying in bed together, Pete had told her how he would be based in Los Angeles and about the apartment the record label was getting for him. But that was where the problem lay; because he had asked her to go with him and Judy couldn't move from Birmingham. Apart from Janine's fantastic offer, she had a disabled mother who she was very close to and wasn't prepared to leave. She still loved Pete and was devastated that they were going to be apart, but she knew in her heart they would be together again one day. She also knew that turning up in America as a new artist ready to be launched to the world with a girlfriend in tow wouldn't go down well with Westoria's marketing department. However, there was one final thing she had to do before Pete left, and pulling on her coat she set off to his apartment. She'd make sure she always had a link to him whether he came back or not.

Pete Peterson was sitting surrounded by his belongings, which didn't really add up to much. He'd always been a man of few possessions with his two guitars, his Martin D12 Acoustic and his 1957 Gibson Les Paul Goldtop taking pride of place. He'd never really been hung up about amplifiers, using what was available instead of having to transport one around all the time. He believed his sound came more from his fingers and the style he played, rather than electronics.

His wardrobe too was quite small: a couple of pairs of Levis, his trademark leather jacket and a collection of T-shirts and various designer shirts he wore on stage. Everything else was disposable. He'd be sorry to leave the place, but he wasn't going to sell it. He remembered Gerry Fortuna's advice that one day it would be worth a lot of money.

He'd asked Janine to contact her estate agent, and through him he was going to rent it out until such time as he either came home or decided he no longer wanted it.

He had received a call from her giving him details of his flight to the States, and he was both excited and terrified at the same time. He wished he wasn't going on his own. He'd have loved Judy to be coming with him. He was still really fond of her even though they'd drifted apart recently. He knew it was his fault; he was being selfish expecting her to drop everything to embark on what could be a huge disaster, and now that Janine had given her such an amazing opportunity he couldn't blame her for turning him down. He would apologise before he left. After all it was she who'd helped him get through his problems so it was the least he could do. But then at the same time he was buzzing with the thought of getting to the States. He reflected for a moment that it was a shame the guys from The Flames wouldn't be there with him. He'd always said he wouldn't do what Bowie had done and get rid of his band as soon as things started to happen, but after the crazy events in the dressing room at The Lexxicon they'd forced his hand. How could he trust them? Tony Waters was a snapper and would always be a liability, his brother Billy and Jess were both great guys and good players, but there were thousands of amazing players over there. The only one he thought he might reconsider was the keyboard player Dave Sanchez. He could be an asset and he would keep him in mind in case he needed him in the future.

His thoughts were interrupted by the buzzer, and when he answered it a familiar voice asked if she could come up. Moments later he opened the door to Judy who stood there with tears in her eyes. He reached out and pulling her to him they embraced, just holding each other as she sobbed into his shoulder. Finally they broke away and Pete kissed her tenderly as she unbuttoned his shirt and then his jeans. She slipped out of her dress and they lay on his bed caressing each other as they used to do. They both felt the intensity of their lovemaking. Stopping and starting again, determined to make it last forever although Pete sensed there was something in the way Judy was acting; that this time it was different. Finally they both held each other tightly as they climaxed together. They didn't say a lot afterwards, and Judy was still tearful as she finally left Pete's apartment, but stopped in the doorway and turned to him with a mysterious look in her eyes.

"There'll always be a part of you with me now," she said as she kissed him goodbye.

Ex-DCI Ray Law was shaking hands with the soon-to-be former-Chief Constable George Williams in his office at police headquarters. His decision to leave had come as a shock to everyone. Ray was a highly regarded police officer, and George had tried to persuade him to change his mind, saying the force could not afford to lose men of his calibre, but he was not really the right person to be speaking to Ray, considering he'd only recently announced he would be leaving himself. It was that news which had started Ray considering his own future, especially as they had become so close. The thought of losing his mentor and having to start again with someone new worried him and after Janine's surprise proposal his mind had been made up, and he handed in his resignation. It bothered him that he was leaving two unsolved cases, both in which he was heavily involved; and one, the murder of Alex Mitchell that he was in possession of relevant information which could possibly lead to two arrests, albeit one posthumously. His dilemma was whether he should reveal it. By doing so it would stain the character of Gerry Fortuna, recently revered at his funeral as being such a wonderful man, but at the same time implicate Bobby McGregor as playing a part in the gruesome murder.

He looked again at George Williams standing there in his immaculate full-dress uniform, and decided he deserved a trouble-free retirement with his wife, probably going on the cruise he'd once mentioned and tending his precious roses. He would keep the information to himself while he forged a new life in Los Angeles with Janine. The only others who knew the truth were Pete and Judy and he was confident they wouldn't say anything.

His parents had been upset at his news, in particular his father, who had initially wanted him to be a lawyer although finally accepting his joining the police force. Ray's rapid rise through the ranks had gone a long way to changing his father's mind, but telling them he was giving it all up to move to the States had not gone down well. He'd done his best to placate them, but despite the fact it was with a millionairess who loved him, they still weren't happy. He was sure they would eventually come around, especially as there would be somewhere fantastic for them to visit in the future.

He'd donated his new Escort to DS Matt Burgess as a farewell gift, which along with Matt's recent promotion to the rank of DCI had been gratefully received. Ray felt sure he would step comfortably into his shoes as a perfect replacement. They promised to keep in touch, although Ray knew that their best intentions wouldn't last once the pressure of the job took its toll. But it was good to see him so happy.

He'd received a short almost curt message from Julia Davies wishing him well. He was relieved she was away on business and too busy to be able to see him in person. That was one complication he was glad he didn't have to deal with.

As he finally left George's office for the last time he smiled to himself. He wasn't big on nostalgia preferring instead to look to the future, and what a future it promised to be.

CHAPTER THREE

Janine had spent a whole morning at the travel agents organising the Trans-Atlantic flights for her, Ray and Pete. As usual Pete had been making things awkward by wanting to fly from Birmingham, but Janine had put her foot down when she found out that it would involve him flying to Paris, and then catching a Pan-Am flight to Los Angeles on his own. She had managed to get three First-Class tickets with TWA on one of their new Boeing 747 Jumbo jets, and she was not accepting any further arguments.

As they were flying from London Heathrow, she had asked Judy to book a minibus to take them down to the airport leaving Birmingham at six o'clock in the morning. That would give them plenty of time for their flight which was leaving at six o'clock that evening. For once in his life Pete was on time, and they had left Birmingham with a tearful Judy the only one there to wave them off.

The journey had been without incident with Pete asleep in the back most of the way, finally waking up as they drove through the tunnel towards their departure terminal at Heathrow. Janine and Ray only had one large suitcase each to check in, deciding anything else they needed they could buy there. As well as his case, Pete had his two guitars which were now labelled up and disappearing down the conveyor belt. They safely navigated their way through passport control and headed for the First-Class lounge. Pete declined a glass of champagne from Janine and sloped off to a seat in the corner with a beer.

Suddenly everyone's attention was drawn to a young man who was entering the lounge followed by a noisy group of reporters and photographers. It was Vince Boyd, one of Janine's all-time favourite heartthrobs who was making straight for the bar. He sat down on the stool next to her giving her an appreciative sideways glance and ordered a Cosmopolitan. Janine had no idea what a Cosmopolitan was, but sat speechless watching him as he took a large gulp.

Pete, in the meantime had wandered over wondering what all the fuss was about. Recognising the man, he introduced himself, striking up a conversation with the pop star. "Hey man I've heard your stuff; I really dig your guitar playing."

Vince Boyd exclaimed. "So what takes you to the States?"

"We're going out to meet Westoria, my new record company in LA. Cool huh?" Pete sounded proud of himself.

"Very cool."

Pete turned to Janine. "Hey Vince, this is Janine Fortuna my personal manager."

Vince Boyd smiled at Janine and she almost fainted. "Hi Janine, good to meet you." He shook her hand. "Westoria's a great company, I was signed to them once. Wish I'd never left."

Janine just about managed to say thanks and held on to his hand far too long, finally letting go, knowing she was blushing a deep pink.

Ray who had been in the restroom while all this was happening returned to find a party going on in the middle of the TWA First-Class lounge. As he was handed a glass filled with champagne he looked around and thought to himself 'I could get used to this!'

During all the commotion they had failed to hear their flight being called, and eventually after one of the TWA attendants had arrived to summon them to the departure gate they all made their way to the giant aircraft. Whilst the bulk of the passengers were being shown into the economy cabin, they were taken upstairs via the winding staircase to their luxury seats and lounge complete with another bar. Pete and Vince Boyd were deep in conversation as they sat down next to each other towards the rear of the cabin, with Ray and Janine just in front of them. As if the excitement of meeting Vince Boyd wasn't enough, into the cabin strolled the actor Charles Morse, who immediately ordered a dry martini from the attractive air-hostess behind the bar.

Ray had been quietly taking all this in and looked over at Janine who had a grin from ear to ear. "Well you did say you wanted some excitement," he reached out and held her hand.

'Hang on to your seat babe, this is just the beginning!' she thought. She leaned over and kissed him as the engines started to whine and they taxied to take-off.

Once in the air the party atmosphere continued with Ray and Janine joining Charles Morse at the bar. He was in a good mood having just finished his first James Black movie, explaining he was on his way to start the endless promotional appearances on American TV. Janine was fascinated listening to him talking until they heard the sound of music coming from the rear of the cabin. Pete and Vince Boyd had found Vince's acoustic guitar, and were singing one of his hits, harmonising perfectly with each other, and laughing loudly when they made a mistake. Janine had never really had any doubts about Pete's ability to make it, but sitting watching him so relaxed in the company of such a big star gave her goose bumps.

'Look out America, here we come' she thought to herself. Even the new James Black was smiling and nodding along.

Later, Charles Morse had graciously retired to his seat, and covered in a blanket with his eye-mask on and ear-plugs in, had slept for the rest of the flight. He now looked immaculate, following a quick trip to the bathroom to freshen up, as they touched down at Los Angeles after the eleven-hour flight. Janine was sure he'd used some make-up especially around his eyes, and felt guilty trying to get a closer look when they shook hands as he said goodbye.

The excitement of their first steps on American soil however was short lived. It soon became apparent that Pete's guitars had been lost. The three of them had waited while the bags from the flight came around on the carousel, and one-by-one had been collected, including their own three suitcases. All apart from the two guitars. After such a long flight with little sleep Pete's temper was becoming frayed, and it had taken all of Ray's diplomacy to stop him causing a scene.

Eventually they managed to find a very attractive lady from TWA called Maud to help them, and to everyone's relief after a couple of phone calls, she came back with the news that the guitars had been found. The only problem was they were still in London and wouldn't be arriving until the following day, but she said she would personally ensure they were delivered to Pete as soon as they arrived, and when she took his address in Venice Beach it turned out she lived in Culver City which was close by. Janine recognised the look on Pete's face when he was talking to her, wondering how long it would be before Maud from TWA was another of his conquests. Still, that wasn't her concern anymore as she turned round and looked at Ray. He was visibly tired, the same as everyone else, but she was so proud of how he had immediately taken control when Pete looked like he might lose it and couldn't wait to lie down with him.

TWA Maud had organised a taxi for Janine and Ray to take them the half-hour journey to Hermosa Beach and had kindly offered to give Pete a lift herself as she was about to get off duty.

'Not that long then!' Janine thought as Pete followed her out to the car park putting his arm around her slim waist.

Their accommodation was everything Manny Oberstein had said it would be, and even though they were exhausted from the journey they still walked around examining everything, marvelling at the place that was to be their home for the next six months. When they finally collapsed into bed in their wonderfully air-conditioned bedroom, they were asleep in seconds.

They spent the next couple of days settling in, relaxing on their fantastic rooftop terrace, and watching the steady stream of trendy West Coast joggers, roller-skaters and cyclists passing by down below. They were situated on the Strand, the wide, twenty-mile-long pathway whose endearing feature is that every construction on it is unique with its own individual style. Theirs was sandwiched between a colonial two-storey clapperboard residence on one side and a traditional brownstone on the other. The jetlag finally went, and they dined out in a couple of wonderful restaurants situated in the nearby Plaza. Janine discovered that what the Americans called shrimp were in fact giant king prawns and not the tiny little things she got back home, while to his dismay Ray had ordered a New York Strip steak, which was so big he had to take half of it home afterwards in a doggie-bag. The weather was so good they'd forgotten it would soon be Christmas.

It wasn't quite the same story for Pete. His guitars still hadn't arrived, although his newfound friend from TWA had done her best to keep him, and more particularly his body occupied while he waited for them to turn up. Her name was Maud Jones and she was an aspiring actress, working for the airline while she looked around for opportunities in the film business although she told him she was really Mildred Johanowitz from Milwaukee and had changed it when she reached LA. He had to admit she was very good looking with long straight blonde hair, bright blue eyes and an incredible body. Her biggest assets however attracted the wrong sort of offers, and although she could make lots of money in the thriving adult-film industry her dream of landing a serious part was still eluding her.

His apartment was smaller than his own back in Birmingham, but its situation was fantastic. At the top of a four-storey block in a side street just off the main drag of Venice Beach, he could hear music day and night. There were street-musicians playing guitars and conga drums on the sidewalk, and new bands playing music he'd never heard before in the numerous bars and clubs. There were so many interesting characters, and while Maud was at work he'd be out exploring and meeting some of the weird and wonderful locals. One guy in particular caught his attention; dressed as an Arab with long flowing white robes and a white turban who roller-skated around while singing and playing an electric guitar. Pete thought to himself he was one guy he'd definitely have to get to know.

Maud had an insatiable appetite for sex, and although Pete always prided himself on his ability in bed, she drained him and then wanted more. He thought if this was the norm for American women he was going to have to up his game. He wasn't sure if she was taking some kind of sexual stimulant, but irrespective of what time it was she always wanted to fuck. She was done with making love, she told him, that was for pussies. She would climb on him and whisper in his ear as she held his erection. "Fuck me, baby, fuck me." And he certainly did his best. In fact by the time the third night was through, he suspected that she had been lying to him all along about the porn films and that they'd been starring in one of their own.

CHAPTER FOUR

Much to his relief Pete's guitars eventually arrived on the fourth day. Despite the continual promises of them always being on the next flight, it had taken the intervention of Manny Oberstein's secretary Mandy to resolve the situation, and the two cases had been delivered by courier to the record company's offices on Sunset Boulevard. It was there that Janine and Pete finally met with Manny face to face. After expressing his condolences about Gerry's death when he greeted them, they sat down in his enormous, air-conditioned office on the top floor of the Westoria Records building. Surrounded by platinum, gold and silver disks covering the walls they began to talk business.

Janine felt nervous being in such a high-powered environment, especially as Manny was a renowned tough character to deal with, but she soon discovered a lot of it was an act, and underneath he had a warm and caring personality. She was wearing a smart new outfit she'd bought from one of the expensive boutiques in Hermosa Beach and looked great. She'd taken the advice of the trendy female assistant and had gone for a slim-line beige linen suit, which although she felt was rather casual had a very expensive look and feel to it. The kitten-heeled shoes matched it perfectly, and for once she didn't tower over everyone. From the flattering looks Manny gave her as she walked in, it had been a good choice. It was obvious he had a lot of respect for Pete, and felt the same as she did, that he had the makings of a huge star. It surprised her that Manny had already heard about Pete and Vince Boyd on the flight over, but when he explained that Vince's manager was a good friend, she realised that the industry was much smaller than it seemed. 'Something to bear in mind for the future,' she thought to herself.

Having finally been reacquainted with his guitars, Pete was in a good mood and looked every bit the star. Janine noticed the three days of Californian sunshine seemed to be having the right effect and he already had a tan.

The first thing on the agenda was setting up some rehearsals with the musicians Manny and his team had chosen for Pete. He explained that the guys had been picked not only on their musical abilities, but also their character. Pete and the band would be living with each other on a tour bus travelling the length and breadth of the country, and in such an environment they all had to get on - something that Pete had experienced on his last tour in the UK.

Manny picked up his phone and asked his secretary to send Don in. "I want you to meet your driver and tour manager, Pete - Don Rosario. He's one of our top guys and I treat him as one of the family."

There was a knock on the door and a tall, handsome, black man walked into the office. He gave Manny a bear hug, before turning to Janine and Pete.

"Guys it's a pleasure to meet you, I've heard so much about you Pete," he shook his hand. "And Mrs. Fortuna. Let's get this out there right from the get-go, Pete, I really dig your music! Manny played me a copy of your album and I love it. It's gonna be a real blast." He gave Pete a wide grin. "But it's gonna be tough, and I mean tough. These guys here are putting together a real mother of a schedule, but with the band they've got you, man, we're gonna rock!"

Pete loved the way he said *we* and was already feeling a good vibe. He looked at Janine and she seemed to be feeling it too.

"So who are the guys, Manny?" he asked.

"Marshall Thomas is the drummer from Chicago, Illinois. He's a great solid player; has done a lot of stuff, jammed with Hendrix at one time; nice guy, you'll like him. Randy Jones from Nashville, Tennessee is the bass player. Randy's a real character, played a lot of sessions and a good singer too."

"Isn't Nashville all country music?" Pete interrupted.

"That's what a lot of people think," Don replied. "Don't worry about Randy, he's a great rock player."

"And he's been on a whole list of top albums," Manny added.

"And then we've managed to get keyboard player Richard Kaye from New York." Don continued. "He's a top, top player and a good writer too. We've organised a studio for you guys to have a jam through some of your stuff, get to know each other. It's booked for ten tomorrow morning."

"What about a rhythm guitarist?" Pete asked.

Don and Manny looked at each other.

"Well that was something we wanted to talk to you about," Manny replied. "We've listened to the album a lot, and to be honest, Richard is such a strong player we don't think you'll need one, plus it's one less mouth to feed. But why don't you see how it goes tomorrow with the guys, and we can talk again after the session. You happy with that?"

Pete didn't look convinced, but before he had chance to reply Janine answered "That sounds great Manny."

"OK. So what's next on the agenda?" Manny looked down at a sheet of paper on his desk.

"We want to rebrand the album with the title *In Flames*. We love that song and the title has energy. Oh, and our marketing guys are loving the band name Peterson. They think it sits with the new breed of rock bands with one name, like Santana. That's their idea not mine by the way, but I get where they're coming from. What d'ya think?"

Pete was silent for a minute deep in thought. "I love the title; it's my favourite song on the album, but I'm not sure about Peterson."

Janine turned to Manny, "How about we live with it for a couple of days and see how we feel?"

"Yeah, I don't have a problem with that, but don't take too long, we need to get moving. We want it released to coincide with the tour. There is one more thing I wanted to run by Pete. Again this is the guys from marketing, and I gotta say they usually come up with the goods when it's down to new launches. They want to smarten up your image a little. Maybe lose the leather jacket and jeans look and go for a cooler white shirt and leather trousers kind of thing, like the guy from The Doors? They came out of Venice Beach, check 'em out."

"I've always worn the leather jacket and jeans; that's my trademark in the UK," Pete said.

"Exactly, you said it. In the UK!" Manny stood up and walked round his desk and stood in front of Pete. Janine thought how he reminded her of Gerry, both in size and his attitude. He was short, about five feet six, slightly rotund and balding on top. "But you're not in the UK now. You're in the States. Trust me there are thousands of guys looking just like you, but we want to make you the best. You met Vince Boyd on the flight over, yeah?"

Pete nodded and Janine sighed.

Manny smiled at her briefly then turned back to Pete. "Well he's all down to our marketing and style guys. If I showed you photos of him when he first signed with us you wouldn't recognise him."

He slapped Pete on the back. "But hey c'mon it's early days, and everything can be sorted out. All I know is we have a hit album on our hands, and the sooner we get working on it the better for all of us. What d'ya say Janine?"

"Can't wait to start Manny, so what's the next step?"

"Well Thanksgiving is almost upon us and we usually take a break. Oh, and then we have a huge party which you guys have to come to. Everybody who's anybody will be there, and it will be great for you to meet some of the movers and shakers. I'll get Mandy my secretary to send you invites."

"Wow that sounds great," Janine said as she stood up to leave. "C'mon Pete we have lots to talk about before tomorrow."

Pete was quiet in the cab on the way back to meet Ray. They'd arranged to have dinner at one of the restaurants in Hermosa Beach to go through what had happened at the meeting. He was waiting for them in the bar wearing a short-sleeved cotton shirt with a psychedelic pattern and white slacks, looking every bit the Californian beach dude.

Pete laughed as they walked up to him. "Well somebody's fitting in already. Looking cool Ray."

Ray looked at Janine who smiled as she gave him a kiss. "So how did it go?"

"Apart from a couple of things, I thought it went really well. How about you Pete?"

"Yeah, I'm cool. Not sure about the name though. The clothes, well let's see what they come up with. To be honest I could do with a new wardrobe, and like Manny said, it didn't do Vince Boyd any harm. I'm just looking forward to hearing these guys play."

"Well that sounds great," Ray said as he called the barman over. "So what are we drinking?"

"I'll have the same as you," Pete said.

"And can I have a Cosmopolitan?" Janine asked.

Pete looked shocked. "What no champagne?"

Janine laughed. "We've got a fridge full back at the house, and they only sell the cheap stuff here."

Ray turned to the barman shaking his head.

Pete laughed. "Hey, wait a minute! Wasn't that what Vince Boyd was drinking at the airport?"

Janine smiled. "If it's good enough for Vince!"

CHAPTER FIVE

Janine arrived as Pete was getting out of his cab the following morning. They were at Whitland Studios where the band was booked to rehearse. She thought he looked a little bit spaced as he came over and gave her a hug, but put it down to the time of morning. Pete didn't do early mornings.

Looking around, Janine thought the area where the studio was situated hardly reflected the image most people had of Hollywood. It was surrounded by run down factory units and boarded up tenement buildings where she wouldn't like to be at night. However once inside it was a completely different story. The place was split into two large rehearsal rooms and a recording studio, all full of the latest equipment, clean, tidy and bustling with energy.

Don was already there waiting in reception and took them through to one of the rooms where Pete's musicians were setting up. The drummer, Marshall Thomas, was tall and black with a large afro hairstyle. He came over and shook hands with Pete and Janine. Randy Jones looked up from behind his amplifier and acknowledged them with a wave. He had long blond hair and when he stood up was about the same height as Pete. Richard Kaye who was playing with the controls of a large sound mixer was shorter than the others and noticeably thin with curly mousey hair. Janine felt he seemed a little shy as he said "Hello."

Don took her by the arm. "What d'ya say we let the guys get to know each other and we grab a cup of coffee?"

They went outside and walked over to the café at the side of reception. It was a bright comfortable area with tables and chairs already half-full of other musicians who were obviously working there.

"Manny happened to mention that there had been some kind of situation with the Rota Bocan, is that true?" Don asked as they sat down with their drinks.

"Well there was a rumour that they could have been involved with the explosion that destroyed Gerry's club," Janine replied.

"And what about the night he was murdered? Wasn't that supposed to be a member of Rota Bocan too?"

Janine looked away and took a sip of her coffee.

"Hey look Janine, I don't want to bring back sad memories, but these guys are bad news and it would be good to know upfront about what happened."

"I think it would be a good idea if you spoke to Ray about all of this."

"Oh hey yeah, you mean your boyfriend right? Didn't he used to be a cop or something?"

"Until recently he was a DCI in the West Midlands Police, and a damn good one."

"Well it would be good to meet him." Don didn't react to her sharp answer. "I'm an ex-cop myself. Retired on medical grounds on account of I was shot trying to stop a robbery. I could have continued after I recovered, but Manny made me an offer and here I am."

She couldn't help but like Don. Somehow she knew they were going to get on.

Back in the rehearsal room the guys were all set up ready to start. Pete had chosen one of the amplifiers available to use, then quickly paid a visit to the restroom as it was called in the States. Using his little fingernail he'd snorted a scoop of the cocaine he'd bought from a guy he'd met the night before in a bar next to his apartment. He'd gone for a nightcap after leaving Janine and Ray and found it easy to buy anything he wanted. It was really good stuff and he was buzzing when he came out again.

Marshall counted them in and they rocked into *Taking Me There*, the opening track from his album. By the time they'd finished the song Pete knew these were the best musicians he'd played with in his life. Everything Manny and Don had said was true. Marshall was the hardest rocking drummer he'd ever heard; Randy just stayed with the groove and sang all the harmonies perfectly, and Richard was incredible. The way he played was so rhythmic they had been right; he didn't need another guitarist. He couldn't wait to play more and started the intro to the second track on the album *It Ain't Worth It* which had a tricky guitar riff. What he was soon to understand though, was Marshall, as well as being a powerful drummer was a perfectionist, and renowned for his timekeeping. So when Pete, buzzing from the coke he'd had and the excitement of the first song came in much too fast, Marshall stopped playing. Pete looked up wondering what had happened.

"Man, you were off the scale there. That tempo was way too fast," he said looking at the others who nodded in agreement. "Maybe you need to chill a little and let me do the counts."

Pete had counted the songs in with his other band and was annoyed to be pulled up. "I've always done it before so what's the problem?"

"Well sticking that shit up your nose before rehearsal ain't a good idea for a start! Listen man, take a tip from us. Manny ain't a fan of drugs, and is not gonna be happy if he finds out his big new star boy likes to indulge in nose candy. You dig what I mean?"

Pete was shocked that Marshall was so perceptive.

"Look man, it don't bother me how you want to fuck yourself up," he carried on. "We all got our own ways, but do it in your own time. You're a great player and this is gonna be a motherfuckin' band, as long as you stay straight. I know the other guys feel the same."

Randy and Richard both nodded. "So let's forget this conversation ever happened and play some music. What d'ya say?"

Pete looked round at the other two and smiled. "I hear you man, loud and clear!"

Three hours later and they'd played every track from his album. It had ended up being a fantastic session, the guys had packed up their equipment and were about to leave when Pete wandered over to Marshall.

"Do you mind if I ask how you knew?"

Marshall turned to him and clapped his hand on Pete's shoulder. "Man I've had enough of the stuff that I should have shares in the whole of Columbia." He leaned close to Pete. "But the secret is to know when it's cool to do it!" He raised his eyebrows and walked out of the room.

While Pete had been playing through his album with the guys in the studio, Janine had called Ray and he'd jumped in a cab to come and meet Don.

The two ex-cops had instantly connected and sat in the café talking about old cases and discussing their wounds. Don had been shot in the shoulder whereas Ray carried a scar across his stomach. After they'd compared wounds and had a laugh about them Don became serious.

"Listen Ray, I really need to talk to you about what happened with the Rota Bocan. Can you give me any more details?"

"Well sure; I mean I can call the UK and get copies of the files sent over, but is it that important?"

Don looked at Ray and Janine. "Important? Man these guys are killers! Benny Mulligan is one of the most feared gang bosses in the country and if he has issues with you we may have a problem."

Ray tried to calm the situation. "Look there were never any charges brought. I interviewed two guys in connection with the explosion but they had a big deal lawyer and we let them go."

"Who was the lawyer?"

"A guy called Silvoni if I remember right."

"Angelo Silvoni! He's one of their top guys! If Angelo Silvoni flies to the UK that's heavy shit man."

"Well as I said no charges were brought and we let them both go. It got very weird though."

Don was still interested in knowing more. "How come?"

"Two officers from Special Branch came up from London and three Irish suspects were brought in for questioning."

Janine went to say something but Ray gave her a look that said keep quiet, and he carried on. "While they were in custody we got a tip off that the man behind the bombing was holed up in a restaurant, and I went with the Chief Constable and two Special Branch officers to see if he was there. That's when I got shot. While I was in hospital and the bomber was singing like a bird, this character from the Home Office appears and all charges are suddenly dropped against the three Irish suspects."

"Any reason why?"

"Evidently some undercover deal between the English and Irish governments."

"And the bomber, what happened to him?" Don was really into the story now.

"Well after I was released from hospital he was due to be transferred back to Ireland to stand trial. I was at the police headquarters as it was happening, except he managed to break free and took me as a hostage." Ray thought back to the day it had happened.

"Wait a minute. He took you as a hostage? Man this is exciting stuff. So then what happened?"

"Well, he made me drive my car, which was a pretty fast rally-spec machine, and he wasn't wearing a seat belt. So I crashed it into a concrete block and he went through the windscreen and I didn't! Wrote my car off in the process though."

"You're kidding me right? You smashed your car into a concrete block and the guy died?" Ray nodded. "Wow man you're a fuckin' hero!" Don jumped up and shook Ray's hand. "Makes my taking a slug trying to stop a bank robbery sound lame. But listen, getting back to Benny Mulligan."

Janine interrupted. "He came out with some statement after Gerry died, saying people who interfered in things they didn't understand usually ended up getting hurt."

Don was thoughtful for a moment. "Hmm, well it's good we're not scheduled to do any gigs in Miami for the time being. He's one evil mother I'm telling you. But look who's here! Hey Pete, how'd it go man?" He stood up and shook Pete's hand as he came over to join them.

"Awesome, they're everything you and Manny said and better." Janine noticed that Pete was visibly excited. "Yeah man, I can't wait to get out on the road, it's gonna be great."

Later that evening Pete had gone out for a drink to relax in Venice

Beach, when he found a little club down a side street called *El Greco*. He could hear live music so he went in to have a look. There was a Mariachi band playing in the corner of a small dimly lit, smoky room. Looking around most of the seats were taken, so Pete walked up to the bar and ordered a beer. He was about to light a cigarette when a female voice asked him for a light. It wasn't an obviously American voice - more Eastern European - and turning to the side Pete looked into the dark eyes of a woman whose wavy black hair hung down to her shoulders. She held a long black cigarette in her fingers which Pete lit for her, and drew deeply on it blowing the smoke up towards the ceiling. She was a strangely attractive woman Pete thought - possibly early thirties and as he lit his own cigarette he noticed she was wearing a black military-style jacket with gold buttons, a short black skirt and high red stilettos.

"My name's Pete," he said picking up his bottle of Bud and taking a mouthful. "That's not an American accent. Where are you from?"

She drained her cocktail glass putting it down on the bar. "Buy me a drink and I'll tell you."

Pete looked at her and then at the barman. "Get her the same again."

"My name is Nadja and I'm from Minsk in the Soviet Union. Nice to meet you Pete, but yours is not an American accent either, so where are you from?"

The barman passed her a full cocktail glass.

Pete noticed a table had just become free. "Let's sit down over there," he pointed to the corner.

They walked over and sat down just as the band stopped playing to take a break.

"Ah that's better, I hate that kind of music. So, Pete, where are you from? Ireland maybe?"

"Haha, No. I'm from a place called Birmingham in England."

"Ah England, a place I'd love to visit, and what brings you to LA?"

"I'm a musician. I've recently signed a record deal with Westoria Records. I've got a new album coming out next year and I'm going to be touring with my band."

She took another deep pull on her cigarette and stubbing it out in the ashtray drank half of her cocktail in one mouthful.

"That sounds very interesting and what is the name of your band?"

"Well it was The Flames, but the record label want it to be my name so Peterson I suppose."

"Peterson," she considered for a moment. "Peterson, yes, I like that name!"

They'd had more drinks and talked about what it was like to live in Russia, what the music scene was like in England and places he should go in Venice Beach, and Pete was beginning to consider taking his leave and getting an early night when she suddenly leaned across the table.

"I need to go home and have sex with you, Pete Peterson. Come with me quickly, I want you now!"

She grabbed his arm pulling him out of his seat and across the club. Pete followed her as she led him outside to an old silver Bentley which was parked just around the corner. She jumped in and started up the engine which coughed and spluttered into life, before putting it in gear with a loud crunch and roaring off down the side street.

Pete sat in the passenger seat, which still felt weird as he was on the wrong side to back home, and looked at Nadja. There was something intriguing about her that he liked. Not least her directness.

Minutes later they pulled up outside the Art Deco frontage of a hotel on Ocean Avenue in Santa Monica overlooking the pier. Nadja tossed the car keys to a valet parking attendant who was standing by the entrance. She walked through the doors and over to the lift with Pete close behind.

"Cool place," he said admiring the elegant décor. The lift took them to the top floor. "Are you staying here?" he asked as the doors opened and Nadja led him across the penthouse apartment to the bedroom.

"Staying here? No darling I live here!"

Pete was stunned and amazed.

"Well don't just stand there admiring the view," she ordered. "Take off your clothes!"

She unbuttoned her black tunic and threw it on an armchair followed by her skirt, and struck a pose in just her skimpy knickers and high red stilettos. Pete lifted her up in his arms and kissed her mouth as he carried her across to the huge bed. She tasted of exotic spices and his excitement showed as he lowered her onto the bed. She lay back and wrapped her legs around him raking her nails down his back, groaning as she pushed her lithe body up to meet his thrusts. 'Maud had been one thing' he thought 'but Nadja's something different altogether.'

Ray and Janine had gone straight home from the studio and decided to have a drink on the rooftop balcony before dinner. Janine had jumped in the shower to freshen herself up and came out wrapped in a towel. She stood at the rail looking down at the usual procession of fitness-mad locals on the Strand below. Ray had just got out of the shower and came up behind her still dripping wet and naked.

"Mmm I wonder if anyone down there knows what you're doing," she said as he lifted her towel and let it fall to the floor. She pushed herself back as he reached around her and gently rolled her nipples between his fingers while she moved against him. Just as she was starting to get excited he took her by the hand and sat her down on the edge of one of the sun-beds. Kneeling in front of her he lifted her legs over his shoulders, and teased her until she started to groan.

"Oh Jesus, you're making me come," she said. "You're making me..." Just at that point he stood up and holding her legs apart pushed himself inside her. She felt as if she was going to explode as he filled her with long deep strokes.

"Ohhhh, you bastard," she squealed. "You feckin' bastaaaaard!"

"You didn't like it then?" He was smiling.

"Oh my God, Ray," she said breathlessly. "You'll be the death of me."

She sat up and started to work on him when the phone rang.

He looked an incredible sight as he walked stark naked over to the phone and picked it up.

"Hello, hey Matt, great to hear from you. Yeah we're both fine. How's things?"

She watched his face change from smiling to attentive and then to a frown as he listened intently.

"Oh my God, that's incredible! No, no you did the right thing. Of course, thanks for letting me know. You'll keep me in the loop, yeah? OK, give my regards to everyone. Thanks Matt, yeah speak to you soon." He put the phone down.

"What was that all about?" Janine asked looking concerned.

"Well, as you probably guessed it was Matt Burgess, or should I say DCI Burgess. He felt I should know that there's been a huge breakthrough in the Alex Mitchell case."

Janine sat down next to him wrapping herself in a large pink fluffy dressing gown.

"It seems a witness has come forward who says on a night during the week of October 24th, she saw two men carry something long and heavy wrapped in a plastic sheet out of the back door of The Lexxicon, and then dump it in the canal down by a wooden dock about a hundred yards away. One of them then threw something in the canal and he - according to the woman he was black - folded the plastic sheet up and dumped it in a skip nearby. Matt's got divers searching the canal around the area and they're checking which company supplied the skip. Evidently she was in a car parked across the other side of the canal, and because the guy she was with is married and she's his secretary, they were nervous about coming forward. Thankfully Matt convinced him he wouldn't have to be involved and so she was happy to help."

Ray was feeling cold and still naked pulled on his own dressing gown wrapping it around himself. "God, Janine this puts a completely different slant on things. I'm gonna have to let Matt know about what you heard."

He turned to her as she let out a loud sob. "What's up, babe?"

Janine wiped away her tears and looked up at him. "Don't you see? If you tell Matt what I heard it will ruin Gerry's name. Everything that's been said about him will mean nothing. He'll be remembered as a murderer. I don't want that."

"But at the time you came to me and told me what you'd heard, he was a murderer Janine, and it's my duty to tell Matt your story."

Janine stood up and shouted at Ray. "No Ray it's NOT your duty. You're no longer a policeman so there's no need for you to say anything."

They both stood and stared at each other in silence. Eventually Ray took her in his arms and they held each other tight.

"Alright babe, I'm sorry, it's difficult for me. I know I'm not a copper anymore, but I'm still getting used to it. There's nothing I can do about the witness, but I won't say anything, I promise."

CHAPTER SIX

Manny Oberstein's penthouse suite overlooking Sunset Boulevard was the venue of the legendary Westoria Records party, held every year at Thanksgiving. It was renowned for the guests who were invited, and a ticket was hot property around Hollywood.

Janine and Ray were sitting in a limo on their way, looking and feeling great. Janine was wearing a stunning backless gown from one of the new designers in LA for which she'd paid a fortune, but it didn't matter. It was important she look the part tonight. She was the personal manager of Pete Peterson one of the most important guests for the evening. She'd chosen an emerald green, silk creation which perfectly matched her eyes, and with her long red hair in an elegant chignon she could have been mistaken for a top model. Ray had bought a stylish evening suit especially for the occasion, and with his black bow tie was the perfectly dressed escort.

Their limo was met at the entrance by a top hatted doorman, who opened their door so they could walk across the red carpet. They were about to enter when Janine heard someone call her name. Turning round she saw that Vince Boyd's limo had just pulled up, and he was waving for her to wait. He came rushing up, and in front of the bank of photographers and reporters gave her a hug and a kiss on her cheek. She almost fainted when he did it, but managed to regain her poise as they entered the foyer. He certainly knew how to work the press, as he posed flashing his smile to everyone. Ray was watching from the side, and thought he'd tell Janine that she should be more outgoing and play to the cameras. After all she was a beautiful woman, and he'd seen how she used her looks before.

They were standing in the reception area waiting for one of the lifts and admiring a huge cake shaped like an old-fashioned record player with a horn. As he, Janine and Vince were ushered in along with about a dozen other guests, there was a commotion at the entrance. Just before the lift doors closed, Ray caught a glimpse of Pete and a woman arguing with the doorman. He decided he wouldn't mention it to Janine; he was sure they would find out about it soon enough. Then they were zooming up to the top floor.

The lift doors hissed open and they were greeted with the sight and sounds of a party in full swing. There were people everywhere, but not ordinary people; David Bowie was sitting on a sofa animatedly talking with Al Green. One of Janine's favourite singers, Sly Stone was mixing cocktails behind the bar, and over in the corner sitting at a white grand piano, Roberta Flack was singing her latest hit. Janine thought how she'd been to a few celebrity parties before with Gerry when they first started seeing each other, but nothing on the scale of this.

Manny spotted them and came over. "Janine, Ray welcome. Has anyone offered you a drink yet?" He beckoned a waiter over. "Have whatever you want guys." He touched Janine's arm and leaned towards her. "Security have just called up to say your artist has arrived." He smiled. "From what they said he's in a bit of a state, but hey, you wouldn't be a star if you didn't make a scene! Don't worry, it'll be cool."

She thought again of how much he reminded her of Gerry as he spotted someone in the crowd and excused himself.

Janine looked at Ray with a frown. "I don't like the sound of this, he's not been returning my calls lately, and Don said he'd been spotted with some Russian heiress driving around in an old Bentley. God, I hope he's not slipping back to his old ways again."

Ray turned to the lift as the doors opened. Pete and an attractive woman, wearing a tight fitting floor-length black silk dress, fell out into the room. Pete had a gleaming white shirt on, hanging loose outside a pair of skintight black leather trousers. Ray had to admit he looked every inch the rock star accompanied by his rock chick, but the state he was in was another matter. He was stumbling about holding on to the woman, who seemed equally unbalanced. Suddenly Pete spotted Janine and made his way over bumping into a couple of guests as he did so.

"Hey guys, cool party. This is Nadja, she's Russian and loaded." He was slurring his words.

Nadja offered her hand to Janine. "I'm pleased to meet you. Pete has told me a lot about you. He told me you were a very beautiful lady, and he was right. Is this your man?" She turned to Ray. "He's very good looking too!"

Janine took Pete by the arm and pulled him over to a quiet corner. "What the fuck are you doing? The biggest opportunity you've ever had in your life and you turn up stoned! And who the hell is she?" Janine turned around just as Nadja was dragging Ray towards the bar. "Don told me she was rumoured to be some kind of Russian heiress. What have you been doing?"

"Mainly fucking," Pete said with a cheeky grin.

"Don't play around Pete. You've been taking some shit again haven't you?"

"Nah, just a little weed and the odd line of coke. I'm cool." He looked round the room. "I need a drink; can we go to the bar?"

Janine shook her head as he pushed past her and made his way through the crowd.

Manny suddenly appeared from nowhere and grabbed his arm. "Pete Peterson, it's good of you to come," he announced in a theatrically loud voice. "Ladies and Gentlemen may I introduce to you our latest signing, from England, Pete Peterson."

There was a ripple of applause from the guests and Pete tried to make an exaggerated bow, but lost his balance and ended up falling flat on his face.

There was a moment's silence and then Manny laughed. "And a future star I think!"

One by one people joined in, and Ray who had been watching, helped Pete up, guiding him to one of the huge leather sofas dotted around the room. Janine was following behind and was about to say something when Bowie sat down next to Pete and shook his hand.

"Nice entrance mate! Manny played me your album. Really cool."

Pete recognised who was talking to him and managed to slur a few thank yous, and then he was gone.

"Was that who I think it was?" Ray said to Janine who seemed to be in a state of shock. All she could do was nod her head.

Don Rosario had joined them and could see Pete was still stoned.

"I think it would be a good idea if we got Pete out of here before he gets any worse. Ray you wanna give me a hand?"

Between them they managed to get Pete back over to the lift without too much fuss, and while they were waiting for it to arrive Nadja appeared. "Don't worry about Pete, I'll get him back home."

Ray was about to object when the lift doors opened and Nadja guided Pete in. Before they could do any more the doors closed.

Don put his arm around Ray. "Don't worry man, he'll be cool. She's a bit of a nut job, but harmless."

"Who is she?" Ray asked as they made their way back to Janine.

"She's called Nadja Romanov, and is reputedly the heiress to some Russian family that makes vodka. She moved out here about five years ago and lives in the big art deco hotel on Ocean Avenue in Santa Monica. Drives an old Bentley about, and supposedly had a scene with Jim Morrison before he became famous with The Doors."

"The guy who died last year?"

"Yeah, they came from the music scene in Venice Beach. I overheard Janine ripping into Pete before; has he had a problem in the past?"

Ray was cautious as he didn't want Don knowing too much about Pete's previous drugs history. "Nothing that Janine can't handle. She's a tough lady when she wants to be."

Don agreed. "Yeah I see that, which is cool to know. Me and Pete gonna be pretty tight once we get underway."

"How are the dates coming on?" Ray was glad to steer the conversation in a different direction.

"Manny was telling me there's about twenty dates in for the first run and a cool TV show," Don replied. "C'mon. Let's grab a beer, I got me a thirst after all that fuss."

They made their way back to the bar, passing Janine who was in conversation with Manny and a couple of important looking guys in suits.

Downstairs the lift doors had opened, and Pete and Nadja made their way out to her car. Just as she started it up Pete jumped out and ran back inside, returning moments later licking his fingers and eating something.

"What is that you?" Nadja asked.

Pete didn't answer her, but had a mischievous grin on his face as they pulled away.

The next morning Janine and Ray were sat having breakfast when the phone rang. Janine answered it and could hear laughing. "Hello who is this?"

The laughing stopped. "Hey Janine it's Manny, how are you? Have you seen Pete today?"

"No, the last we saw of him was when Ray and Don put him in the lift last night. What were you laughing at?"

He started to laugh again. "Well evidently around about the time he left, someone peed in the ashtray in the lift and filled it to the brim, and then took a huge bite out of the cake in reception."

"Oh God, Manny I'm so sorry. Do you think it was Pete?" She sounded horrified.

"Look, it's no problem, I just think it's so funny. Pure Rock and Roll. Hey did you see David Bowie talking to him? David loves the album. I'm getting really good vibes about *In Flames*. Listen, I've got a meeting later with Don to discuss the tour dates. It's a pretty hectic schedule, but we're hitting all the best cities and we have a cool TV show lined up. Let's speak tomorrow when I have the complete list. Have a good day."

He rang off. Janine sat down shaking her head. "You're not going to believe what Manny just told me."

She sat down as Ray poured her a cup of coffee and relayed what Manny had just said with a serious expression on her face, but Ray started to giggle.

"Yeah well, thank fuck Manny thought it was funny too. I'm gonna kill him when I get hold of him!"

CHAPTER SEVEN

Matt Burgess was having a meeting with DS Tony Carter and DS Jackie Rose in Ray's old office. All three had benefitted from his leaving with promotions and were discussing the rapid developments in the Alex Mitchell murder case. Since the witness had come forward, forensics had searched the canal at the back of the club, and using a team of trained divers had recovered a pistol by the wooden jetty. Then with a real stroke of luck, Matt's team had identified the company whose skip the plastic sheeting had been dumped in. For some reason the skip hadn't been taken to the tip, and the folded plastic sheet had been found tucked under a length of plywood. Both pieces of evidence were now with Ginger Thompson, and he was sounding hopeful they might have some good news soon.

The new Acting Chief Constable, Charles Mainwaring who had taken over from George Williams, appeared in the doorway. He was a tall, distinguished man with a full head of greying hair, always immaculately dressed in tailored suits. Today's was a dark grey pinstripe with a white shirt and red and blue striped Guards tie. He was also more hands-on in his approach than his predecessor, often dropping in on meetings unannounced.

"How are we doing with forensics?"

Matt stood up. "Ginger's pretty confident we may have something, Sir. Especially from the plastic sheeting."

"Good, good keep me in the loop," Mainwaring said as he left the room. "Carry on."

Matt looked at the other two with raised eyebrows and sat down again. "So what have we got so far? Tony?"

DS Tony Carter took out his notebook. "The female witness is pretty sure one of the men she saw was Bobby McGregor. She identified him from a photo we showed her, and the other one she's certain was Gerry Fortuna."

"Damn, are you sure? Ray's not gonna like that when I tell him."

"Well she was at the opening night of The Lexxicon and recognised him from that. Standing right at the front, she reckoned. Big fan of Pete Peterson."

"What about the guy?"

"Trouble is boss, he's married and shit scared because it's his secretary," DS Jackie Rose added. "Says his wife is the jealous kind. He's quite paranoid in case she finds out."

"Well he should learn to keep it in his trousers then! He does know we're investigating a murder?"

Tony and Jackie both nodded.

"Well we've got one positive ID so we'll have to go with that." Matt's phone rang.

"Yes Ginger. It is? Brilliant, you're a genius. I'll tell him straight away. I owe you one."

Matt put the phone down and addressed the other two officers. "They've got a bloody fingerprint match on the plastic sheet with Bobby McGregor. Fortunately we had his prints on record after he had a fight at The Hideout one night and got arrested. There was also a blood smear, but it isn't Gerry Fortuna's and as yet unidentified. Ginger's working on it. The gun is clean, been in the water too long. I'll tell Mainwaring; give him some good news. You two get an APB out on Bobby McGregor right away, I'll give Ray a call. Anyone know what time it is in LA?"

Janine had finally caught up with Pete at the rehearsal studios. Don had organised another run through with the band, and she saw him sitting with Nadja in the café area as she walked through the door.

Pete waved to her as she walked across. "Hey Jan, how's things?" he said cheerfully.

"You and I need to have a talk," she said sitting down at their table. She looked at Nadja. "Will you excuse us please."

Nadja looked at Pete and paused, before Pete answered. "Nadja's cool."

"I don't give a fuck what she is; this is our private business." Janine exploded.

Without a word Nadja stood up and walked away.

Janine watched her go then turned round and stared at Pete. "Don't you ever do that again. Just remember who got you here."

"Yeah Gerry!" Pete replied with a smirk.

"Gerry! Listen here you ungrateful piece of shit, I negotiated that deal, and for your information Gerry's dead, and I'm in charge now!" She was blazing.

"Well Nadja's a powerful woman with a lot of money."

"Yeah and you're just the latest in a long line of naïve singers she's screwed, and you won't be the last. Ask Don, he'll tell you all about Miss Romanov. Oh and another thing, thank your lucky stars Manny Oberstein has a sense of humour. Those little pranks of yours the other night, pissing in the lift and then eating the cake, very funny. But don't push it Pete. You're not there yet. One wrong move and you're on the next plane back home."

She stood up and strode out of the studio slamming the door as she left.

Don, who'd been standing back watching, thought to himself as he looked across at Pete. 'Wow, that's one lady I wouldn't like to get on the wrong side of, and that's a fact!'

Matt had called Ray to tell him the latest news. Fortunately Janine was still out at the studio, and they'd been able to have a long talk without being overheard.

"And there's no doubt it's Bobby's print?" Ray asked.

"No doubt. His prints were on file already."

"And the woman who identified Gerry; is she positive it was him?"

"Definitely. She was standing right at the front when Gerry made his speech. We've got an APB out to bring Bobby in for questioning. Look I know this is going to be difficult for you Ray, but how do you feel about coming back; I mean it was your case?"

Ray was thinking, sitting in the lounge on his own. Janine had already made it plain she didn't want Ray involved in any way and he could see her point. The trouble was, he knew with the information she'd given him along with the new evidence Matt now had, Bobby McGregor would certainly be put on trial for murder.

But if that happened Gerry Fortuna's name would be dragged in and that would jeopardise his relationship with Janine. Wouldn't it?

"You're gonna have to leave that with me mate. Look I gotta go." He put the phone down as he heard Janine's key in the door.

She came in and threw her handbag down on the sofa.

"Hey babe, how're you?" She walked into the kitchen and poured herself a glass of Bollinger. "I think I'm gonna have to keep an eye on this Nadja woman. She's getting a little too cosy with Pete, and he's easily lead where his dick's concerned!" She swallowed a mouthful of champagne and looked over to Ray. "What's up? You look bothered."

"Matt Burgess was on the phone again just before you got back. They've got a witness who has identified Bobby McGregor and Gerry as the two men who dumped Alex's body in the canal, and forensics have confirmed Bobby's fingerprint is on the plastic sheet that they used to wrap him in. He's being brought in for questioning."

Janine slammed her glass down on the table. "So what's it got to do with you Ray? You're over here with me and no longer in the force. Why can't you just leave it and walk away?"

"Because it was my case, Janine, and when I left it wasn't finished. Now there's a chance it will be." He stood up and walked over to the window. "I don't expect you to understand, but I need to put an end to this."

Janine took another drink and paused before she spoke.

"No, you're right, I don't understand, but if that's how you feel, you need to go and finish it. But don't bother coming back if you do!"

She picked up her bag and walked out of the door slamming it behind her. Ray stood silently looking out at the Pacific as the waves rolled in relentlessly. He eventually picked up the phone and booked a single ticket to London on the first available flight.

Janine had left the house in a blind fury. Driving around aimlessly, she found herself heading along Sunset Boulevard. She pulled into the car park of the Beverly Hills Hotel, and after handing her keys to the parking attendant, walked into the bar and ordered herself a Cosmopolitan. She bought a pack of twenty Marlboro, and as she put one into her lips a hand appeared at the side of her with a lighter.

"May I?" a man said as he flicked it and lit her cigarette. She thought she recognised the voice, and turning, found herself looking into the smiling face of Charles Morse. He gave her one of his trademark looks, raising one of his eyebrows just how he used to do when he was *The Avenger.*

"I recognised you from the plane when you walked in, and thought you might like some company; you seemed a little bothered."

Janine inhaled deeply on her cigarette, blowing the smoke up towards the fan slowly rotating above her head, as Charles Morse lit one for himself. He was immaculately dressed in a navy-blue double-breasted suit with a pale blue shirt and beige loafers.

"I don't like to pry, but you look like you've lost a fiver and found a ten-shilling note."

Janine started to laugh and then to cry.

"My dear lady," he said handing her a handkerchief which he took from his top pocket. "It would be bad form for James Black to be seen with a mysterious woman in tears. Perhaps you'd care to join me for dinner, and we could try to sort out your problem a little more privately."

He ushered her into the restaurant where the Maître D' made a great fuss of him, showing them to a secluded table in the corner. Over oysters bonne femme, followed by beautifully cooked medium rare filet steaks accompanied by a bottle of Chateau Mouton Rothschild, Janine poured out her woes. Charles turned out to be a wonderful listener, nodding and frowning in all the right places as her story unfolded. At the end he put down his knife and fork, dabbed his mouth with his napkin and looked at her for a few moments.

"So what are you going to do then?"

"What can I do? He has to go back and be there when my ex-husband is found guilty of murder, and I have to be here to make sure my artist behaves himself. I've told Ray if he goes, he doesn't come back, and right now I think that's still how I feel."

She leaned forward as Charles Morse lit another cigarette for her, and lighting his own he leaned back in his chair.

"Well I think only time will tell. You're both obviously strong-minded people who are used to having their own way. My advice would be to book yourself into the hotel, have a few more drinks in the bar, and by the time you go home tomorrow everything will be fine. Now can I get you another one of those disgusting Cosmopolitans or would you like a Dry Martini the same as me?" He gave her another one of those irresistible smiles.

"Thank you James," she replied as she took his arm. "That would be wonderful."

The following morning she arrived back at the house in Hermosa Beach with a hangover, after having at least three more cocktails with Charles Morse who had been joined by his secretary and his publicist. Janine hadn't been too drunk to ensure she described herself as 'up and coming rock star Pete Peterson's manager', when quizzed who she was. She also managed to be in at least one photograph taken by the ever-present paparazzi.

She called out as she opened the door, but finding the apartment empty noticed a letter addressed to her on the table. It was from Ray.

> *My darling Janine,*
> *I'm sorry but this is something I have to do. Please forgive me. I love you with all my heart,*
> *Ray.*

She read it, and as tears began to roll down her cheeks she tore it into little pieces and threw them over the edge of the balcony, watching as they fluttered to the ground.

At that very moment in the clear blue sky above, a Pan Am Boeing 747 was climbing over the Los Angeles coast turning sharp right and then heading north towards Canada, before making its way across the Atlantic en-route to London Heathrow. Sitting in it, Ray turned away from the window and closed his eyes wondering if he'd just made the biggest mistake of his life.

CHAPTER EIGHT

Bobby McGregor had done his best to maintain a low profile in the aftermath of Gerry Fortuna's death. He had blamed himself for not being at Gerry's side when he left the club. He always made a point of making sure he was safe when there was a crowd of people, but on this occasion he had been occupied trying to sort out the row in the dressing room between Pete Peterson and his band. The bass player Tony Waters had started it by aiming a blow at Bobby, but as an ex-boxer he'd easily side-stepped and dispatched his assailant with a swift jab. Unfortunately whilst this was taking place, Gerry and Janine had decided to leave the club. As they made their way to Gerry's Rolls Royce they were surrounded by an excited crowd of well-wishers, one of whom had a sinister motive. In the confusion he had fatally stabbed Gerry then disappeared back into the throng, leaving him dying in Janine's arms

The subsequent fruitless investigation, and then high-profile funeral had largely overshadowed the murder of Alex Mitchell, and Bobby had tried to slip back into Birmingham's underworld. He'd been staying at a run-down old house with Errol, the uncle of Mr. C, the DJ who had died as a result of injuries he'd sustained after Gerry's previous music club, Rudi's had been blown up. When the word spread that he was wanted in connection with the murder of Alex Mitchell, he had panicked and tried to flee the country. He'd been apprehended at Dover, when an observant customs official spotted him trying to board a ferry to Calais.

After the long journey back to the Midlands handcuffed to an officer in the back of a cramped police car, he was now sitting in an interview room at police headquarters, faced by DCI Matt Burgess and DC Tony Carter. Unseen in the observation room, Ray Law watched on. To Ray's surprise, the door to the interview room swung open and Bobby's solicitor strode in. None other than Julia Davies.

Dressed in her customary tailored suit and high heels she sat down and lit a cigarette. "I'd be obliged if you would allow me to consult with my client in private, gentlemen," she said opening her leather briefcase and blowing smoke across the desk in their direction. Matt indicated for Tony to follow him, and they left the room closing the door behind them.

Julia removed a folder and spread a few sheets across the table before turning to Bobby.

"You my friend, are well and truly up shit creek without a paddle! Looking at the evidence against you and the fact you tried to do a runner, things do not look good. Plus the fact that the only supporting witness you had is no longer with us." She drew deeply on her cigarette before crushing it in the metal ashtray on the table. "Unless this mystery man who Gerry mentioned to me, some agent or other comes forward. Do you have any idea where he is?"

"I don't even know his name," Bobby replied. "Gerry bunged him a wad of cash and he arranged to meet Alex at the club. Then once he'd got him in the dressing room talking and Gerry and I came in, he just disappeared."

"Terrific! In that case. I suggest you stick to "No comment" for now and let me handle it," she said as the door opened and Matt and Tony returned.

Matt remained standing and addressed Bobby. "I assume you have had time to consult with your solicitor, Mr. McGregor?"

Bobby nodded.

"In that case Robert McGregor, I am arresting you for the murder of Alex Mitchell on or around the 22nd of October 1971. You do not have to say anything, but it may harm your defence if you do not mention when questioned something which you later rely on in court. Anything you do say may be given in evidence." Tony Carter moved across and holding Bobby's arm handcuffed himself to him. Julia looked slightly taken aback as Bobby was led out of the room. There was to be no interrogation it seemed.

"Looks like we'll be meeting in court, DCI Burgess" Julia said as she packed up her papers.

Ray Law had been sitting in the shadows taking in the events happening on the other side of the two-way mirror, and remained seated as Julia left the room. She was the last person he wanted to see right now. He'd tried calling Janine when he landed at Heathrow, but there was no reply at the house, and when he'd called the studio they'd said she wasn't there. Eventually he'd allowed Matt to drive him to his hotel to try and sleep off the jetlag which was making him feel dreadful.

At ten o'clock the next morning, Janine was in Manny Oberstein's office with Don Rosario, going through the first part of Pete's tour itinerary. It was going to be a gruelling schedule starting off further up the West Coast in Oakland, followed by a string of club dates taking in places such as Salt Lake City, Denver, Phoenix, the Fillmore in San Fransisco and eventually finishing back in LA at the Whisky A Go-Go, just a short way down Sunset Boulevard from where they were sitting. Don had organised the tour bus; a converted Greyhound with six bunks, kitchen facilities, a lounge complete with TV, a video player and a small bathroom. This was going to be home for the band, and Don was at pains to point out he'd chosen the best to ensure the guys were comfortable. The musicians were used to touring so he didn't foresee any problems. Although Pete's experience, as Janine explained had only been in a small bus back home, which had been fine for the short distances between each venue. Here in the US, some of the states were as big as the UK, so a few of the journeys between gigs were huge.

She had thought about going on the tour herself now that she was on her own, but she resisted the temptation. She needed to concentrate on other aspects of Pete's career, such as the promotion and distribution of his album. Manny had already mentioned they were working on getting Pete a TV show at the end of the first run, and if she was to become the successful manager she was aiming to be, she would have to start learning how the business worked, and fast. So far Westoria had been more than helpful, but she knew their benevolence couldn't go on forever, and she wanted to make sure she was ready for the challenge.

It was the first day of the tour and the band had assembled at Whitland Studios at ten o'clock to meet Don and the bus. All the back-line equipment, keyboards and guitars had been loaded, and they were waiting for Pete to arrive. He eventually turned up driven by Nadja in her old Bentley, with his possessions packed in a hold-all. As he left her she made a spectacle of kissing him passionately, then wiping the tears away as he climbed on the silver Greyhound bus to join the others.

Don was already sitting in the driver's seat ready to go, and started the engine, closing the door with a hiss of the hydraulics. "You guys all set?" he called out revving the engine. "Then let's do this thing." He let out the clutch and the bus pulled smoothly away from the studio car park.

Inside, the guys were relaxing in the lounge area, which was furnished with two large grey couches and a couple of swiveling armchairs. They'd already chosen their bunks in the rear and filled up the fridge with beers ready for the journey. The first run to Oakland was a five-hour trip, and they had planned to discuss the set with Pete in preparation for the opening night, but as soon as he arrived he'd gone straight to the back of the bus with his bag and hadn't returned. After about an hour, Marshall the drummer made a visit to the cramped bathroom and poking his head through the door which separated the bunks and the rest of the bus, he saw that Pete was fast asleep. So much for the planned discussion he thought, as he headed back to the others. Realistically there was no need to go through what they'd already rehearsed. It had sounded great at the last run through, but Marshall was a perfectionist, and along with the other two wanted everything to be right.

In the end he needn't have worried. The venue was an old-established club called *The Decade* that both Marshall and Randy had played many times, which had a great reputation for its sound system. It hadn't taken long for them to set up, and a rejuvenated Pete was running through the opening number in front of the club owner and a few onlookers. They were just getting into it when Pete stopped playing.

"OK, that's good for me, how is it for you guys?" he said turning to the others. They all nodded, seemingly happy with their monitors and individual sound.

The sound engineer appeared as they started to leave the stage. "Hey guys is that all OK for you? That was pretty short for a sound check."

Pete stopped and walked over. "Why do we want to play our set?" he said taking off his guitar. "It sounds great from where we are. You just ride those faders and we'll do the rest, OK!"

He turned to the others. "Time for a beer guys. You with me?"

Marshall smiled at Randy and Richard as they followed him to the bar.

The show was a great success. Everything had gone according to plan, and the packed audience had rocked along to every song. Pete had been on top form strutting about the stage, interacting with the girls at the front, posing and pouting and at times using his guitar more like a phallus. The band had followed his every move, and when they eventually left the stage the crowd were ecstatic still shouting for more. Pete was first off, and had collapsed into an armchair in the dressing room, his clothes soaked and stuck to him. The others came in slapping each other on the back and laughing. Don had followed behind them and was about to join in the celebrations, when he noticed Pete was about to snort something he had in a small plastic bottle. He moved quickly and caught his hand pulling it away from his nose.

"Man, we got to get a few things straight before we go any further," he said to Pete as the others stopped what they were doing. "You start sticking that shit up your nose and we gonna have a problem."

He licked his fingertip and dipped it into the white powder tasting the small amount sticking to it.

He grimaced. "Man, it ain't even good shit. Where d'you get this?"

Pete was now looking embarrassed. "Nadja scored it for me before we left."

"Nadja!" Don exclaimed loudly. "What's she tryin' to do, kill you? Listen Pete, didn't my brother Marshall here talk to you back in LA?" Pete nodded. "Yeah, I know he did, 'cos I told him to. So let's be cool, and we'll all have a real good time. You wanna party, we'll have our own private party back on the bus. We don't want any club owners knowing our business, and if Manny finds out then you may as well pack your bag and get the fuck back home! Now there's some real pretty ladies out there dyin' to give you the best blowjob you've ever had, so why don't you dry yourself off and let's go get ourselves some real nice Oakland hospitality." He gave a huge beaming smile. "You dig what I mean!"

Pete knew exactly what he meant and peeling off his shirt and trousers towelled himself down ready to meet his adoring public.

Back in the UK, Ray had arranged to meet his friend, DCI Matt Burgess for a drink. He was feeling slightly better since he'd had a good sleep, although his body clock was still playing games and he wasn't sure what time it was. Matt had arranged to meet him in the bar of the hotel where he was staying. It was right in the centre of Birmingham, just a short distance away from the site of Rudi's where they had both witnessed the aftermath of the terrible explosion that had taken so many lives. Even though it was being rebuilt as offices he noticed, the memories would always remain.

The Crowne Plaza was a busy hotel and popular with international tourists, which explained why Ray could hear so many foreign accents as he sat waiting for Matt to arrive. He was about to order a drink when he heard a female voice he instantly recognised, and turning he saw Julia Davies with another woman and two men walking into the bar. He didn't have time to escape before they were upon him and he came face to face with her again. She looked surprised to see him but didn't show it to the others. Instead she smiled and offered him her hand.

"Well, Well, Well! DCI, or should I say ex-DCI Law. How nice to see you again. But I heard you were residing in Los Angeles, so what brings you back from the sunshine state?"

Just at that moment Matt Burgess came rushing into the bar with a flustered look on his face.

"Sorry mate, I got held up." He suddenly recognised who was standing next to Ray.

"Ah Ms. Davies, this is..." but Ray interrupted him before he went any further.

"Nice to see you again Julia, sorry we can't stay," and before he had chance to say anything more, Ray steered Matt back out of the bar.

"Phew, thanks mate. That could have been embarrassing," Matt said as they headed to the underground car park.

"Yeah, but I'm not sure for who; you or me," Ray said as they climbed into Matt's car. He thought for a moment how good Julia still looked, then found himself wondering what Janine was doing back in LA.

Janine had decided she wasn't going to sit at home on her own feeling sorry for herself now that Ray had left. She had been spending a lot of time at Westoria's offices, talking to the various departments involved with Pete, and whilst there she'd struck up a friendship with Mandy

Valasquez, Manny Oberstein's secretary. A seemingly tough character who had recently gone through a separation from a rock guitarist she'd met when his band signed to Westoria, Janine liked her. They'd arranged to go to the opening of one of Santa Monica's newest clubs for which Mandy, as the secretary of one of the biggest record company executives in LA had been given VIP tickets.

Janine was dressed quite conservatively in a cool cream linen shirt and beige flared trousers with flat white pumps. She was sitting at the bar waiting for Mandy to arrive when a man sat down next to her. Her initial impulse was to turn away and ignore him, but he was wearing the most intoxicating aftershave she'd ever smelled, and she couldn't help but accept his offer to light her cigarette. She was conscious of how, since Ray had left, she'd started to smoke again, and made a mental note to keep an eye on how many a day she was smoking.

The man was attractive with a Middle Eastern appearance but with a strong American accent, and asked her if she was on her own. He was smartly dressed in a dark grey silk jacket with an Indian styled stand-up collar and a crisp white shirt.

Janine explained that she was waiting for a friend trying not to offend him, but at the same time glancing anxiously around to see if Mandy had arrived.

Just as she was starting to feel worried, Mandy breezed in and pushed in between her and the man giving her a kiss full on the lips. Janine was so shocked she almost fell off her stool, and as the man stood up and walked away Mandy leaned in close to her and winked. "Usually does the trick," she said taking his place.

Janine was momentarily lost for words. She watched as Mandy caught the attention of the barman and ordered two glasses of champagne, then reached over and took Janine's cigarette from her fingers and drew on it deeply letting the smoke out slowly. She was wearing a multi-coloured silk blouse which was open to show off her ample cleavage, and a blue mini skirt barely long enough to be decent with matching blue high heels. Her hair was a mass of curls in a loose kind of Afro-style with a silk headband which matched her blouse.

They took their drinks and found a table away from the bustle of the bar where they could sit and talk. Janine was still reeling from the unorthodox greeting when Mandy reached over and held her hand.

"You're a good-looking lady, Janine. Don't look so surprised. I know a few women who would like to do more than kiss you, me included."

"But I thought you were, er..." Janine stumbled over her words.

"Hey listen, it's no big deal; a lot of us swing both ways. Just look around. I've just pissed off a few who were watching you."

Janine found herself relaxing a little as the champagne started to work. "So tell me about yourself. I only really know about you from the office."

"I met José Valasquez who played lead guitar in a band that Manny signed. At the beginning it all seemed cool and we ended up getting married. The band started getting known, so we were invited to all the rock and roll parties around LA. I began to notice more and more, after a few lines of coke how he would disappear, leaving me alone with some of the other wives and girlfriends. Then one time at this big important do in some famous film star's mansion on Mulholland Drive, I followed him and found him upstairs in the master bedroom screwing the wife of the drummer. After that we drifted apart and eventually split. According to Manny, José became disillusioned with the band and got more and more into guns and watching films about violence. The band split up and he moved down to somewhere in Miami. So instead of getting hung up about it, I decided I would get myself some real fun. Don't get me wrong, if the right guy came along I wouldn't turn him down, but let me tell you honey, until you've been made love to by another woman, you've not lived."

Janine thought back to the time in the hotel suite in London with Pete and the receptionist, but they'd drunk so much champagne it was all a bit of a blur. Mandy was certainly an attractive and sexy lady, and maybe it was the fact Janine hadn't eaten and the champagne was going straight to her head but that kiss had certainly had an effect on her she hadn't experienced before, and she was curious to find out more. The atmosphere in the club was becoming louder and more oppressive, so she made up her mind and taking Mandy by the hand led her outside.

As they sat in the back of the cab on the way to Hermosa Beach their lips met again. This time it was Janine who was in charge.

CHAPTER NINE

Ray was lying in his king-sized bed in the Crowne Plaza the next morning wondering what to do. He'd decided to take a day off from following Matt and his team. Having arrested Bobby McGregor, they were concentrating on getting all the paperwork in order before he appeared in court. He suddenly remembered Janine had mentioned she hadn't heard from Judy Watson for a while, and thought it would be the ideal opportunity to pay her a visit to see how she was getting on in the new office at The Lexxicon.

The club was only a ten-minute walk from the hotel and as it was a nice day, Ray decided to take a stroll down the canal and observe all the new building that was going on. He remembered Gerry had once mentioned how the area around the canal basin would one day be a desirable place to live, and judging from the number of cranes and new building sites that had sprung up since he was last here, he seemed to be right. If he remembered correctly Pete Peterson still owned a small apartment overlooking the canal which might soon be worth a lot of money.

He'd been walking for a while and was aware he'd arrived at the back of The Lexxicon. In front of him was the wooden jetty where Alex Mitchell had allegedly been thrown into the canal along with the pistol used to shoot him. A few strands of the police tape that had been used to cordon off the area still fluttering in the breeze. He spotted the back door to the club was ajar, and pulled it open allowing him to enter through the dressing rooms. Could this have been where Alex had been murdered by Gerry and Bobby? He glanced around the rooms as he made his way into the main part of the club, calling out to anyone who was there. There was a cleaner and a barman who were talking and smoking by the bar, and they looked up as he walked across the dance floor to them.

"Hi, I'm looking for Judy Watson, is she in?" Ray asked.

The barman pointed to a door at the back of the room. "If you go through there and turn right you'll see a door marked FAM Office. You're in luck she's just got back from the hospital."

Ray followed his instructions and knocked on the office door.

"Come in," a voice called out, and he walked in to see Judy sitting behind a huge desk surrounded by photos of bands and singers covering the walls.

"Oh my God, Ray!" she said jumping up out of her chair and running round the desk to give him a hug and kissing his cheek. "Why didn't you call to say you were coming? Where's Janine, is she here?"

"Well one thing at a time," he replied. "I'm over on my own. I'm sure you're aware of the situation with Bobby McGregor and the Alex Mitchell case, and I was invited over by DCI Matt Burgess who's now in charge. Trouble is Janine and I had - how can I say - a difference of opinion whether I should get involved again, which resulted in her giving me an ultimatum that if I came not to bother going back."

"Oh that's heavy," Judy said. "Look, Janine always was headstrong, she'll get over it. Have you spoken to her since you've got back?"

"No that's the trouble, I've tried on numerous occasions but with no luck."

"Tell you what, I'll give her a call later. I've been really busy here and haven't had time to speak to her recently, so it'll be a good excuse to get in touch."

"That would be great if you could. Anyway how are you? The barman said you'd just got back from the hospital, but you look amazing. I don't think I can remember seeing you looking so well. Is everything alright?"

Judy smiled. "Yeah everything's fine. It was just a checkup."

"And how's it all going here? Looks like you've settled in. What have you done? I can't work out what's different?" Ray was trying to think what had changed.

Judy opened the door and walked out into the corridor. "Come on I'll show you. We decided to cut the Lexx2 room in half, getting rid of the grand piano, and making one half my office and the other a cocktail bar. It does really good business with the older crowd," she said leading the way into the small bar. Ray remembered standing in there with George Williams the night Gerry was murdered. It was a lot smaller now and almost reminiscent of Georgie's where he had first met Janine.

He followed Judy as she led him out and across the corridor to the big room Lexx1.

"And in here is where all the bands play. It's incredible how popular it's become," she explained. "We're getting all the top bands from both the UK and the States queuing up to appear here. I can't believe how lucky I am that Janine asked me to take charge of all this. You know we've got ten top bands signed to FAM now."

"Well she wouldn't have asked you if she didn't think you could do it."

"So how's it going in LA with Pete? From what I've heard he's about to head out on tour."

"Yeah, well round about the time I left, Janine was sorting it out. You know what Pete's like. There were a few minor problems, but I think she was dealing with them. His band sounds amazing and there's a great team behind him."

"Look, when I speak to her I'll tell her you dropped in and you've been trying to contact her. And don't worry, it'll be fine." She gave him a peck on the cheek. "I'm sorry, but I have to make a few calls. Why don't you come and see the show tonight. We've got Argent on; they're really good."

"Yeah, I might do that. I'll give Matt Burgess a call; he's into that kind of stuff."

She walked off back to her office, and Ray couldn't help thinking how well she looked, almost glowing.

Janine woke to the smell of coffee permeating through the house in Hermosa Beach. It was a sunny Californian day, and outside she could hear the locals passing by down below on The Strand. The door swung open and Mandy came in wearing Janine's silk kimono and carrying two mugs of steaming Java. "Good morning, how are you feeling?" she said as she passed one of the mugs to Janine.

"A little hung over, but I've been worse!"

They went outside on the balcony and lay naked on the sun loungers, sipping their coffees. Janine's mind went back to the events of last night when she had brought Mandy back to the house. She was aware that something had happened between them at the club earlier but then after they had drunk more champagne, Mandy had undressed her slowly exploring her body, touching and kissing her as Janine lay back on the bed. She wasn't quite sure when, but Mandy had tied her wrists to the bed posts with her stockings and removing her headband she'd blindfolded her. It seemed like Mandy had taken forever as Janine lay unable to see what she was doing, until she finally climbed on the bed straddling her and then unexpectedly her nipples were being stroked with something really cold. She had realised they were ice cubes and Mandy was slowly taking her to the point where the ache of the coldness was making them erect and hard, when, just as suddenly, Mandy's hot mouth was sucking them, her tongue teasing them. Janine had been writhing and groaning softly when she'd felt Mandy's hand feeling between her legs stroking and teasing her. She hadn't noticed the buzzing sound at first - she was concentrating on what Mandy's fingers were doing to her - until the vibrating tip touched her moist lips and then slowly entered her as Mandy's mouth covered hers. Holding her tight as Janine's body bucked beneath her, Mandy had orchestrated her orgasm as Janine pulled on the ties holding her to the bed and she was gasping for breath as Mandy removed the stockings and blindfold and slowly climbed off her.

Janine grinned at the memory. "Jeesus, I thought you were trying to give me a heart attack for a moment there."

Mandy propped herself up on one elbow, looking at her. "So how did that feel?" She leaned over and licked Janine's left nipple making her jump.

"Well I have to say I don't think I've ever come like that before," she said. "But there's something about feeling yer man's lad doing the business, if you know what I mean."

Mandy rolled back on the bed laughing. "You know something Janine? I think you and I are gonna be great friends." She sat back up and, holding her close, kissed her on the lips. Janine didn't resist and wrapping her arms around her kissed her back.

They were just getting interested in each other again when the phone rang. Janine stood up and went to answer it. When she noticed the number display showed it was from the UK she thought did she really want to speak to Ray right now? She knew she would have to sooner or later and picked the handset up expecting to hear his voice, but she was surprised to hear it was Judy Watson.

"Hey Judy, how are you? I was only thinking the other day we haven't spoken for ages. How's things?"

"Hi Janine. Yes I'm sorry, I've been so busy here lately. Things are great. The club is really doing fantastic business and the agency is flying. How's things there? I believe Pete has just set out on tour." She paused briefly. "Ray dropped by earlier today and he was saying it was going well."

Janine picked up on her hesitation. "Oh did he! And did he get you to call me?" she snapped back, then regretted her reaction. "Sorry Judy, I didn't mean that. As he's probably told you we had a disagreement which sadly got out of hand. Right now I'm not sure what the outcome will be. But as regards Pete, everything's going great. There's been the odd disagreement, as I'm sure knowing Pete like you do you'll understand, but the record label is brilliant, the band are unbelievable and so far the gigs are going really well."

"That sounds amazing. So what are you up to today?"

Janine glanced round at Mandy who was lighting a cigarette. "Well me and my girlfriend Mandy are doing brunch in a while. Oh hang on, that sounded wrong. Mandy is my friend, she's Manny Oberstein's secretary. Oh well you know what I mean."

"Well it sounds like you're having fun."

"You know what I miss most though, a full English breakfast. I'd just love a plate of eggs, bacon, sausage, beans, fried bread. All you get here is these fancy dishes - *Eggs Benedict* and stuff like that!"

Judy sensed the time to finish the call before it cost her a fortune. "Listen Janine, I have to go. I'll send you the accounts for the club and what I've been doing at FAM. Let's speak again soon. Bye."

Janine put the phone down and stood for a moment wondering whether she really missed all that. Then she saw the cloudless sky and the waves breaking on the sun-drenched beach as she walked out to her friend on the balcony. "Come on Mandy, how about we try that new bar in the Plaza with the great brunch menu?"

The band had finally got back on the bus after the gig in Oakland. Pete had been the perfect gentleman meeting all the fans who had patiently queued for his autograph. His English accent was a huge hit with all the females, and one or two had made it plain they wanted more than just a photograph with him. He'd managed to slip backstage with one particularly sexy blonde lady in an *In Flames* t-shirt and tight blue jeans, who had returned to her friends ten minutes later with a broad grin on her face wiping her mouth with the necktie Pete had been wearing on stage. He appeared moments later fastening his belt, and thought he was going to have to buy in a supply of neckties for future gigs.

Don had been supervising the loading of the equipment and after checking the dressing room one final time they pulled away from the club en-route to their next destination, a nine-and-a-half-hour drive to Boise, Idaho. Just as Don had said earlier, the private party was about to begin.

Once underway Marshall took responsibility to chop out the lines of coke for the guys, while Randy was in charge of the bar. They'd even managed to get some fried chicken from the club, and as they settled down on the next leg of the tour, Pete began to understand he might have been doing this all wrong. The guys were seasoned touring musicians and had everything under control. He momentarily thought about the last night he'd spent with Nadja in her penthouse apartment, where they'd had sex in the open air on her balcony overlooking the Santa Monica pier. He'd promised to keep in touch with her while he was away to let her know how things were going, but then he remembered the look on the face of the blonde in the dressing room and his thoughts turned to the next gig.

CHAPTER TEN

Ray had called Matt Burgess, and they'd taken Judy up on her offer of free entry in The Lexxicon to see Argent that night. It was really busy especiallyas the band hd a single, *Hold Your Head Up* in the top ten, and they'd stood at the back of Lexx1 to watch. Although he wasn't a keen rock fan - he preferred more soul and R'n'B - Ray really enjoyed the show. They'd spotted Judy towards the end of the set and she took them backstage afterwards and introduced them to the guys.

Ray thought it was great to see how Judy interacted with the band and their respect for her considering how young she was, and once again noticed how well she looked. He couldn't put his finger on it but there was definitely something different about her.

Matt apologised for being a party pooper, but he had an early start the next morning and had left Ray on his own with Judy and the band. She had organised them a hotel nearby, and they invited her and Ray back for a drink. Sitting in the bar later with the members of the band and a few of their groupies, Ray and Judy found themselves separated from the main crowd and Judy suddenly remembered her conversation earlier with Janine.

"She sounded fine, and was with someone called Mandy, Manny Oberstein's secretary. They were off out for brunch or something. Honestly Ray, give it time, she'll come round."

He decided to make a move back to his hotel, and thanking her for a great night kissed her cheek, shook hands with the members of the band and left. As he was collecting his room key from reception a well-dressed group of people were leaving the bar. Standing waiting by the lifts, he didn't taking much notice of them until he became aware of a distinctive perfume. The lift doors pinged as it arrived and he was about to step inside, when he recognised the elegant lady in a shimmering black cocktail dress covered in sequins, high black stiletto, her hair pinned up, who was standing with the group. He walked over and linked arms with her.

Julia Davies' startled expression changed to a warm smile as she saw who it was. He mouthed "Sorry," to her friends while guiding her into the lift, pressing the button to his floor. As the lift started to ascend he pushed her up against the side wall of the lift and kissed her forcefully on the mouth holding her there until the lift reached his floor. Her crimson lips tasted sweet and the intoxicating perfume she wore invaded his senses.

He pulled away from her as the doors opened. "You and I have unfinished business," he said taking her by the hand.

She unpinned her shoulder length hair shaking it out as she followed him down the corridor to his room.

Once inside they left a trail of discarded clothes as they undressed each other on the way across the room. He kicked off his loafers and unzipped her designer black dress dropping it on top of his black leather jacket and jeans and her skimpy silk underwear was thrown aside along with his t-shirt and boxers. She lay back on the king-sized bed and pulled him to her still wearing her stockings and stilettos which she wrapped around his waist. She'd forgotten how big he was as she held his enormous erection in her hands when with a low groan she guided him deep inside her.

Later as they lay on the bed drinking the bottle of champagne Ray had ordered from room service, Julia broached the delicate subject of why he was here on his own.

"It's a bit complicated," he replied. "Even more so that I'm here in bed with you."

She looked confused.

"Matt Burgess called to tell me there had been major developments in the Alex Mitchell murder case. He suggested as I had been involved that I might like to come back and see it through to a conclusion."

Julia began to have an inkling of what was coming.

"Trouble was Janine hit the roof when I told her what I was planning to do. She couldn't understand why I still wanted to be involved considering I'm no longer on the force. I tried to explain it didn't work like that and how I still felt part of the investigation."

"So what you're telling me is you've just screwed the defence solicitor in a case that you're going to be part of the prosecution team!" She started to laugh. "Shit, Ray you don't do things by half do you!"

"Well I won't actually be involved. I'm really only here to observe, but in a way, yes!" He stood up naked and walked over to the pile of clothes picking them up and arranging them in a neat pile.

"Looks like you're getting ready to throw me out," she said as he folded her dress over the back of a chair.

He gave her an impish grin and climbed back into bed.

"I wasn't thinking quite yet," he said as she pulled him down on top of her.

Sitting behind the wheel of her Porsche in the hotel's underground car park, Julia Davies wondered how many legal rules they'd broken over the past few hours. She turned the key in the ignition of her red 911 and revved the engine. It was a sound that never ceased to send a shiver through her body - even though some parts were a little sore - and slipping it into gear she roared out into the street just as the new day was dawning.

Upstairs Ray lay in bed smelling her perfume on the bedclothes, wondering what he'd got himself into. He knew in his heart he still loved and missed Janine, but Julia had a way of getting to him he could never understand. What had Judy said, 'Give it time, she'll come round'. He hoped he hadn't just done something else that might finish it altogether.

CHAPTER ELEVEN

Bobby McGregor's trial attracted huge media attention, and court Number One at Birmingham Crown Court was full to capacity. He was accused of the murder of Alex Mitchell in October of the previous year and was standing in the dock with a forlorn expression watching as the action began to unfold.

Ray remembered him as an outgoing friendly guy who worshipped Gerry, always supremely fit from his time as a boxer, although due to recent events he appeared to have put on a fair amount of weight. He was dressed in a suit that had seen better days, and appeared badly in need of a shave. His solicitor, Julia Davies, was sitting near the front, behind the defence QC, Wendy Garner, who Julia had recommended. They were old friends and colleagues, and made a powerful team, exuding confidence.

High up in the public gallery watching the proceedings while trying to be as unobtrusive as possible, Ray noticed how immaculately Julia was dressed, and thought back to how she had looked in her little black dress the other night.

His friend DCI Burgess had called him earlier that morning to make sure he was going to be there. They hadn't spoken since Matt had left Ray at the Argent party, and he wasn't aware what happened when Ray had arrived back at his hotel. Ray had decided the less Matt knew the better, and was snapped out of his reverie when the words, "All rise" announced the arrival of the judge.

He looked down to see Matt talking to James Muirhead QC who would be prosecuting on behalf of the Crown. He was a venerable old character who had been around for years, judging by the state of his wig which looked like it had seen better days. Wendy Garner's on the other hand had the appearance of having just come straight from the cleaners, it was so bright.

The jury who had been previously sworn in had filed into their seats, and the proceedings began with an opening statement from the prosecution explaining how they would endeavour to prove beyond a shadow of a doubt that the accused had murdered Alex Mitchell. This was followed by Wendy Garner QC standing up and announcing how she would prove that her client had not murdered Alex Mitchell, and was innocent.

Various exhibits were referred to, and after a short delay when both councils were asked to approach the judge, James Muirhead began his cross examination of the first witness. It was the person who had been walking his dog alongside the canal when he had spotted the body of Alex Mitchell floating by the lock gates. All quite straightforward, and Julia had declined to question the witness.

The next witness to take the stand was the owner of the hire company, in whose skip the plastic sheet with Bobby McGregor's bloody fingerprint on had been found. By this time it was midway through the afternoon and as is customary with the legal profession, an early adjournment was agreed. The witness was stood down until the following morning, and after the judge left the courtroom the day's proceedings were over.

Ray made his way down to the foyer where he was waiting to speak to Matt when the thunderous sound of two pairs of high heels shattered the relative silence, and Julia and Wendy Garner came striding through. They made a formidable pair with Wendy's long blonde hair and Julia's chestnut brown mane. He froze as they approached but they walked straight past without acknowledging him. Ray breathed a sigh of relief as Matt arrived, and they left heading for the nearest pub which was just across the road. They battled their way through the crowded room to the bar where they ordered two pint turning to find Julia and Wendy closing in on them.

"DCI Burgess and Ex-DCI Law, so nice to see you again," Julia said. "Let me introduce you to my friend, Wendy Garner QC."

They both said "Hello" but Wendy Garner gave them only a slight nod of her head before pushing past them.

Ray and Matt managed to squeeze away from the bar and found a space in the corner where they could stand.

"Don't seem to be able to go anywhere without bumping into Ms. Davies," Matt said as he swallowed half of his beer in one long draught.

Ray remained silent, but was keeping an eye on where the two women had gone.

"So this witness of yours; is she reliable?" Ray asked Matt feeling a little more relaxed.

"She should be. James Muirhead's been working with her the past few days, although I wouldn't put anything past this Wendy Garner to try something dirty, if she's anything like Julia Davies." He aimed that at Ray with a knowing look.

"What's that supposed to mean?"

"Nothing, nothing, but well you know what happened back at the King's Head. She didn't beat around the bush that night, and she has a reputation for getting what she wants however she does it."

Matt could see Ray was uncomfortable with the way the conversation was going. "Anyway, it'll probably be a couple of days before she takes the stand the way things are going. The judge seems a bit of a stickler for detail."

Ray decided he'd had enough and made an excuse to leave before Matt said anything else. Anyway, he felt he could do with an early night after the exertions of the weekend.

Pete Peterson was wide awake lying in his bunk at the back of the tour bus as they hurtled down the highway towards Portland, when he noticed they'd slowed down and were pulling into a truck stop to get some gas. He got up to stretch his legs and saw Don going to get a coffee, so he decided to join him. He hadn't really spoken to Don much since they'd first met back in Manny's office, so it was a good opportunity. He found him sitting in a booth in the diner and grabbing himself a coffee slid onto the long seat opposite him.

"Hey Don, how's it going? Where the hell are we?"

Don looked tired. "We're about twenty miles outside of Boise, nearly halfway there."

Pete thought a moment. "Boise, weren't we there the other night?"

"Yeah I know. Sometimes the schedules get crazy man. Seems like they couldn't book the shows close together, so we had to go a couple hundred miles down the road then all the way back again. That's the way it works." Don looked at him. "How you getting on with the guys? Everything OK?"

"Yeah man, the guys are cool. Great players. Weird thing though. I was feeling hungry before and went to get a sandwich from the fridge. The chef at the last club gave it to me. But it was gone, and so was just about everything else. I mean I went to bed the same time as the others so I don't get it."

Don laughed. "Ah you're talking about the phantom ice box raider. There's usually one on every bus."

"Any idea who it is?"

"Nah man I'm too busy driving." Don gave him a mischievous look. "But if it bothers you, you could easily find out who it is."

"Oh what, you mean maybe we should set a trap."

Don smiled at Pete and explained. The conspirators finished their coffees and made their way back to the bus.

Later that day before everyone had woken up, Pete left the bus on his own to have a look around Downtown Portland, and eventually returned with a full bag of groceries from one of the major supermarkets. The rest of the band had all gone out to a local bar for some food, so Pete set about making himself a huge bowl of salad with the bits and pieces he'd bought earlier. By the time the guys arrived back to get ready for sound check he'd finished, and was just putting the container in the fridge. He'd covered it with cling film and written a note saying *Pete's salad, don't touch*, in large letters which he left on top.

It was a storming gig that night. The Portland crowd loved him and the band, especially the cute little red-haired girl who'd asked him to sign her breasts after the show. Of course Pete obliged and managed to make sure all the guys were there in the dressing room when he did it. In fact Randy the bass player joined him afterwards when she volunteered to give both of them her speciality Double BJ, which involved amazing manual dexterity using her hands and mouth, the like of which Pete had never witnessed before in his life.

They'd all had a good laugh listening to Pete and Randy's description of the experience, and settled down for another long trip back down the coast to San Fransisco where they were playing the legendary Fillmore the following night.

One by one they started to drift off to bed and Pete noticed that Richard the keyboard player was always the last one up. He'd wait until they were all getting tired, and then suggest watching an awful video, which usually triggered an exodus to their bunks. Pete decided to watch what happened and opened the door to the rear bunks section just wide enough to see. Sure enough once Richard was satisfied he was on his own, he went over to the kitchen section and opened up the fridge.

Pete chuckled to himself as he watched Richard sit down, carefully remove the covering from his bowl of salad and start to devour the contents. He'd had a few mouthfuls and was contentedly munching away, when suddenly he jumped up and ran back to the fridge, frantically opening the door and rapidly swallowing the best part of a large bottle of beer. He finished it with the next gulp clearly in some distress.

Pete lay back in his bunk trying not to laugh out loud, deciding he'd wait until the next day before saying anything, leaving Richard to suffer.

The following morning as they were all sitting around eating breakfast, Richard wandered out from the sleeping section at the back of the bus looking a little pale.

Don, who figured that Pete must have set the trap noticed Richard didn't look too good. "Hey man, you OK? You don't look too well?"

"Ah yeah man, I got bad guts. I ate some salad shit last night and I think someone spiked it."

Pete looked up. "Which salad was that?"

"Dunno man, just some salad in a bowl." Richard replied.

"The one that said *Pete's salad, don't touch* on it?"

Richard looked slightly annoyed as the others, understanding what Pete had done started to giggle. "Yeah, but that's not on. I mean you deliberately put all sorts of stuff in it. My ass is on fire this morning; you could've poisoned me, man!"

Pete was desperately trying to keep a straight face as Don and the others were now laughing out loud, but he couldn't resist keeping it going.

"So what you're saying is, you're pissed off with me because I spiked my salad which belonged to me that you ate."

By now Richard was aware that he had to admit defeat and sloped off back to his bed mumbling, as Randy played *Ring of Fire* by Johnny Cash on his acoustic guitar accompanied by gales of laughter.

CHAPTER TWELVE

Janine was at the Westoria offices meeting with Manny and the sales & marketing department. They'd released the album on the day Pete and the band had set out on tour, and sales figures were already looking good. The album was picking up airplay on the West Coast radio stations, and there was a TV show booked in for when they got back to LA for the Whiskey A Go-Go gig.

Mandy said she had a few days holiday owed, and suggested she and Janine take a trip up to San Fransisco to see the Fillmore show and stay over afterwards for a couple of days to do a bit of sight seeing. She had found them a deal in a hotel called The Golden Gate with great views across the Bay. It was midway between the Golden Gate Bridge and Fisherman's Wharf, where she promised to take Janine to eat the best seafood she'd ever tasted.

They set off early the following morning on the six-hour road trip in Mandy's yellow Mustang, and were soon cruising with the hood down.

Janine had gone for the rock-chick look wearing an *In Flames* t-shirt she'd been given by marketing and a pair of tight blue jeans, red suede ankle boots and aviator shades, topped off with a cream Stetson which she'd bought from a local store in Hermosa Beach.

Mandy, who always looked cool and sexy, was wearing a denim shirt tied in a knot under her breasts to reveal her tanned stomach with a pair of faded denim shorts, brown leather cowboy boots and round hippy-style sunglasses. She'd tied her hair back with a headband, which Janine noticed was different from the one she'd used as a blindfold the other night. The memory gave Janine a little quiver of excitement, and although she hadn't talked about it to Mandy, she sensed there was a sexual undercurrent still flowing between them. She wasn't sure how she was going to deal with it, but knew it would resurface sometime, especially as they were sharing a double room at the hotel.

Pete and the band had arrived early at the Fillmore, with the bus parked up in the alleyway at the back of the venue. As they were unloading the equipment they were approached by two well-built black guys wearing long coats and sunglasses. For some reason Don was immediately suspicious, and challenged them as they stood by the rear of the bus.

"Can I help you gentlemen?" He seemed agitated by their presence.

"Hey man, no problem, we're just here to make sure everything runs smoothly," the taller of the two replied.

"Well we got it all under control, thanks." Don said although he still looked bothered.

The two men started to move away slowly, still watching what was happening so Don followed them down the alley. "Say guys who d'you work for?" he called out as they reached the end.

"We work for the promoter, Mr. Graham," the shorter of the two replied as they turned the corner.

Don walked back to the bus opening the front door and disappeared inside. Moments later he reappeared tucking a large revolver into the back of his trousers.

Pete had been watching what was happening and looked shocked. Don gave him a reassuring smile.

"Can't be too careful. Something about those two I didn't like."

Eventually the sound check was underway, and the band were rocking into the opening number when Pete looked out into the auditorium and saw two women sitting halfway down the stalls nodding along to the rhythm. As they finished the song the house lights came on, and he recognised who they were.

"Hey Janine," he shouted as they stood up and made their way down to the front. He took off his guitar and jumped off the stage, giving her a hug and kiss, before turning to Mandy. "Who's this?"

"Pete, you remember Mandy, Manny's secretary?" she said untangling herself from his arms.

Pete gave Mandy one of his trademark smiles. "Hey Mandy, how's it going? You two look great. Why didn't you tell me you were coming?"

"We only decided yesterday, and thought we'd come up for a couple of days and take in some of the sights."

"Well that's cool," he replied and turned round to the band. "Hey guys look who's here," he shouted up to the stage. "Listen we just need to go through a couple more songs and then we're finished. Maybe we can grab a beer before the show?"

"Yeah that sounds cool," Mandy said taking Janine's hand. "We'll meet you backstage."

Pete stood watching as they walked over to the exit. 'Strange,' he thought to himself.

Janine and Mandy had checked into their hotel earlier, and as Janine had thought, their room had just the one king-sized bed. She had to admit it was a beautiful room, with amazing views across the bay from their balcony. Janine had been nervous about raising the subject with Mandy, but knew it had to be done.

"Hey look Janine, it's no big deal. You know I dig you, and I also know you dig guys. This was the best room I could find and it came with one bed. So let's just see how it goes, huh?"

Janine gave her a hug. "I'm glad we've cleared that up."

Mandy looked away hiding a hurt expression which said *lover scorned*. She'd let it go for now, but knew there would be another time to requite her feelings.

Back at the gig, Don had gone to look for the promoter Bill Graham, and eventually found him in his office tucked away at the back of the building. He'd worked at the venue before with other artists and had met him on a number of previous occasions.

Bill looked up as he came in the office. "Hey Don, good to see you again. I'm looking forward to the show tonight, I've been hearing some great reports about your artist."

"Hey Bill, good to see you too. Yeah man, Pete Peterson's the real deal alright. Listen Bill, do you have a couple of black guys working for you on security?"

Bill thought for a moment. "Don't think so. What makes you ask?"

"When we arrived these two black dudes wearing shades came and checked us out. When I asked them who they were they said they worked for you."

Bill picked his phone up and dialled a number. "Hey Carlo, you got any new guys working for you on Security? Two black guys?" He listened to the reply. "OK thanks." He replaced the receiver. "That was Carlo my head of security. He hasn't taken on any new staff for tonight. Can you describe these guys?"

Don thought. "They had on long coats and shades, and they had southern accents which I found kinda strange."

Bill looked concerned. "What kind of southern accents? Texas, Tennessee?"

Don thought a moment. "More like Florida, Miami." He suddenly realised what he'd said. "Shit!"

"Yeah, shit alright!" Bill agreed. "We've been having trouble with some Miami-based gang trying to muscle in on the drugs scene here recently. They're called Rota Bocan. Guy named Benny Mulligan runs the show. Bit of a nasty bastard by all accounts. You heard of him?"

Don nodded slowly. "Yeah I've heard of him alright." He stopped. He didn't think it a good idea for Bill to get wind of Benny Mulligan's previous history with Gerry Fortuna. "Should I be worried?"

Bill shook his head. "Don't think so. I'll get Carlo to increase the security, but it shouldn't be a problem. They've been concentrating on small clubs and bars mainly."

Don left the office thinking he'd have to be extra cautious tonight especially as Janine and Mandy were there. But then he remembered thinking Janine was a tough lady. He'd had experience of her in action having a go at Pete, so maybe it might not be a bad thing.

CHAPTER THIRTEEN

Christine Atherton the female witness for the prosecution had been called to the stand and sworn in. James Muirhead stood up and smiled at her. Although he'd spent hours going through everything, he knew it was a daunting experience, especially with an adversary such as Wendy Garner waiting to attempt to rip her testimony to shreds.

"Good morning Miss Atherton, please don't be nervous. It is very commendable of you to come forward as a witness. Now I want you to tell me and the jury, exactly what you saw on the night in question back in October. Take your time."

Christine had done as James Muirhead requested and worn a smart two-piece suit, but her hands were shaking and her throat felt dry as she started to speak.

"I was sitting in a car on the other side of the canal when I saw the back door to The Lexxicon open, and two men come out carrying something long wrapped up in plastic sheeting. It was heavy because they were struggling to carry it, and then when they got to the jetty further down the canal one of them dropped his end. He picked it up again and then they threw it in the canal."

James Muirhead interrupted her. "Could you see what it was they threw into the canal?"

"It looked like a body," she replied.

"Objection!" Wendy Garner stood up. "Supposition."

"Sustained," the judge ruled.

James Muirhead carried on. "What happened next?"

"One of them folded up the sheeting and the other one dropped something into the canal. Then as they walked back to the club, the one with the plastic sheeting pushed it into a skip on the side of the canal."

"What happened then?"

"They both went back into the club and closed the door."

James Muirhead looked at her. "And are either of the men who you saw that night in court today?"

Christine looked at Bobby McGregor and pointed at him. "Yes him," she said.

There was a loud murmur from the packed court and the judge asked for order.

"Thank you Miss Atherton." James Muirhead nodded at her and sat down again.

Wendy Garner seemed to take forever arranging her papers on the desk in front of her, and finally slowly stood up looking at Christine.

"What time was it when you saw this take place Miss Atherton? I assume it is Miss Atherton?" She gave her a condescending look emphasising the word *Miss*.

Christine was noticeably rattled by Wendy's attitude. "It was about nine o'clock," she replied, her voice wavering slightly.

Wendy looked down at her notes. "Correct me if I'm wrong Miss Atherton but wouldn't it be dark at nine o'clock especially down by the side of the canal?"

"I saw them clearly when the door opened. There was a light on inside the club." Christine answered.

"And you said you saw them carry the rolled-up sheeting down to a jetty which is what, fifty yards away. Then you saw one of them drop something in the water? Is that correct, Miss Atherton?" Wendy emphasised the *Miss* again.

"I could clearly see them. There was some light coming from the windows in the warehouses overlooking the canal. And also it was a clear night and the moon was shining." Christine was more positive this time.

Wendy smiled, and then paused referring to her notes again.

"Were you on your own in the car, Miss Atherton?"

Christine looked shocked and her face reddened. She seemed to take an age before answering.

"Yes."

Wendy studied Christine. "I'm sorry could you repeat that."

"Yes." Christine answered.

Wendy turned to the judge. "No more questions."

The judge looked up at the clock and turning to the clerk said

"As it's almost one o'clock I suggest we adjourn for lunch."

The court all rose and James Muirhead urgently beckoned Matt Burgess to speak to him, watched closely by Julia Davies sitting at the side of Wendy Garner.

"What the hell is she doing? She might just have blown the case by lying. Wendy Garner will rip her to shreds if she finds out who was in the car with her."

Matt tried to calm him down. "Look, the fact she was with her boss never got revealed. He refused to be a witness and so it's not on record."

James Muirhead was still unhappy. "I still don't like it. All it takes is for someone to leak that information and Wendy Garner will crucify us."

He picked up his notes sliding them into his bulging leather briefcase, and strode out of the courtroom, leaving Matt standing on his own.

Matt looked up at the public gallery where Ray was still sitting, and mimed the universal action for a drink.

Ray nodded and made his way to the exit.

Once again they were in the pub just across from the courts, when Julia Davies came bustling in with a group of her colleagues this time. She looked far from concerned about the case, as she pushed her way through the crowd to the front and began ordering drinks.

Matt and Ray managed to find a corner where they could stand and talk without being overheard.

"James Muirhead's going mental," Matt said. "You know she was in the car with her boss having a bit of nookie?"

"Shit, no I didn't. So how come he's not a witness then?" Ray asked.

"Got a case of guilt. Won't come forward in case his wife throws a strop and kicks him out. Not the first time evidently." Matt drained his glass.

"Time for another?" Ray asked Matt.

Matt shook his head. "Better not. It could get messy later."

Ray thought for a moment. "Yeah but if he refused to be a witness and was never interviewed, how will anyone know. It's not on record is it?"

"No." Matt replied.

"So unless you've got a leak, the defence won't know about it." Ray spotted Julia approaching them. "Talk of the devil."

"Hello boys, this is becoming a habit," she said as she wafted past on her way back to court.

As he took his place back in the public gallery, Ray thought he recognised one of the team who had been with Julia sitting down the other end of the balcony. Once the judge had returned and they all sat down, the man opened his briefcase and took out a small pair of opera glasses. Very discreetly he trained them on Matt Burgess and James Muirhead as they sat at the front of the court. Ray watched as the man jotted down notes on a small notepad, and suddenly remembered where he'd seen him before. He had been brought in as an expert lip reader on a case he had once worked on. So Julia and Wendy had hired him to report on what was being said between Matt and James Muirhead. His instant reaction was to try to get a note to Matt, but before he had time to do anything Wendy Garner was on her feet and addressing the judge.

"Your honour, before we continue I would ask for an adjournment as I have recently been made aware of information relevant to our defence."

The judge asked the clerk to remove the jury and called both Julia and James Muirhead to approach the bench.

"Are you aware of this Mr. Muirhead?"

"No, your honour, and I find it highly irregular."

Wendy Garner turned to him. "Please accept my apologies, but this information has only just surfaced and I need extra time to be able to substantiate it before we continue."

"Very well Ms. Garner, but I expect you to have everything ready for a prompt start tomorrow."

He requested the clerk to bring the jury back and then after adjourning the session for the day, left the court.

Julia had a smug expression on her face as she and Wendy left the courtroom. At the same time Ray noticed the man disappear from the Public Gallery.

He ran down the stairs and met Matt as he came out of the court.

"Listen mate there's something you should know that might cause you problems," he said pulling him to one side. "They've got a trained lip reader sat up in the public gallery writing down everything you and James Muirhead say. Did you mention the other witness in the car?"

Matt thought for a moment, recalling the conversation with James Muirhead after Christine Atherton had lied in the witness box.

"Shit! Yes we did. James was really annoyed but I calmed him down by saying he'd declined to give a statement."

"Did you say anything else about him?"

Matt's eyes widened as he remembered something. "Yes, I said he was her boss. Damn!"

"I think you need to speak to James Muirhead ASAP mate."

Matt Burgess followed James Muirhead to his chambers where he was removing his robes.

"My ex-colleague Ray Law who I don't think you've met, but he was in charge of this case originally, has told me that the defence has had a lip reader in the public gallery watching our every move. He has probably our *read* conversation about Christine Atherton's boss being in the car with her."

"Damn!" The Barrister was shocked. "Where's Christine Atherton?"

"She went home as soon as the court was dismissed."

"Went home!" James Muirhead exploded. "She's just dropped us right in the shit and she's gone home! We'll need to speak to her first thing in the morning. Can you arrange for her to meet us here at nine o'clock. I need to run through everything again. We don't want any more slip ups. I've a feeling Ms. Garner smells blood."

After they left the court, Julia and Wendy Garner met in her chambers. Wendy had instructed Julia to rush straight back to her office and task one of the female members of her team to find out as much as possible about Christine Atherton's boss.

It was easy enough to find the factory he owned, which was Prestons Manufacturing based in the Arts Quarter. There was a workforce of about thirty according to the investigator, and she watched as a few of them went into the local pub, the *Lord Clifford* after they left off.

There were a couple of young women about the same age as Christine Atherton at the bar, and she approached them. "Hi Ladies, sorry to interrupt but do you work at Prestons?"

"Yeah what about it?" one of the women answered.

"Well I was told there might be some vacancies," she replied. "Is Mr. Preston around do you know?"

The two women looked at each other. "Yeah he's next door, but a word of warning. You want to keep your hand on your cherry. He's a bit of a one is Mr. Preston." They both laughed.

The girl played innocent trying to get more information. "I'm not sure what you mean."

"Listen babe, John Preston's had more female workers than I've had hot dinners. He charms 'em, promises 'em the world, screws 'em then dumps 'em. Look at his latest conquest Christine Atherton. She told us he'd said he was leaving his wife for her. Silly girl; his wife's the major shareholder in the company. Why would he lose all that for a screw in the back seat of his car. She'll learn!" They laughed again and finished their drinks.

"Can I buy you another?" the investigator asked.

"Why not?" the other one replied. "Two large Gin and Its, thanks."

The investigator called the barman over and ordered for the women and had an orange juice herself.

"So what do you know about Christine Atherton?" she said as she passed them their drinks.

One of them paused as she sipped her drink. "Not a lot really. Keeps herself to herself. She's got a disabled brother who she cares for. Had some sort of accident in a club a few years ago. That's about it, other than she's John Preston's latest screw. Anyway why you asking all these questions, you're not a copper are you?"

"No, just interested before I apply for the job. Though I might not bother now." She finished her drink and left the two women at the bar. Driving back to the office she thought about what she'd just found out and knew Julia Davies would be very interested in speaking to John Preston.

Julia didn't waste a minute after listening to her investigator's report. She gathered the team together and gave them their individual tasks before leaving with one of her male colleagues. She'd called ahead saying she was a buyer from a new company interested in doing business with Prestons Manufacturing, and John Preston had agreed to meet her straight away.

She was immediately taken to the boss who was sitting behind a large glass topped desk in his office. It wasn't the traditional factory office which she'd expected, with wall-to-wall shelves full of lever files and an old-fashioned wooden desk. This office reflected his style, with modern light wood fittings and smart leather furniture. His eyes lit up as she walked in and he immediately turned on the charm. He was immaculately dressed in an expensive dark grey business suit, white shirt and light grey tie. She thought the matching light grey silk handkerchief in his top pocket was a subtle finishing touch. He was obviously someone who took a lot of time with his appearance, and she knew straight away that her plan of playing to his vanity would work. She sat down and seductively crossed her legs. He couldn't help but notice her short skirt and long legs complete with the stilettos she'd changed into before leaving the office. Deliberately making no attempt to pull her skirt down, she accepted a cigarette which she allowed him to light for her. She knew the gentle stroke of her fingers on his hand as he flicked his lighter would have the desired effect, and started to play him along. 'It never fails', she thought in her cold calculated way.

"I won't beat about the bush; I've done my homework and I think we can do business together." She gave him one of her best *come on* looks. "I also hear you're a bit of a *ladies' man* if you know what I mean."

"I'm sure I really don't know what you're talking about," he said attempting to sound coy.

"Oh I'm sure you do," Julia replied. "So why don't we stop playing games and go somewhere where we can seal the deal."

She stood up and crushed her cigarette out in the ashtray on his desk.

He jumped up, grabbing his car keys and told her to follow him. He led her down a back staircase which opened out into the car park. Julia took a quick glance around hoping her plan would work. He drove out of the car park in his silver Aston Martin registration JP10, with Julia following closely behind. Minutes later he turned down a secluded side street flanked by old derelict warehouses. It ended in an abandoned car park alongside the canal on the opposite side to the rear of The Lexxicon. Before she had chance to turn off the ignition he jumped out of his car and got in alongside her.

She quickly dropped something in her handbag and put it behind her seat as he sat down.

"A little bird told me this is where you always come with your latest conquest," she said.

He started to take off his jacket. "Who told you that?"

"My friend Christine said you were here with her." Julia glanced in her rear-view mirror.

"Christine Atherton? She's just a silly little girl. Not like you. You're a real woman."

"She told me you'd been with her when that musician guy was killed." She reached over and stroked his trouser leg moving her hand slowly up towards his rapidly bulging crotch.

"Yeah but we didn't see anything though. She was too busy with her head down my trousers. You wanna try?" He started to pull down his zip.

Julia reached over to the back of her seat pulling out a small recorder from her handbag and with a click switched it off.

"I think I'll pass on that," she said looking past him as her male colleague walked up to the passenger door and opened it.

"Thanks for your information John, now if you'll put your brains back in your trousers, I have some pressing business back at my office."

She kissed the tip of her finger and pressed it on the end of his nose. "Bye bye lover."

He was pulled out of the Porsche by Julia's colleague, and spraying grit across the car park she roared off.

CHAPTER FOURTEEN

Pete and the band were in the dressing room getting themselves ready for the show in San Francisco. It was a packed house, and Pete was going through his usual ritual of visiting the toilet for a pee at least half a dozen times before he went on stage. The guys in the band accepted all frontmen had their own routines before the show, and just left them alone. Some threw up, some like Pete had to use the bathroom, and some just locked themselves in a room and yelled at the top of their voice to get themselves in the vibe.

Janine and Mandy were sitting towards the back to the side of the sound desk, when they heard a commotion in the foyer. There was lots of shouting and screaming, as two men wearing balaclavas with eye and mouth holes cut in them burst into the auditorium. One had what looked like a sawn-off shotgun in his hand, which he pointed to the ceiling and fired. The crowd panicked and started running blindly in every direction trying to escape. Janine sat quite still, taken back to the night in Georgie's when two men had raided the club threatening Gerry. That time Gerry and Bobby McGregor had taken care of them using violence, which had ultimately turned her on so much that she and Gerry had wild sex in the back of Rollie. She still never knew what had caused those feelings, but something inside her was stirring again.

Suddenly from nowhere Don appeared holding a huge pistol and fired at the man holding the shotgun, hitting him in the shoulder. The other man fired back at Don causing him to duck behind a pillar and as he did so the two attackers made their exit through the front doors, shooting and wounding one of the security guards. Don checked Janine was OK then ran through the foyer after them, but they had driven off before he managed to get outside.

Mandy who had lain on the floor while the action was happening, finally got up and sat down next to Janine putting her arm around her.

"You alright Janine?" Janine seemed in a daze staring into space. "Janine, Janine you OK?" she asked.

Suddenly Janine snapped back to the present and looked around her.

"Pete, where's Pete?" she said jumping up, and climbing over the seats in front of her. She raced down the aisle to the front, clambered onto the stage and ran across to the dressing room where Pete and the guys were in a state of shock.

"Pete, are you alright?" Janine called as she ran into the room.

"Yeah, yeah, no problem. What the hell was all that about?"

They were all still ready and dressed to go on stage.

She gave him a hug and kissed him. "Doesn't matter, as long as you're OK." She looked round at the rest of the band. "You guys all OK?" They nodded back to her.

The door opened and Don and Mandy came in, relieved to see everyone was unhurt. Don had a large envelope in his hand which he handed to Janine.

"I think something strange is going on. This is for you; it was delivered to the box office earlier this afternoon."

The envelope was addressed to Mrs. Fortuna and she ripped it open. Inside was a sheet of paper on which was drawn a dollar sign and the words *BEWARE THE ROTA BOCAN* written in large letters underneath. Janine suddenly felt the blood drain from her face. She knew exactly what she was holding, and at that moment knew she needed Ray Law standing by her side. But he was in the UK, and so it was up to her to be strong and deal with the situation.

'What would Gerry do?' she thought to herself. 'Well for one thing he wouldn't panic, and he certainly wouldn't let anyone think he was frightened.' She turned to Don. "Don what's the situation outside, is there a chance we can still do the show?"

"Well the cops are here, but I think it's all under control now. The security guy they shot was only winged and he's being seen to by a doctor."

She turned to the guys. "Any of you guys got a problem with playing a show?" She scanned their faces.

Marshall the drummer spoke out. "Bring it on, man. Right guys?"

As one they all shouted "Yeah!"

Janine turned to Don. "OK Don let's get this show on the road. No one fucks with Pete Peterson, whatever they call themselves."

Don reached out and gave Janine a huge bear hug. "You got it!"

The word went round the crowd still gathered outside, that the band were going to play, and within minutes the excitement level was going through the roof. When Pete and the band walked out on stage the roar was deafening.

Janine stood next to Mandy sidestage and watched as Pete performed an incredible show. She found herself reaching for Mandy, and in the shadows she wrapped her arms around her and kissed her with a force so strong she'd only experienced once before - in the back of Gerry's Rollie.

Bill Graham was backstage after the show grinning from ear to ear. "Best fuckin' show I've ever seen. Wow! You guys are awesome. Where's Pete?" He looked round and saw Pete standing in the corner next to Janine. "Man you are something else." He shook his hand and slapped his shoulder. "Manny's got himself a winner with you, I tell you. I ain't ever seen nothing like it. Man, you fuckin' rock!"

He turned to Janine. "You got a whole load of reporters waitin' outside. Soon as word got out about what happened they all high-tailed it down here. You gonna be front page news tomorrow!"

Janine grabbed Pete's arm and looked over to Don who was packing up clothes and equipment. "Don I need you to come with me and Pete to meet the press. It will look good to have our own security, you get what I mean?"

"Sure do. You ready, Pete? C'mon let's go."

"Just a minute, I need to change my shirt," Pete said, slipping on a clean white shirt and necktie from out of his bag. Janine smiled and felt proud with the way he was so cool and looking every bit the star.

They walked back out onto the stage to be confronted by a mass of photographers and reporters, all jostling to speak to Pete and get the best photo. Don automatically slipped into his tour manager role and organised them so they all got chance to ask a question which Pete answered. Then he made sure the other members of the band were on hand for a photo shoot.

"Manny is gonna cream himself when he hears about this," he whispered in Janine's ear. "You couldn't buy this kind of exposure. I got to say that was a brave decision you made earlier to still play the gig."

She whispered back. "We have a saying back home. 'The show must go on!'"

CHAPTER FIFTEEN

Wendy Garner and Julia Davies sat at the front of the court at ten o'clock waiting patiently for the judge to enter. They'd spent most of the previous evening and late into the night preparing Wendy's cross examination of Christine Atherton. They now knew for definite she had lied the day before when asked if she was alone in the car, and she had the proof on a recording of John Preston admitting he was with her. Although it would probably be ruled inadmissible it didn't matter. She knew she had enough ammunition to scare the witness into admitting her lie.

Julia turned round and looked up to the public gallery where Ray Law was sitting and acknowledged his presence with the ghost of a smile. They'd dispensed with the lip reader for the time being, suspecting Ray had worked out what they were doing, but they had enough information to be going on with.

Her thoughts were disturbed by the clerk calling "All rise" as the judge entered.

He immediately asked both Wendy Garner and James Muirhead to approach the bench.

"I trust we're both ready this morning, I could do without any tiresome interruptions today. It's my wedding anniversary and my wife has arranged a party for later."

"Congratulations, your honour," Wendy said with a nod of her head.

James Muirhead just smiled, mainly as he'd been invited to the party, but he wasn't going to let Ms. Garner know that.

He was not happy that Matt Burgess hadn't been able to contact the witness Christine Atherton before she had turned up that morning just before the start of proceedings. It meant he hadn't had the opportunity to give her any pointers on what and what not to say.

They returned to their seats and Christine Atherton was called. She returned to the witness box where she was reminded she was still under oath.

Wendy was immediately on her feet and began before Christine had time to catch her breath.

"Miss Atherton if you will recall, I asked you yesterday if you were alone in your car when you witnessed two men carrying a roll of plastic sheeting out of the rear door to The Lexxicon. And you answered, *Yes*. I will repeat the question. Were you alone in your car?"

Christine looked across at James Muirhead and Matt Burgess before she turned back to Julia.

"Yes." she replied.

Wendy shook her head and looked down at her papers on the desk in front of her. She flicked her gown back revealing a fitted cream silk blouse with just a hint of cleavage showing. She addressed the witness again.

"Well you see Miss Atherton, I'm afraid I don't believe you. In fact I know you weren't in that car on your own. Do you know a Mr. John Preston?"

James Muirhead stood up. "Objection! Relevance?"

Wendy put her hand up. "If you'll allow me I'll prove the relevance."

The judge sat forward. "I'll allow it. Please continue, Ms. Garner."

"You see, my colleague had a rather interesting meeting with Mr. John Preston yesterday afternoon, when in the process of their conversation he admitted to her that not only were you with him in the back seat of your car at the time in question, but your head was so far down the front of his trousers you would have been unable to see anything that was happening!"

James Muirhead was on his feet shouting red-faced. "Objection your honour. I strongly object to this defamation of my client's character by the defence!"

"Sustained! Ms. Garner you will refrain from such inflammatory language," the judge said looking across at her.

"My apologies, your honour," she replied turning back to Christine Atherton who by now resembled a frightened rabbit caught in a car's headlights.

"Miss Atherton, is it true that Mr. John Preston is your boss?"

Christine nodded her head. "Would you reply for the benefit of the jury." Wendy asked.

"Yes." Christine replied.

"And is it also true that you were having a sexual relationship with Mr. Preston at the time of the incident?"

Christine hesitated before answering. "Yes."

Wendy continued, not letting her relax. "Can you tell the court the reason why Mr. Preston declined to be a witness to the incident?"

"He didn't want his wife to know about us," Christine answered.

"But wasn't it just a fling like all the others he'd had with female members of staff? Surely you were aware you weren't the first to satisfy Mr. Preston's inflated ego?" Wendy was in full flow, with Julia sitting at her side smiling and enjoying watching the witness suffer.

James Muirhead was standing again. "Objection. I have to ask the relevance of this line of questioning."

Wendy changed tack. "Do you have a brother Miss Atherton?"

James Muirhead was now like a Jack in a Box. "Objection! Relevance?"

Wendy looked up at the judge. "If you'll allow me, your honour, I believe this question is highly relevant."

The judge waved his hand. "OK Ms. Garner you may continue but be brief."

Wendy looked back at Christine. "Please answer the question."

Christine answered almost under her breath. "Yes I do."

Wendy pushed her again. "And is it true you look after him because he is disabled?"

"Your honour! I fail to see what Miss Atherton's brother has to do with this case." James Muirhead was starting to lose his cool.

Wendy looked at the judge again. "Ms. Garner will you get to the point."

She paused deliberately, knowing she was about to drop a bombshell on the prosecution.

"And was his disability caused by being thrown down the stairs at Georgie's club in 1968 by three men, one of whom was the defendant, Bobby McGregor?"

Christine Atherton immediately burst into tears as James Muirhead turned around to stare at Matt Burgess.

Wendy Garner sat down and straightened her papers smiling at Julia Davies. "No further questions."

The judge seeing that the case had suddenly turned in a different direction hammered his gavel and called for an adjournment.

Back in his chambers James Muirhead was pacing up and down incandescent with rage as Matt Burgess entered accompanied by Ray Law.

"What the hell was that about!" he yelled. "Why didn't we know about her brother?"

Matt was lost for words. Ray tried to calm everything down by suggesting it might not have been brought to the attention of the police at the time.

James Muirhead still carried on pacing. "Well Wendy Garner and Julia Davies found out about it. And who the hell are you?"

Matt spoke up. "I'm sorry James this is ex-DCI Ray Law who I mentioned before. He was originally in charge of the case."

James Muirhead stopped pacing and shook Ray's hand.

"I'm sorry for being so rude Mr. Law. Please accept my apologies. But I have to admit this has completely caught me off guard. It's put a whole new complexion on the case. First of all she's lied about this John Preston character, and now the defence can infer she had a vendetta against the defendant because of what he did to her brother." He sat down at his desk and took a pad of paper from his battered leather briefcase.

"So what do we do now?" Matt asked.

"Anything those two damn women can do, so can we. Gentlemen, and Mr. Law I include you in this, it's time to play them at their own game!"

In Manny Oberstein's office at Westoria Records everyone was buzzing. Janine had called him from her room in San Fransisco after she'd seen a copy of the San Fransisco morning paper, which had a half page photo of Pete and the band, along with a rave review of the gig. It was the same on all the other broadsheets, with the LA Times devoting two pages to the *Hero of the Fillmore* complete with photos of Pete and the band, plus an in-depth review of the show.

"Janine, you are a star, what on earth prompted you to get the guys to play the show after what went on?" Manny asked.

"Like I said to Don, back home we have a saying, *The show must go on'* and I knew Pete wanted to play for the fans and so did the others. Manny I've got to tell you those three guys are awesome. The show is blowing everyone away."

"I know. Bill Graham was on the phone first thing. He wants the guys back for another show as soon as possible. The newspaper reviews have given the album sales a huge boost, and we've just confirmed a run of dates in Europe and the UK." She'd never heard Manny so excited. "How long are you staying in Frisco? I could do with you and Mandy back here ASAP."

Janine looked across at Mandy, who was propped up in bed reading one of the newspapers Janine had ordered to be delivered to their room.

"Well we're booked for another couple of nights, and I'm definitely having dinner down at Fisherman's Wharf tonight, but we'll keep in touch. You've got my number in case you need me urgently. Pete's in Reno tonight, then they've got Santa Fe and Phoenix before they play the Whisky A Go-Go."

"Look we might pull the Santa Fe and Phoenix gigs and reschedule. I need Pete and the band back here to do a TV show which has just been confirmed. It'll be aired the night before the LA gig. In the meantime you take care and enjoy your seafood, it's the best. And Janine, watch your back. That Benny Mulligan is one evil bastard. He's not gonna be too pleased when he sees all this great publicity going down. We need to talk as soon as you get back."

He ended the call and Janine sat down on the bed.

Mandy folded the paper she was reading and dropped it on the floor. "Manny sounds pretty vibed up from what I could hear," she said.

Janine slipped back under the bedclothes. "Yeah, he's desperate for us to get back." She cuddled up to Mandy pulling her night shirt up over her head. "But I was thinking we might continue from where we left off last night. That is if you're not too tired."

CHAPTER SIXTEEN

Bobby McGregor was called to the witness box and sworn in. James Muirhead stood up and looked at him for a while before referring to his notes.

"Where were you on the night in question, Mr. McGregor?"

Bobby was looking pale and tired. "I was with Gerry Fortuna; we'd been to visit an agent friend of his."

"And did you visit The Lexxicon that night with Mr. Fortuna?"

"Yes we did, but there was nobody else there. Gerry wanted to check up on some work that the carpenters had been doing in the dressing rooms." Bobby seemed confident in his reply.

"According to the witness, she saw you and Mr. Fortuna carry something wrapped in plastic sheeting out of the back door of The Lexxicon. What was in the plastic sheeting?" James Muirhead was stopped by Wendy Garner's voice.

"Objection! Mr. Fortuna's name was never mentioned in the witness statement."

"My apologies," James Muirhead replied. "I'll rephrase the question. Did someone else help you carry the plastic sheeting?"

"Yes."

"And was that person Gerry Fortuna?"

Bobby looked at Wendy Garner then back at James Muirhead. "Yes."

"And what was inside the plastic sheeting that was so heavy?" James Muirhead asked.

Bobby hesitated. "What was in the plastic sheeting Mr. McGregor?" James Muirhead repeated his question.

Bobby looked at Wendy Garner again.

"Mr. McGregor would you kindly answer the question, or would you prefer your defence team to do it for you?"

"It was, erm, it was some off cuts of wood and carpet the workmen had left behind," Bobby finally answered.

"And are you usually in the habit of dumping off-cuts of wood and carpet in the canal?" James Muirhead asked with a smirk.

"Erm actually no. We put it in the skip at the side of the canal." Bobby answered.

"I put it to you Mr. McGregor you had the body of Alex Mitchell in the plastic sheet which you dumped in the canal. You then folded the plastic sheet up and put that in the skip."

"Objection!" Wendy's voice rang out.

"Sustained," said the judge.

"Can you explain how a bloody fingerprint happened to get onto the plastic sheet which was later recovered from the skip, Mr. McGregor?"

"I cut my finger on a nail which was sticking out of one of the pieces of wood." Bobby answered.

"Are you sure of that Mr. McGregor?" James Muirhead continued to pester Bobby trying to confuse him with minor details.

"Yes, yes. I, er caught it as we were picking the wood up in the dressing room. I remember Gerry was annoyed that the workmen had left it in a mess." He seemed satisfied with his answer.

James Muirhead paused. "So would it surprise you to know according to the forensic results that it wasn't only your blood on the sheet but also Alex Mitchell's, Mr. McGregor?" The loud murmur from the public sitting in the gallery caused the judge to call for order.

James Muirhead allowed the noise to die down.

"Now Mr. McGregor, going back to what you said earlier, that you and Gerry Fortuna were alone in the club, are you sure this was the case?" James Muirhead was leading him down a dangerous path. "Wasn't Alex Mitchell there as well?"

"Objection! The prosecution is leading the witness." Wendy was on her feet.

"I'll rephrase. Did you see Alex Mitchell or anyone else in the club that night?"

James Muirhead was intent on getting Bobby to admit that Alex was there.

"No!" Bobby almost shouted his answer. "And it couldn't have been his blood. He wasn't there."

Sensing the opportune moment for a break, the judge announced an adjournment for lunch and left the court as everyone stood.

Janine and Mandy were seated in Alioto's on Fisherman's Wharf, an Italian-owned seafood restaurant established in 1925. They had decided after Manny's reaction to Janine's call earlier, that it might be a good idea to get back to LA sooner than they had planned. Although Janine had insisted she wasn't coming all the way up to Frisco without eating some of her favourite seafood. They'd foregone starters in favour of a Negroni for Janine and a Manhattan for Mandy, which they sat sipping whilst taking in the magnificent view of the Golden Gate Bridge.

Janine had decided on a Cioppino which the waiter had described as a delightful seafood stew containing mussels, clams, prawns, scallops and calamari served in a seafood broth with carrots, fennel, Roma tomatoes, celery and saffron, topped with garlic croutons. She could hardly contain her excitement. Mandy who had admitted she was not a huge fan of seafood had decided on a Prime New York strip cooked medium rare served with fries.

Janine's face was a picture of joy as she savoured each mouthful of her seafood stew, whilst Mandy methodically set about her huge piece of beef. They'd chosen a bottle of the house Chardonnay from a local vineyard to go with their food, and finished off with coffees. The atmosphere between them was erotic as they walked back to their hotel, but Janine was aware that they were being followed by two suspicious looking men. She'd noticed them as they left the restaurant.

Without alarming Mandy she flagged down a taxi and pushed her inside, despite her complaining they were only a few minutes from the hotel. Janine asked the driver to take them to the Ashbury Heights area, and sat back as they sped off, leaving the two men standing on the sidewalk. Mandy was still looking confused as the taxi dropped them five minutes later, but Janine made the excuse of fancying a coffee and Mandy seemed to believe her.

While they were sitting drinking their coffees, Janine thought back to what she could remember of the two men. They were both black, well-built and wearing long coats and sunglasses, similar to the two men who had caused the disturbance at the Fillmore the previous night. She would have to talk to Don as soon as he got back to LA, which thankfully would be tomorrow thanks to Manny cancelling the two dates Pete was due to play. She wished Ray was here; he'd know what to do. She made up her mind to call him as soon as she got back to the hotel. She hated to admit it, but she missed him and needed him more than ever.

Ray was in James Muirhead's chambers with Matt Burgess, reflecting on the morning's events. Bobby McGregor had started off quite confidently, obviously having been well coached by Wendy and Julia, but as the questions from the prosecution got more intense he started to crack under pressure, resulting in the outburst at the end.

"What's your plan for the next session?" Ray asked.

"I need him to admit that Alex was there." James was thoughtful for a few seconds. "To be honest, I don't think he killed Alex Mitchell. He probably helped, but if you look at his record, it's only ever for violence using his hands. Killing someone with a gun just doesn't fit for me."

Matt joined in. "So what you're saying is Gerry Fortuna was the one who pulled the trigger?"

"Of the two of them, I'd say it was more likely to be him," James Muirhead replied. "Trouble is he's not here to defend himself, so we have to make do with what we've got."

Ray was faced with a major dilemma. Should he tell them what Janine had overheard, which would surely involve bringing her back as a witness, and almost certainly end their relationship? Or should he remain quiet, and hope that James Muirhead's skill as a prosecutor would be enough? The one thing he did know was he needed a drink, and so he made an excuse and left Muirhead's chambers heading for the pub across the road. As he was walking down the corridor, one of his old friends who worked as a secretary in the courts spotted him and called his name.

"Hey, Ray Law?"

Ray turned and recognised her from the many times he'd been in court.

"I'm glad I've caught you. There's a message for you from America. It was left first thing this morning but no one could find you. Come to my office, it's written down there."

The secretary gave Ray the piece of paper with the number written on it. The message said 'Please call me. Urgent. Janine.' But Ray didn't recognise the area code. It certainly wasn't LA, so he asked if there was an International telephone directory he could use. The secretary found a dog-eared copy, and he looked up the number which was for San Fransisco. 'What was Janine doing in San Fransisco, and what was so urgent for her to phone?'

He asked if it would be alright to use the phone in the office, and although it was highly irregular according to his friend, she said as long as he wasn't on for ever it would be OK, just this once. He dialled the number and felt his heart beating fast as he heard it ringing in the States.

The phone was answered by a female voice, but it wasn't Janine.

"Hi can I speak to Janine Fortuna please," he said nervously.

"Oh hey yeah, is that Ray? I'm Mandy, Janine's friend. Hang on I'll fetch her for you."

He heard Mandy calling Janine and footsteps, then she was there. "Hey Ray, it's Janine, how are you? Can you hear me?"

Ray smiled at her question. "Of course I can hear you. I'm fine, but what's the urgency? I've just received your message. I'm at the Law Courts using their phone, so I can't talk for long."

"Ray I miss you," she said. "I think I'm in trouble and I need you here now. When can you come back?"

"Hang on, what do you mean, you're in trouble? What's going on? Is it Pete? What's he done now?"

He was aware his friend hovering nearby looking at her watch.

"No, it's nothing to do with Pete, he's great. It's just there was an incident at the gig here in San Fransisco here last night, and I think it's the Rota Bocan again. There was a letter with my name on, the same as Gerry received. Then two guys were following me and Mandy earlier. I'm scared Ray."

Ray could detect the tenseness in her voice.

"Look the case is almost finished here, and I was wondering what I was going to do after what you said. Do you mean you've changed your mind about me not coming back?"

She laughed at the other end of the phone. "You are an idiot Ray Law. Of course I didn't mean it! We say stupid things when we're angry, and I was angry. But everything's changed. So get your arse back over here, I need you, and I love you."

Ray's friend was getting agitated and he nodded to her he understood.

"Look Janine I have to go; can I call you later? Where will you be tonight?"

"Mandy and I are driving back to LA in a few hour's time, it's the middle of the night here at the moment, but I'll be home later."

"OK I'll call you then. And I love you too." Ray put the phone down and apologised to his friend feeling slightly embarrassed.

"Don't worry about it," she said with a smile. "And good luck with the case, I hear it's pretty tough going."

"Yeah thanks," he replied as he thought he needed that drink more than ever now.

CHAPTER SEVENTEEN

Matt was standing in the corner of the bar on his own. He looked up as Ray approached. "Hey man, where've you been, I got you a pint." He passed Ray the glass.

"You're not going to believe this, but I've just been talking to Janine in the States. She wants me to go back as soon as possible."

"That's great news. With a bit of luck James reckons he'll have the case all wrapped up in the next day or so. So how's Janine then?"

"Well that's just it, she called because she's got some trouble with those Miami guys again, the Rota Bocan, I'm calling her tonight so I'll know more then, but it sounds worrying."

Matt glanced at his watch and finished the rest of his pint. "Listen we'd better get back, I don't like keeping James Muirhead waiting, he's a bit of a stickler for time."

They both left the bar just as the defence team were heading back to court.

"Ray, hold on a minute," he heard Julia's voice from behind as he was about to enter the front doors. She came up to him as Wendy Garner carried on into the court building.

"We haven't spoken since the hotel, and I was wondering if we could get a drink later. Maybe have something to eat back at my place?" She gave him a sultry smile.

"You don't cook at your place," Ray replied, guessing where the conversation was leading.

"Well I was thinking of eating you if the truth be told," she said lowering her voice and leaning in to him.

Ray moved away slightly. "Julia. You know as well as I do, it would be completely out of order to be with you whilst the case was proceeding."

"It's never stopped us before," she replied looking slightly hurt.

"Well this time it's different." Matt was at the door waving to him.

"Look I have to go."

He ran up the steps and disappeared inside leaving her standing on her own. She lit a cigarette angrily puffing on it before dropping it on the floor and stomping on it with her high-heeled shoe.

Bobby McGregor had been reminded he was still under oath after the prosecution's cross-examination and Wendy Garner stood up for her rebuttal, looking across the courtroom at him.

"Mr. McGregor can you tell the court your movements on the day in question?"

Bobby thought for a moment. "Gerry Fortuna rang me in the afternoon and said he wanted to go to meet an agent about booking the artists for The Lexxicon."

"And where was this agent?" Wendy asked.

"In Leicester."

"Please continue."

"Then when we came back, Gerry wanted to go to The Lexxicon to check up on some work the builders had been doing in the dressing rooms. The opening night was only a few days away, and he wanted to make sure everything was finished."

"And was it finished?"

"It was finished, but they'd left a load of wood and carpet pieces lying about, so Gerry and I gathered them up and took them out the back to throw in a skip." Bobby sounded confident.

"And whilst you were in the club you didn't see anyone else?"

"No, there was just me and Gerry."

Wendy sat down.

"Mr. McGregor," James Muirhead was on his feet again. "You say you drove to Leicester to see an agent with Gerry Fortuna. Can you remember where you went?"

Bobby shook his head. "No, I can't remember, Gerry was driving."

James Muirhead continued. "And when you got back to The Lexxicon you helped Gerry take out the rubbish, and the club was empty apart from the two of you. Is that correct?"

"Yes," Bobby replied.

James Muirhead shuffled his notes separating a sheet of paper which he laid down on the table in front of him.

"I think you're lying, Mr. McGregor! I'll tell you what really happened. Gerry Fortuna rang you in the afternoon and told you to meet him at The Lexxicon that evening. He said he'd spoken to an agent friend of his who would ring Alex Mitchell and arrange to meet him at the club on the pretence of showing him around. Once there, he would get Alex in the dressing room and encourage him to describe the scam they could set up similar to the one he had at Rudi's, while you and Gerry Fortuna listened in the next room. After he'd done that, and with ten thousand pounds cash in his pocket, he would conveniently disappear. Leaving you and Gerry to deal with Alex. How am I doing so far?" James Muirhead looked at Bobby who shook his head.

"That's not true. We were on our own!"

James Muirhead picked up the sheet of paper on his desk and waved it at Bobby.

"Not according to the statement by the agent from Leicester!"

Wendy stood up. "Objection! What statement? The defence has not seen the statement."

"Sustained" The judge said.

James Muirhead waited calmly, and when she sat down he continued.

"You see Mr. McGregor, I think this is where things started to go wrong. You went along with Gerry Fortuna wanting to teach Alex Mitchell a lesson. He was the kind of person who didn't like people ripping him off, and once he heard Alex admit he'd done it to him at Rudi's, you knew he was in trouble. What you didn't expect was for Alex to produce a gun. And the moment you saw him threaten your boss you intervened, and in the struggle the gun went off and Alex Mitchell died."

Bobby was looking highly agitated. "No! No! That's not what happened. He was pointing the gun at Gerry and when I punched him he dropped it. Gerry wanted to hurt him, and hit him a few times with a piece of wood while I held him. But then he went mad and really started to smash his hands, and I said I thought that was enough. Gerry had this weird look on his face and when he spotted the gun he just picked it up and shot him. I couldn't believe it."

James Muirhead had been standing listening intently. "And what happened next?"

"Gerry suddenly became calm and told me to help him wrap the body in the plastic sheeting he'd found. Then we dumped him in the canal along with the gun. I noticed the skip, and hid the plastic sheet in there afterwards. I didn't kill him I swear." Bobby broke down in tears.

Wendy Garner looked at Julia Davies, who just sat shaking her head slowly from side to side looking shell shocked.

The judge loudly banged his gavel, and announced he was adjourning the session for the day, leaving the court as everyone stood.

Ray made his way down from the Public Gallery and knocked on James Muirhead's chambers as Julia Davies walked slowly past.

"A drink across the road?" she asked. "Help me drown my sorrows?"

"Where's your friend Ms. Garner when you need her?"

"Oh her! Well when I dropped by her chambers to ask if she wanted to join us, I caught the right honourable lady in flagrante delicto with an extremely well-endowed young clerk from Court Two," she replied.

The door opened and Ray smiled. "OK but just the one, I've got a plane to catch tomorrow," he said before turning and heading for the prosecutor's chambers.

James Muirhead was pouring out the whisky as Ray walked in. Matt Burgess was already there with a glass in his hand.

"So what do you think the verdict will be?" Ray asked accepting a very large cut glass tumbler of James Muirhead's deliciously peaty Highland Park Single Malt.

"It's down to the judge and jury now, but I'd suggest conspiracy to commit murder. You and Matt here did a great job finding that agent, I have to say."

After the shock of the revelation about Christine Atherton's brother, James Muirhead had asked Matt and Ray to find the phone records of Gerry Fortuna from the day that Alex Mitchell was killed. According to Ray's log, he knew Alex was interviewed at the police headquarters by the two of them on the same morning, with Gerry Fortuna watching in the observation room.

"Yes, that's correct. I remember him not being too happy when he left," Ray had said.

"So we need to find a connection between Gerry leaving the police station and the events of that night." James Muirhead had scribbled a note down on his pad. "Why did he go to the club, and what happened there? If we can find a link we may have a chance of derailing the defence."

Matt and Ray had set off back to Matt's office to make some calls.

First, Matt had contacted the telephone engineer he knew, who had recorded the phone call that helped catch Sergeant Seamus Byrne during the enquiry into the bombing of Rudi's, and asked if he could help them with Gerry's phone records. While they were waiting for him to call back, Matt contacted Gerry's bank. After explaining to a very cautious manager why they wanted to see the account details and how it was linked to a murder case, he reluctantly agreed to give them a copy.

Fortunately the telephone engineer was able to come up with what they wanted pretty quickly, and Ray noticed something straight away. There had only been four calls that day to and from the FAM office phone. An incoming call first thing, which was when George Williams had called to invite Gerry to hear the interview with Alex Mitchell, an outgoing call to an unknown number, an incoming call from the same number and another outgoing call which he identified as being Bobby McGregor. He traced the unknown number to an entertainment agent based in Leicester. When he called, he was told by his secretary that the man was not available. Ray wasn't to be put off, and explained he was trying to contact him about a very important show he was organising, and the agent had been highly recommended. He also said there was an awful lot of money involved, at which point the secretary said she would call him back.

By that time the trace which Matt had organised had given them the address of the office. Ray had a hunch, and Matt called the telephone engineer again and asked if he could get them the records of the Leicester number, and once again he replied within minutes. Matt was going to owe him a big drink he thought, as he read the message. It only took Ray a short time to find the incoming call from Gerry's office and then the return call, but in between was an outgoing call to another number which he thought he knew but couldn't place. Then it dawned on him. It was Alex Mitchell's number. He remembered calling him to arrange the meeting. It was all starting to fall into place.

At the same time, Matt had been checking Gerry's bank account, and on the day in question there was a cash withdrawal for ten thousand pounds. Maybe this was just what James Muirhead was looking for. They both grabbed their coats and headed out to Matt's car.

The agent's office was in a converted garage attached to his house, situated on a rough-looking housing estate just outside Leicester city centre. After showing his warrant card, Matt and Ray were invited in by a lady, who's voice Ray recognised as the secretary he'd spoken to earlier. She led them through to a small room with walls covered in photographs of artists, the majority of whom Ray had never heard of.

The agent looked nervous and was initially cagey about answering any questions concerning Gerry Fortuna, but when Matt explained they had records of the calls between him and Gerry on the day of Alex Mitchell's murder, and were investigating a sum of cash totalling ten thousand pounds, he visibly paled. He admitted he'd accepted the money from Gerry but had only agreed to entice Alex to the club. He said Gerry had told him he suspected Alex had ripped him off before at Rudi's, and wanted to get the truth. He said he'd done as Gerry had asked. He tricked Alex into offering him a deal to set up a fictitious company that would book the artists. Then they would cream money off the top and split it between them without Gerry knowing. But he said he left the minute Gerry and Bobby had entered the dressing room, and had no idea what had happened until he saw the reports in the English newspapers a few days later. He was in Spain at the time, having spent a good chunk of the money on a holiday. He'd kept his head down ever since, hoping he wouldn't be implicated.

Matt got him to sign a statement of what he'd just told them, and he and

Ray left him in his office with a warning not to think of leaving the country again for the foreseeable future.

"So what's your next move mate?" Matt asked Ray as he savoured the burn of the single malt.

"I'll be on the first available flight to LA in the morning, but if you'll excuse me there's just one more thing I need to do before I go."

He shook hands with James Muirhead and Matt and subtly placed the glass containing the rest of his whisky behind a vase of flowers as he left the room.

Julia Davies was waiting for him at the bar across the road, and waved as he entered. She was on her own nursing a half empty flute of champagne.

"Can I get you another one of those?" Ray asked.

"Well I was hoping I could persuade you to come back to my place," Julia said stroking his arm suggestively. "I'm going to need some comforting after the defeat we've suffered today."

"Sorry, I can't oblige you Julia. I'm off down to London tonight. I have an early flight back to LA first thing tomorrow. I just thought I'd say goodbye one last time."

Julia drank the champagne back in one.

"In that case, good luck, Ray, you're gonna need it." She kissed him on the cheek. "Now where's that charming solicitor I met earlier?" she said as she turned away and disappeared into the mass of people at the bar.

CHAPTER EIGHTEEN

Ray had driven down to Heathrow Airport, and checked into the Holiday Inn about the same time as Janine was arriving home at Hermosa Beach. She and Mandy had left straight after breakfast, and had had a trouble-free drive back home. Janine noticed Mandy was a little quiet on the journey.

"You really dig this guy, Ray?" she asked as they arrived at Janine's house.

"Yeah, I really do, and it wasn't until the events of the past few days that I realised just how much." Janine replied. "Hey look, don't get me wrong, what you and I have had is amazing and I'll never forget it. You've introduced me to a part of myself that I didn't know existed. But Ray is someone special, and right now I need him more than ever. What happened in the Fillmore frightened me, and then being followed by those two guys. He'll know what to do, and I need to speak to Don as well. There's something not right and I don't know what it is, but once he's back I'll feel better."

Mandy gave her a hug and was just leaving when the phone rang.

Janine closed the door and ran to pick up the receiver.

"Hey it's me. I'll be with you tomorrow evening." Ray's voice sounded so reassuring she almost cried.

"Baby, just get here, I need you so much," she said. "Where are you?"

"I'm at the Holiday Inn at Heathrow. The flight's early tomorrow morning. Is everything alright? You sounded worried when we spoke earlier."

"Everything will be fine once you're back here."

"Who was the girl who answered the phone at your hotel when I phoned? Why was she in your room in the middle of the night?"

"Oh that was Mandy, she's Manny Oberstein's secretary and a good friend. We went up to San Fransisco together to watch Pete."

"Oh well at least it wasn't another guy I suppose," he said jokingly.

"Look this call must be costing a fortune, I'll tell you everything when I see you tomorrow. I love you!"

"And I love you too," Ray said as he ended the call.

Mandy had driven away from Janine's house but stopped just around the corner to make a call lasting two minutes. When she finished she drove back to her apartment in West Hollywood, stopping off to pick up a chilli dog from Pinks on La Brea.

Pete and the band travelled from San Fransisco to Reno which was only a short trip for a change, spending most of the journey watching movies and drinking the large box of beers that Bill Graham had given them. Don was relieved that Manny had pulled the next couple of shows, happy to be heading back to LA after the gig.

They had a day off and then a TV show before the Whisky A Go-Go gig, which he knew was going to be massive. All the press and movers and shakers would be there, and it was the gig that would boost their profile and record sales. The one dark cloud on the horizon was what had happened at the Fillmore. Don was suspicious that the problem he had talked to Janine and Ray about back at the studio in LA could be rearing its ugly head once more, only this time on home soil. He would have to speak to Janine and make sure they kept it away from Manny as much as possible.

The sound check at the club in Reno hadn't gone as smoothly as usual, and there seemed to be an atmosphere amongst the guys which Don noticed as he sat by the sound desk. Although he wouldn't normally interfere, he took Marshall the drummer to one side after they finished. "What's the problem? I'm picking up a strange vibe from you guys tonight."

"Man I think we need to keep an eye on Pete. He seems to be in a mood for some reason. I saw him make a phone call earlier, then after that he went weird."

"I'll be glad to get back to LA," Don said. "Leave it to me, I'll have a word with him."

Don saw Pete coming out of the dressing room and called him. "Hey man, what's happening?" Don said cheerily.

Pete looked troubled. "Just spoke to Nadja on the phone and she's giving me grief 'cos I haven't called her. Wants to know what I'm doing and when we're getting back."

Don patted him on the shoulder. "Listen you don't need that kind of shit going on, especially just before a gig. Tell her to chill out until you get back. Anyway, I know for a fact there's a lady here tonight who will definitely make your troubles go away." He smiled at Pete. "Better get some rest, she just loves lead singers, you get what I'm sayin'!"

And he was right. Carole was a thirty-year-old blonde with a great figure, who took no time in letting Pete know she was his for after the show. She stood at the front of the stage and never took her eyes off him for a second during the whole set. She wore an *In Flames* T-shirt deliberately a size too small, to accentuate her voluptuous breasts, and skin-tight blue Levis that looked like they'd been sprayed on, with a pair of high-heeled black leather boots.

The gig was great, although the crowd wasn't as big as usual due to some kind of political rally happening the same night in the Town Hall. Pete wasn't too bothered for once when Don introduced him to Carole who he'd brought backstage after the show. She explained she always liked to collect a souvenir from the lead singer, as she led Pete out of the dressing room to the privacy of her large RV on the parking lot out the back of the venue. Pete's eyes nearly popped out of his head when she opened the sliding side-door, to reveal a double bed, soft lighting and a drinks cabinet, with the inside covered in luxurious shag carpet. He opened them a couple of bottles of beer as she pulled her T-shirt over her head allowing her breasts to flop free. The next minute she had wriggled out of her jeans, and was now concentrating on Pete's belt. She certainly knew how to operate in confined spaces he thought to himself, as she soon had his jeans and shorts off. Pinning him down on the mattress she lowered herself on to him. He wasn't sure what she wanted as a souvenir, but right now she could have anything she wished, watching her breasts bouncing up and down while she rode him. He couldn't help but laugh to himself, imagining the sight from the dressing room of the van lurching on its springs. The sound of her groaning was getting louder the more excited she got until finally she came with a squeal that could be heard in the next street.

Ten minutes later as he walked back into the dressing room, Don couldn't wait to ask Pete what souvenir she'd claimed.

"She wanted my boxer shorts," he said as Don and the guys started to laugh. "And she nicked my neckerchief as well."

"You know we ought to have a conversation about your neckerchiefs man. We should get them on the merchandise stall. We could make a fortune."

Pete looked at him. "Yeah but at whose expense?"

"Wait until we get up to Chicago and you get to meet the Plaster Caster," Marshall the drummer said laughing. "You better be on top form that night."

Pete looked confused.

"Don't worry man you'll find out soon enough." Randy the bass player added.

Janine had driven to meet Ray at LAX. He'd managed to sleep for some of the flight, although being in Economy instead of First Class he'd noticed the difference in comfort. He'd got through Passport Control, and found his bag quickly as it came round on the carousel. He walked through the doorway into the Arrivals hall scanning the sea of faces waiting for their loved ones. He heard a scream, and suddenly Janine rushed up and launched herself at him, throwing her arms around him and covering his face with kisses. When they eventually untangled themselves he had chance to stand back and look at her.

"Wow, you look fantastic, the sun really suits you."

"Just wait until you see my tan marks," she replied taking his hand as they walked towards the car park.

Neither of them noticed the tall olive-skinned man wearing sunglasses as he followed them across the concourse.

Pete arrived back about the same time at Whitland Studios, where Don had arranged to drop everyone. He'd phoned Nadja as soon as he got off the bus and she'd told him to wait there until she picked him up. Both the drummer and the keyboard player had left their cars at the studios, and had driven off, while Randy the bass player was having a scene with the studio receptionist and was waiting for her to finish her shift. While he was waiting for Nadja, Pete had called Janine, but there was no reply, so he'd got himself a coffee and settled down in the cafe. Eventually Nadja arrived in her Bentley, looking slightly dishevelled as if she'd just got out of bed.

Pete was in a foul mood by this time, and threw his bag on the back seat, slamming the door as he got in.

"I'm sorry baby, I was tied up and couldn't get away," she said apologetically, reaching over to kiss him, but Pete pulled away.

"Don't you mean you were in bed," he said accusingly. "Who was it this time, another new singer!"

"Baby, how can you think like that?" she replied looking sad. "You know how much I've missed you. I told you the other night when you called."

"Don't you mean how much grief you gave me when I called," he stared out of the side window looking away from her.

"I know what you need," she said as she started up the Bentley, "And I'm taking you home to give it to you right now."

She crunched the car into gear and slipped her hand across to his crotch stroking him as she pulled away.

Janine and Ray had celebrated his return with sex and champagne in equal measures, and were lying back on their bed listening to the ocean as the waves dashed against the beach below. It had been an idyllic homecoming and Ray felt great to be back, but at the same time noticed something about Janine had changed. He couldn't quite figure out what it was, but he knew she was somehow different. Maybe it wasn't the right time to broach the subject so soon after getting back, so he decided to let it ride for now, but there would come a time to talk.

Janine had put on her kimono and walked over to the balcony looking out to sea. "I'm so glad you're back. There was an incident up in San Fransisco that really frightened me." She picked up an envelope that was lying on the table. "There were two masked men who burst into the venue and fired a shotgun into the ceiling. I was so scared; it was just like the time at Georgie's. Don was amazing, he shot one of the guys in the shoulder and they ran off. Then this was left for me at the box office, it's exactly the same as the one that Gerry received."

She passed the envelope to Ray who took the sheet of paper out and studied it.

"Don was worried about this when we spoke at the studios before the tour started," he said concerned. "I think we need to have a meeting with him and see what he thinks. Maybe we don't involve Manny just yet. We don't want him panicking and pulling the tour. In fact didn't he cancel a couple of gigs already?"

"Yeah but that was because of the distance they had to travel, and there's a TV show tomorrow that he said is more important. He wants the Whisky gig to be sold out. That reminds me, I need to call Pete to make sure he's OK. They should be back by now."

She picked up the phone and dialled Pete's number letting it ring until she replaced it.

"I bet I know where he is," she said smiling. "Up to his balls in Nadja if I know Pete."

Ray seized the opportunity. "Do you miss him?"

"Miss him? What makes you ask that?"

"Well you did have a pretty intense scene with him at one time, remember."

She looked at him with a hurt expression. "Look babe, that was a long time ago, and believe me I have no feelings for Pete whatsoever, apart from him making me a lot of money. Do you think I would have asked you to come here with me if I still had something going with him?"

"Well, I don't know what it is, but since I've been away you've changed. I can feel it in the way we made love. I mean, tell me I'm wrong." He held her hands in his and looked into her eyes.

She started to cry and he pulled her to him.

"I'm sorry, so sorry," she uttered into his shoulder. She pulled away. "I didn't know what I was doing. Manny's secretary and I went out for a drink at this bar and when we met she kissed me."

"Lots of women kiss each other when they meet."

"No Ray I mean kissed me! Full on, her lips on mine, kissed me."

"Ah right. So what did you think?" he asked trying to be delicate.

"Well to be honest I didn't know what to think. At first I was shocked, but then I found myself feeling excited and the next thing I knew we were in a taxi on our way back here. Oh my god, Ray it was the most erotic night of sex I've had in my life! And don't look like that, this was completely different. She did things to me that I could never imagine."

"So where does that leave us?" he asked looking slightly puzzled.

"It leaves us exactly where we were before you left. I need you more than ever. It was fun, amazing, sexual, but not you! When we're together there's nothing like it in the world. And it was only after doing what I did I realised how much I loved you. Now take me back to bed and show me what I missed so much," she said kissing him.

CHAPTER NINETEEN

Don had arranged for the band and Pete to meet at Whitland studios so they could all travel together to the TV studio. He'd called Janine first thing to let her know the address and time they were arriving. She and Ray were already there sitting in reception when the coach pulled up, and she was surprised and secretly thrilled that there was a crowd of about a hundred girls waiting outside for Pete and the band. Her mood changed rapidly when she saw a dishevelled Pete climbing off the coach with Nadja alongside him holding his hand. He looked a wreck, and was hardly paying attention to the fans who were calling to him. She was on her feet waiting at the entrance as he walked in, and gave Nadja a stare that left her in doubt as to what she was thinking. Nadja excused herself, leaving Pete to face Janine's wrath as she pulled him to one side out of earshot.

"What the fuck do you think you're doing?"

Pete had seen her annoyed before, but even he was afraid.

"Just look at the state of you, you look like a bag of shit, and you don't smell much different. Have you been home since you got back?" She was shaking with rage.

"Er no, Nadja picked me up from the studios and took me back to her place." He was shuffling from side to side.

"Why the hell didn't you call me?"

"I did but there was no reply, and I couldn't leave a message," he said defensively.

She remembered she must have been at the airport meeting Ray.

"Look Pete, this show is really important. Manny cancelled two gigs so you could do it. You need to go and get yourself together. Then afterwards we need to have a serious talk; there's things happening I don't like. And promise me when you've finished rehearsing, you'll go straight over to those girls who've been waiting outside all day. You just totally ignored them. They buy your records, and don't forget that!"

Don appeared looking flustered and beckoned Pete to follow him.

"Hey Janine, let's grab a coffee once I've got the guys sorted," he said as he disappeared down a corridor with Pete following behind him.

He returned five minutes later more relaxed, and suggested they go to the Green Room where it was a bit more private.

Finally he sat down with a coffee in his hand and breathed a sigh of relief.

"Man those guys are hard work some days," he blew across his cup. "So did Janine tell you what happened up in 'Frisco, Ray?"

Ray sat up in his seat. He'd been transfixed watching what was happening in the studio on the monitor.

"Yeah, the two guys who tried to sabotage the gig and then the message. I've seen the sheet of paper. It's the same as Gerry received in Birmingham before the club was blown up. But I'm having difficulty linking the two, because the Rota Bocan had no connection to the bombing, so why are they getting involved now?"

"According to Bill Graham they've been trying to take over the drugs scene up there for a while. Maybe it was just a coincidence. But how did they know Janine was going to be there?" Don was puzzled.

"And why the message?" Ray asked. "She's got nothing to do with their business."

Don thought for a moment. "I don't want to mention this to Manny right now, he's got far too much on his plate. I think he might freak out and we don't want that happening."

"Yeah I agree, we were talking about it before." Ray said. "Janine told me you had a bit of a cannon you shot one of the two guys with, is that right?

Don reached round his back. "You mean this?" He pulled his Smith and Wesson Model 28 Magnum from the waistband of his trousers and offered it to Ray, holding it by the barrel.

"I hate guns," Janine had been quiet up to now but pulled a face.

"Yeah well sometimes nothin' else will do," Don said.

Ray was holding the gun very cautiously. "In a way I'm glad the police over in the UK don't carry firearms, although more and more criminals are starting to get hold of them."

"I'm just glad you're out of it and over here," Janine said.

"So what do we know so far?" Ray asked changing the subject back to the reason they were there.

"Two guys up in 'Frisco approached me as we were unloading, and I'm sure it was the same two who came in and tried to shoot the place up. I winged one of them, so maybe we could find out if anyone turned up at any of the hospitals in the region with a gunshot wound to his left shoulder. Someone had left the envelope at the box office during the afternoon, but it wasn't discovered until after the shooting."

Janine suddenly remembered something. "Oh god I forgot. Mandy and I went for a meal on Fisherman's Wharf the next night and because it was only a short distance from the hotel we decided to walk. Then on the way back two guys were following us. I wouldn't swear to it but they looked pretty similar in height to the two in the club."

"What did you do? You never told me about this." Ray asked.

"I just flagged down a cab and we went up to Ashbury Heights and had a coffee before going back later."

"What did Mandy say about all this?" Don asked. "Wasn't she worried or frightened?"

Janine thought a moment. "Well she was concerned about the guns in the Fillmore. In fact she laid down on the floor when it was all happening. But I didn't tell her why we'd jumped in a cab, I just said I wanted a coffee."

"And how did you leave it when you got back?" Don asked.

"Cool I suppose. She dropped me back to my place and left saying she'd catch up next time I was in Westoria." She gave Ray a look which Don picked up on but decided not to comment.

"I gotta say one thing right now which I think needs sorting out before we go any further." Don announced.

"Nadja!" Both Janine and Don said it together.

"Man she's fucking with his brain, apart from anything else." Don seemed concerned.

"Yeah I'm aware of that situation, leave it with me, I'll deal with Pete. We have history," Janine said staring at Ray.

Suddenly the door burst open and the band all came in looking for beers and food which was laid out in the corner. Ray surreptitiously passed the gun back to Don who slipped it back under his shirt as he walked out of the door.

The show that Pete was appearing on was a new addition to the network, and featured news and events with a live music slot at the end. It was hosted by Alan Brookstein, the latest in a long line of young chat show hosts all desperate to get on the ladder to success. Janine was fascinated by how the production team all carried out their roles, ensuring everything ran according to the tight schedule. It was being broadcast in front of a live audience so there was no room for mistakes, and the pressure on the studio floor was intense. Pete and the band were to perform *In Flames* as the single taken from the album. The presenter would talk briefly to Pete before introducing the song, and they would play the show out with the credits rolling over the ending.

Janine didn't think she'd ever been so nervous in her life. Her hands were shaking so much she could hardly drink from the glass she held in her hand. And when she looked at the studio audience she nearly had a heart attack. Sitting in the front row was Manny Oberstein, Mandy and the rest of the sales and promotion team along with most of Westoria's staff.

Pete strolled onto the set just before his section, looking cool in his gleaming white shirt and black leather trousers. Janine had never seen him so focussed, and as she watched him talking to the presenter in the short interview and then playing the song, she couldn't help but shed a tear. She hoped wherever he was, Gerry could see that he'd been right. But now it was up to her to make sure he went all the way.

For once Pete had listened to Janine when they sat down together after the TV show. She had explained how important it was for Pete's image that he looked great at all times. He was now being photographed on a regular basis, and although she agreed with him that he was fundamentally a rock star, Manny and his team wanted more of a Vince Boyd persona than a rebel. He'd gone home that night and slept alone in his apartment. As a consequence he had turned up at the club looking rested, healthy and fit. Even the band had commented how much better he looked when he walked on stage for the sound check. The Alan Brookstein Show had done the trick. Any remaining tickets were snapped up, and the queue of excited rock fans stretched down Sunset Boulevard. Don was busy sorting out the tickets for Manny and the team when all hell broke loose at the stage door. He knew without looking who it would be, and he wasn't wrong. Nadja was screaming at the security guard whose job it was to make sure only people with the correct pass could get backstage to the dressing rooms. He was patiently trying to tell her that she had a guest pass, but not an access all areas pass, which meant she could watch the show but nothing else. She was demanding to see Pete, who was in the middle of the run through, and the irritated guard had found Don to see if he could help.

"Hey Nadja," he said trying to appear calm. "I'm sorry but Pete's busy right now. As soon as he's finished I'll let him know you're here." He turned to go.

"But I have to see him urgently," she said sounding agitated.

He stopped and explained again. "Like I just said he's busy at the moment. As you know, he's got a very important show tonight and they're getting the sound together which is why he can't be disturbed."

"I don't give a shit what he's doing," she screeched. "You get him now. I tell him what he does. He listens to what I say. I have the plans ready for the show."

Don laughed. "Well I think Janine Fortuna might have something to say about that."

He walked away as she shouted after him. "He does what I say, not her. She knows nothing."

Don raised his eyebrows and chuckled to himself as he thought he'd pay good money to be a fly on the wall during the confrontation between Nadja and Janine.

Pete wisely remained backstage after Don told him about Nadja. He was beginning to find her a nuisance, especially as he was becoming so popular with all the women after the shows. She'd run her course of being useful, and it was time to draw a line and move on. He wasn't quite sure how he was going to do it, but he'd cross that bridge when he came to it. Right now there were some interviews with the press to do and he was starving, so he grabbed a sandwich while he had chance.

Janine was in the foyer with Manny, Ray and Don when Nadja came striding up.

"What the fuck is going on?" she demanded. "Why can't I see Pete? I have the plans all ready for his show which I have to discuss."

Manny and Janine looked at each other.

"I think we need to talk," Janine said as she guided Nadja towards the Ladies Restroom gripping her arm tightly. The door slammed open against the wall as Janine propelled Nadja in before her. She grabbed her by the throat and pushed her up against the wall.

"Let's get one thing straight you Russian piece of shit. You have nothing to do with Pete Peterson unless I say so." She was yelling inches away from Nadja's face. "Get it? Now before I do something I'll regret, get the fuck out of here. And don't even think of trying to speak to Pete again. Do I make myself perfectly clear?"

She let go of Nadja who ran out of the door crying.

Janine slowly walked to the hand basin and washed her hands, meticulously drying them on the paper towels. She stood looking at her reflection in the mirror for a few moments before returning to the guys.

Don gave her a hug. "I said to Pete I didn't ever want to get on the wrong side of you."

Janine smiled but was glad they hadn't seen the tears she'd shed before she left the restroom. 'What they don't know won't do them any harm' she thought.

Finally it was showtime, and the buzz around the packed room was deafening. Pete and the band absolutely tore the place apart. From the first minute he strutted on stage the crowd were with him every step of the way. It was amazing how many were singing along to every song, knowing all the words, even better than Pete on a couple of occasions. Manny was standing next to Janine and Ray with a wide grin on his face, and she could have sworn there were dollar signs in his eyes when he looked at her. There was a large contingent of music press who were frantically writing notes after every song, and surprisingly quite a few celebrities from other bands as well as a couple of film stars who Janine thought she recognised.

The band played two encores and finally left the stage to roars of approval. The crowd was slowly starting to make their way out, when Janine noticed a well-known actress walking across the room waving to her. She was transfixed as Kathy Blake, who she'd recently seen in a film on TV, came over and introduced herself. She was dressed in a psychedelic kaftan with a matching headband in her long straight blond hair, and large round rose-tinted sunglasses.

"Hi, excuse me, I hope you don't mind, but I'm told you're Pete Peterson's manager?"

"Er, yes I am." Janine stuttered.

"I'm Kathy Blake and I wondered if it would be possible to meet him. It was an amazing show."

"Of course, come with me, I'm Janine Fortuna," she said trying to be cool, while at the same time not believing she was with the Kathy Blake. Ray was watching her walking backstage with the famous actress, feeling proud of how she was becoming so strong and confident.

There was lots of laughter coming from the dressing room as Janine and Kathy walked down the corridor, and having experienced previous embarrassing scenes involving semi-naked bodies, Janine knocked loudly on the door before entering. There were one or two jaws dropped when she walked in with Kathy Blake who seemed totally unfazed by the whole situation. She walked over to Pete and took his hand.

"That was one of the most amazing shows I've ever seen," she gushed. "I just had to come and meet you."

Pete wasn't quite sure who she was, although he knew she was famous, so he played along. "Well thanks for coming to tell us," he replied graciously.

"I'm having a party this weekend at my place in Malibu and I'd love you all to come," she said. "Janine, I'll contact you with the details if that's OK." She was still holding Pete's hand. She pulled him closer. "I think you and I could have some fun," she whispered and kissed his cheek.

The room was totally silent as she and Janine walked out.

"Holy shit! Kathy Blake wants to fuck you man!" Randy Jones was the first to speak after the door closed.

Pete was stunned. "Wow! I better check out some of her films," he said as he realised what had just happened.

Marshall the drummer looked up from packing his clothes away. "Hey Pete, a word of advice. One thing you gotta bear in mind about Kathy Blake. She's got a reputation for having trophy boyfriends. A good-looking guy on her arm to show off at all the awards."

"It'll be cool to see her place down in Malibu though," Richard the keyboard player added. "I wonder who'll be there. Hope there's some stars, I might take my film camera."

"That might not be cool, Rich," Marshall said. "Sometimes these people don't wanna be photographed when they're partying."

"I'll be discreet," he replied.

CHAPTER TWENTY

Janine was sipping a glass of champagne sitting on the balcony watching the waves as they gently lapped the shore. She found it so relaxing, as opposed to Ray, who had recently taken up jogging on The Strand, along with the other fitness junkies who constantly passed by down below. He'd bought himself a trendy outfit complete with a headband, and he set off every morning before breakfast to run up to the pier at Manhattan Beach and back. In his favour he was looking trim and fit again.

It occurred to her that since they had returned from San Fransisco, Mandy had become a little distant. She hadn't called and she'd barely spoken to her at the gig. Although to be fair, Janine had been running around most of the time speaking to journalists and friends of Manny. Perhaps the fact that Ray had returned had something to do with it, but it would be a shame if that's how she was thinking, Janine thought to herself. She'd told her after their first time that she preferred men but if she had a problem, so be it. Perhaps she would invite her to come to Kathy Blake's party with the guys. It sounded like it was going to be fun.

Kathy had called Janine earlier with the address of her place. Shed said there would be lots of her friends there who were dying to meet Pete. She'd also asked her to tell the guys to keep the details secret as she didn't want the press to find out, otherwise they would be besieged with paparazzi. Her place was right on the beach, so she suggested they should all bring their swimming costumes.

Janine had called Mandy and excitedly told her about the party, inviting her to come with them, but she said she was busy and couldn't make it. There was definitely something different about her that Janine couldn't work out. Maybe she'd have a chat to Manny next time she saw him.

Janine and Ray picked Pete up on the way to Kathy Blake's house in Malibu, and arrived at the same time as Don and the rest of the band. It was exactly as she'd described to Janine, a two-storey wooden construction built right on the beach, where she'd arranged rows of sun loungers. It was a beautiful sunny day and the guys had dressed accordingly in T-shirts and shorts. Janine had opted for a short emerald green silk dress with a pair of flat cream pumps, and Ray was wearing another loud short-sleeved Hawaiian shirt he'd bought in a local men's boutique and a pair of faded denim shorts. Pete on the other hand had found a stall just down from his apartment on Venice Beach which was selling the latest trendy hippy fashions, and had on a collarless cheesecloth shirt with wide flared denims, sandals and small round John Lennon sunglasses.

Kathy welcomed them all with hugs and kisses. She was wearing a long see-through sun dress over a bright red skimpy bikini which left nothing to the imagination. She ushered them all into the impressive marble-floored hallway hung with various canvases of modern art. It led into an enormous lounge with a fire pit in the centre, surrounded by bean bags and brightly coloured Persian rugs. French windows down one side opened out into the garden, which had a magnificent vista of the Pacific Ocean. It was full of exotic plants and scarlet bougainvillea bushes, and in the corner she'd had a small stage erected where a Mariachi band were playing.

Ray stood taking in everything around him wondering how much this sort of place would cost. But when you were the latest glamorous film star in Hollywood that everybody wanted, you probably didn't care about money. He watched Pete doing exactly the same thing and smiled to himself. 'If he plays his cards right, according to Janine, he could be tasting a bit of all this. Lucky bastard!'

Kathy was introducing Janine and Pete to the guests who were eager to make his acquaintance, so Ray wandered over to the well-stocked bar.

She certainly knew how to throw a party; he thought as he helped himself to a chilled bottle of Schlitz from one of the huge tubs full of every kind of cold beer you could imagine. There was an impressive spread of food which was being cooked in the outdoor kitchen by two chefs, and the smell of steaks on the grill reminded him he hadn't had much for breakfast. He could see Janine was deep in conversation with a group of people across the garden, so he went over and ordered himself a medium-rare fillet steak.

By mid-afternoon the sun was beating down and the party was in full swing. After many requests and a pleading kiss on the cheek from Kathy, Pete finally agreed to sing a few songs. He borrowed an acoustic guitar from one of the Mexican musicians and sat down on the edge of the stage. With Randy the bass player alongside him to sing the harmonies and Marshall the drummer who had found a pair of bongos which he used to provide a rhythm, they performed acoustic versions of some of the songs from *In Flames*. Janine was standing at the back with Richard the keyboard player, who was surreptitiously filming them with his camera. She thought they sounded great playing in this style, and made a mental note to mention it to Manny as a possible new recording. She looked around the garden and was amazed at how all the guests were held spellbound by Pete's voice.

When he finally stood up they went crazy, whistling and shouting. Kathy Blake made a point of going up to Pete and embracing him, planting a long kiss on his lips. Her intent was plain for all to see.

'I'm going to have to keep an eye on that situation,' Janine thought to herself. She'd just dealt with a crazy Russian, but a Hollywood actress was a different kettle of fish altogether.

As an ex-policeman Ray couldn't believe how many people were taking drugs. There were long lines of cocaine on a glass coffee table in the lounge, constantly being replenished as soon as any of the guests wandered over and snorted them, and the strong smell of marijuana was pervading the atmosphere. He noticed Don was observing one of the female guests, a pretty young actress friend of Kathy Blake, as she enthusiastically hoovered up a couple of generous portions of the white powder.

"Doesn't this bother you, being an ex-cop?" Ray asked him.

"Ah hey, look man. It's Miss Blake's private house and she can do what she wants. As long as it doesn't interfere with anyone else it's OK. The cops all know her around these parts and turn a blind eye to what she gets up to." He paused. "She's got a bit of a reputation as a party animal though, so Pete had better be careful if he's thinking of getting involved, although I don't think he's stupid. I've got to know him over the last few weeks and he seems a pretty cool guy. But Kathy Blake!"

He raised his eyebrows as Pete came into the lounge with his arm around Kathy Blake's waist. They wandered over to the coke table and both snorted a line each, kissed briefly, before she grabbed his hand leading him upstairs. Ray smiled as they disappeared, and turned to see Janine watching from the doorway. 'I wonder if this is what having kids is like' he thought to himself.

A lot of the guests had done as Kathy had suggested, and now stripped down to their swimming costumes, were going for a dip in the ocean. It was too good an opportunity to miss and Ray had changed into his trunks along with the guys from the band, heading across the sand towards the waves. Don had decided he didn't fancy it and was sitting under a large umbrella finally talking to the young actress.

Someone had produced a frisbee, and there was lots of shouting and laughter as it was tossed around. Janine had eventually joined him, looking amazing as she walked across the beach in her luminous green bikini, which Ray had to admit rivalled Kathy Blake's for style and sheer sexiness. She seemed bothered though. "I'm worried about Pete. He's starting to slip back into his old ways again," she said.

"Look babe, he's a grown man and can take care of himself. I'm beginning to feel like a parent with a naughty son. I think you should cut him some slack. Don's on his case so let's us just have a bit of fun, what do you say?"

"That's all well and good, but Pete thinks with his dick and I'm getting fed up of having to bail him out."

"Look forget it for now. Anyway, who were those people you were talking to before? It looked pretty intense," he asked trying to change the subject.

"They were Kathy's manager and a couple of her production team. They were really blown away when Pete was singing. They want him to go for a screen test." She didn't look as enthusiastic as Ray thought she should.

"Wow, that's amazing!"

"Well it will be if they're not bullshitting me. Let's just wait to see if the phone rings," she said. "So are we going for a swim or what?" She grabbed his arm and pushed him backwards into the warm water, laughing as he sat up spluttering, the water running in rivulets down his face.

By the time nightfall came the guests were starting to drift off. It had been a fantastic party, and surprisingly there had been no incidents considering the amount of alcohol and drugs that had been consumed.

Pete and Kathy had reappeared looking flushed from their bedroom antics, and with a shy look Pete had told Janine that he wouldn't be going back with them but would call her tomorrow. Don had left earlier with the young actress, and the guys from the band were leaving together.

Ray and Janine were about to call a cab to take them back to Hermosa Beach when Kathy suggested they stay and have a nightcap before they left. It seemed like a good idea, so they agreed and went into the lounge where the fire pit had been lit. Pete was relaxing on one of the bean bags smoking a joint, and Kathy asked Ray if he'd help her in the kitchen with the drinks while Janine announced she needed to go to the bathroom.

As Ray bent down to pick up a box of beer Kathy came up behind him and grabbed his crotch.

"Oh my God, you're so big!" she exclaimed. "I couldn't help but notice when you had your swimming trunks on before. I'd love to get me some of that!"

Ray was speechless and worried Janine might walk in at any moment.

Here he was, alone with Hollywood film star Kathy Blake and she was propositioning him. He remained calm. "I don't think Janine would be too keen, do you?"

"If it's a problem she can join in, she's a good-looking woman. All three of us, don't you think it would be fun?"

"Ah no, actually we're not into that kind of thing," he replied, but in the back of his mind he remembered what Janine had told him about her and Mandy.

"What about Pete? I got the impression you and he were getting on pretty well," he asked trying to put a bit of space between them.

"Yeah Pete's cool. We're gonna have some fun I can tell, and he'll look great on my arm at a couple of awards ceremonies I've got coming up." She looked him up and down. "But from that bulge in your trousers you look like you're packing some serious cock, and I thought I'd test the water. After all there's no harm in asking is there?"

"I think it's time we took the drinks in before someone wonders where we are," Ray said picking up the beers and heading back into the lounge. 'I might keep this conversation to myself' he thought as Janine came back from the bathroom.

Pete woke the next morning to the sound of loud music coming from outside in the garden. He and Kathy had gone back to bed after Janine and Ray had eventually left, and screwed until the sun was starting to come up. Pete was learning that American women, or certainly the ones he'd experienced so far had an insatiable appetite for sex. He wasn't complaining, but concluded he needed to get himself fit to keep up with their stamina. Kathy was a demanding lover, and loved cocaine which she took in abundance. Pete however had learned his lesson after the episode at the Dominion in London, so he was a lot more cautious where hard drugs were concerned.

He found a robe his size in Kathy's closet and came downstairs to find her outside with her personal trainer, going through fitness routines to the sound of the latest tunes on her portable stereo system. Considering what they'd got up to last night, he was amazed how good she looked at this time in the morning. But then again that was why she was one of the top actresses here in Tinseltown, where it was all down to looks and who you knew.

He sat in the lounge with a cup of coffee and a cigarette watching her, until she finished and joined him dripping with sweat. She took the cigarette out of his mouth and threw it into the garden.

"Those have got to stop," she said kissing him. "And you need to get yourself one of these." She towelled herself down and nodded towards her trainer as he came in from the garden.

The guy came over to give her a kiss goodbye and let himself out. As the door closed behind him, she untied the belt on Pete's robe and knelt down in front of him. He threw his head back and closed his eyes as his new favourite Hollywood film star went to work.

True to their word the production team behind Kathy Blake had called Janine first thing the next morning and asked her to come into their office for a meeting. It was on Sunset Boulevard and a short distance from Manny Oberstein's office, so she thought she would drop in to see him after she had finished.

The meeting went well, and ended with the promise of a date for a screen test to be arranged around Pete's current touring schedule. Janine was pleased with herself and how she'd handled the questions that had been thrown at her. She got the impression that Kathy Blake had asked them to meet with her as a favour, but either way at some point in the future, Pete would have a screen test. Then who knew what would happen.

With that in mind, she walked into Westoria Records and asked to speak to Manny, to be told he was very busy. She knew that one day their relationship would be on a more business footing, but the harshness of the response took her by surprise. After all hadn't Pete just sold out the Whisky A Go-Go and been the hit of the chat show? She asked to speak to Mandy but was told she wasn't in the office. So instead of getting annoyed she sat down and said she would wait until he was free.

This seemed to have the desired effect, as minutes later Manny appeared and invited her into his office. She noticed he looked a little more flustered than usual and asked if there was a problem.

Manny beckoned her to sit down. "Look Janine, I know you're doing a great job with Pete, but I gotta tell you, something I heard this morning has got me real pissed."

She looked at him confused. "I don't understand, what are you talking about?"

"The fact you're going behind my back and arranging a screen test for Pete. We're doing great business with the band and the album right now, and he's slowly becoming the star that we both knew he could be. So why all of a sudden are you getting him a screen test for God's sake? We need to concentrate on one thing at a time. Keep him focussed. I know it's all down to Kathy Blake. She's picked him as her latest piece of eye candy, perfect for the awards ceremonies coming up. She'll screw his brains out until she finds the next good-looking guy who she takes a fancy to, and then he'll be out the door along with his screen test."

Janine went to speak but he carried on. "Don't you think we have the resources already here to get him into films as soon as we think he's ready?"

"Manny I'm sorry, I just didn't think it would do any harm," she apologised.

"Look I'm sorry too. I've been having a bad day, Mandy has resigned, so I'm without a secretary and..."

"Hang on, Mandy's resigned?" Janine interrupted him.

"Yeah, said something about a problem with her ex-husband. Can't understand it; she's always been so reliable."

"But I spoke to her last week and invited her to Kathy Blake's party. She never mentioned it then. Hey, wasn't her ex in a band that you signed?"

"Yeah, pretty short-lived. They had one minor hit and then split. He ended up moving to Miami. Shame really, he could have been the next Santana but he just didn't have the dedication."

Janine thought for a moment. "Look is there anything I can do to help? I'm pretty good at office work and it'll be a way of saying sorry for the misunderstanding."

"OK, look. I'm gonna say yes because I haven't got any other options, but it'll only be for today. And the first thing I want you to do is find Don. He's disappeared."

"I know where he is," Janine said with a grin. "I saw him leaving Kathy Blake's party with a young actress yesterday. I'll give Ray a call, I'm pretty sure Don told him her name."

"I believe Pete did an amazing little set at the party," Manny said.

"Ah now, you've just reminded me why I came to see you in the first place," Janine said. "It was incredible. Just Pete with an acoustic guitar, Marshall playing bongos and Randy singing harmonies. So I thought why can't we record an acoustic version of *In Flames*? With a bit of work by the guys on the arrangements it could appeal to a whole new market."

Manny sat and thought. "You know something, that's a great idea. I should get you working in my Promotions department."

Janine smiled. "You couldn't afford me!"

CHAPTER TWENTY-ONE

Pete had said he needed to get back to his place in Venice Beach to change his clothes, but Kathy had other ideas.

She was in the small bedroom she'd had converted into her office making phone calls. "I want to introduce you to an incredible guy I've met who'll blow your mind. But first we'll go and get you some new clothes. There's a really cool shop I use all the time, they have some amazing stuff for guys. Then we'll grab something to eat in a little deli I love in Santa Monica, and then we'll go to his *Gathering*."

Pete was just happy to go along with events as they happened. The whole weekend had been amazing; the party, singing with the acoustic, making love to a Hollywood actress, and now she was taking him to God knows where to get him some new clothes, have lunch and then to meet some guy who was going to blow his mind. 'Not bad for a Birmingham muso! If only Johnny Rhodes could see me now,' he thought as they drove off in her bright pink Mini. It occurred to him as they sped down the Pacific Highway that he'd never be seen dead in a Mini back home, but here in LA sitting in one next to one of the hottest women in Hollywood, it didn't seem so bad.

Janine had called Ray at home to see if he remembered who the actress was that Don had left the party with. He'd just come in after his morning run along The Strand. As it turned out he couldn't remember the name, but it didn't matter as Don had called earlier to say he was going down to Whitland Studios after lunch, and would he meet him there for a coffee. Janine mentioned that Mandy had resigned suddenly, which piqued Ray's ex-policeman's curiosity. He'd always had a strange feeling about Mandy which he couldn't quite work out, especially after Janine had told him about what had happened between them. So her leaving without saying anything set his radar in motion. He'd have a chat with Don later when he met him at the studios.

Manny was explaining to Janine how the booking system worked for the next set of gigs for Pete and the band. This leg was predominantly in the North and Northeast coast, at great venues in places such as Kansas City, Chicago, Boston and Minneapolis, starting with a prestigious appearance on the Johnny Carlton Show in New York.

"This is so important for the tour and the album," he explained. "It's almost impossible to get on that show without a top ten hit, but one of the producers was at the Whisky last week, and he's a big fan of Pete's. He loves the album and he's managed to fix it. It also helps that someone's leaked to the press that Pete is seeing Kathy Blake, and they're trying to get her on the show as well. I'm not a great fan of her and how she uses people, but you know, whatever it takes babe!"

Janine sat up as he said the very words that Gerry always used.

"Yes, Manny I totally agree. Whatever it takes!"

Pete and Kathy had just left the little deli where they'd had lunch. It was run by an Italian family, situated down a narrow side-street serving amazing seafood and pasta dishes that Pete had never heard of before. They had sat in the courtyard surrounded by an abundance of plants growing in weird and wonderful containers hanging on whitewashed walls. Kathy had chosen a bottle of Sicilian Rosé to accompany their shrimp grilled on rosemary skewers which was incredible, and by the time they'd finished their lamb cutlets with garlic and lemon, Pete was in heaven. He was feeling cool in the red Sergeant Pepper-style military jacket, black jeans and white grandad shirt she'd bought him from her favourite boutique *Granny's Trip*, and they were walking across to Kathy's car when they were besieged by a posse of photographers all calling her name. She stopped and held Pete's hand, pulling him close to her as the paparazzi did their jobs. She gave Pete a kiss on the cheek as the shutters clicked away, holding him tight while posing for the lenses. Pete thought back to the time he and Anders Neckermann had ambushed Sophia Loren at the hotel in London to get a single publicity shot. This time there would be hundreds and it was for real. He actually was with a film star and he was beginning to enjoy it.

She'd already mentioned while they were in bed last night that she wanted him to accompany her to the Oscars. They were being held next month and she was nominated for Best Actress. Pete knew there were more tour dates coming up, so he would have to call Janine as soon as possible, but there was no way he was going to miss out going to the Oscars. No way!

Before he had time to think about anything else he and Kathy were running over to her car, and they screeched off down the road leaving the press pack desperately trying to run after them.

They were now driving up into the canyons behind Malibu. She told him they were on their way to see Surinam Chandra the charismatic leader of The Supreme Enlightenment. Pete had heard of Chandra before because Nadja had mentioned him. She had tried unsuccessfully to convince Pete to attend one of his so called *Gatherings*, where he extolled the virtues of higher consciousness. He'd been sceptical before, and even though Kathy was talking enthusiastically about his teachings Pete was yet to be convinced.

They drove for about twenty minutes through the dry brush and steep clay slopes lining the road into the Saratoga Hills, until she turned down a narrow dirt track that ended at a pair of solid wooden gates built into a high wall. An armed guard opened the gates, and they drove into an oasis of verdant foliage surrounding a large modern house built of wooden beams and glass.

Kathy parked her Mini alongside the rows of cars presumably belonging to other followers, and they made their way through the fragrant bushes to join them, already sitting cross legged on the grass waiting for the *Gathering* to begin. Surinam certainly had some money, judging by the collection of sports cars that Pete could see parked up at the side of the house. A red Ferrari Daytona GTS/4, a vintage silver Porsche 911 and a bright yellow Lamborghini Miura which took pride of place. According to rumours, Chandra enjoyed the attentions of a bevy of beautiful women wherever he went, at least half a dozen of whom were sitting next to him on the podium. Kathy sat down entranced, and since she was driving and the only way he was going to get back, he could only play along and listen.

Surinam started to speak in a low monotone which seemed to have an almost hypnotic effect on the crowd. Maybe Pete was missing the point, but he was totally unaffected and found himself bored. He started looking around at the upturned faces absorbing everything that was being said. After ten minutes of inane waffle he had yet to hear anything that blew his min d and then Surinam finally got down to the real nitty gritty; the financial contributions to be made by his followers. Now it was starting to make sense, Pete thought to himself. But if this was supposed to be a meeting of Supreme Enlightenment, he couldn't work out what part the proliferation of heavily armed guards played. He felt it was more like a meeting of a secret army than a peaceful mind-expanding session, and the more he watched Surinam spouting his rhetoric the more uncomfortable he began to feel.

Finally the *Gathering* came to an end, and everyone began standing up and walking towards the podium where Surinam was standing. He was shaking their hands and graciously accepting an envelope each follower gave to him which he passed to one of his female assistants who placed it into a large wooden box. Kathy had joined the orderly queue, and when it came to her turn to meet him, Surinam made a fuss of her, bending down to kiss her cheek. He talked to her for much longer than any of the others, finally kissing her again as she handed over her envelope. Pete's attention had been drawn to the group of women on the stage and one in particular. Even though she was wearing a large pair of sunglasses and a floppy felt hat he thought he recognised her. He was too far back to get a good view and before he had chance to get any closer she left the podium and disappeared inside the house but then it came to him who she was. Mandy, Manny's secretary who had come up to San Fransisco with Janine. He was positive it was her; he'd know those legs and that butt anywhere. But what was she doing with Surinam Chandra? Perhaps he should mention it to Janine and Ray when he spoke to them next.

As they were driving back down the road towards Malibu, Pete asked Kathy what was in the envelopes that everyone had given to Surinam.

"It is a contribution towards his work in freeing our minds from the daily oppression we suffer at the hands of the Establishment," she said taking her eyes off the road and looking at him as she made her point rather too forcibly for Pete's liking.

"Wow, that's pretty heavy stuff. But would you mind keeping your eyes on the road, I don't want to end up at the bottom of the canyon. So how much is the contribution?"

"A thousand dollars," she said quite nonchalantly.

Pete was visibly shocked. "A thousand dollars! There must have been a hundred people there. If everyone gave him a thousand dollars that's a hundred thousand dollars in one go. Shit, I'm in the wrong business!"

Kathy carried on driving, unaffected by his outburst.

"So what does he do with all the money, besides buying sports cars?"

"It all goes to the greater good," Kathy replied.

"Yeah and running his own private army judging from the number of armed guards I saw. What does a man supposedly talking about peace and all that other stuff he was waffling on about need with so much muscle and firepower?" Pete asked.

She glanced at him but returned her eyes to the road, steering carefully past a steep drop on one side of the road.

"Look, all I want is a release from the crap I take at the studio. Day in day out I get people yelling at me, 'Do this, Do that! You're saying that wrong! Lose weight, you're looking fat!' Man I could scream sometimes, but I keep my mouth shut, do as I'm told and take my pay check. It ain't easy at times believe me. I envy you. You go out there, playing what you love. So what if I blow a grand here and there? It's only money."

She pulled over to a lay-by which overlooked the Malibu coastline and switched off the engine, turned to him and said, "Kiss me."

Pete obeyed and she responded pulling him to her.

She sat back up again. "That's better. Now I'm going to drive home and I want you to take me to bed and fuck my brains out," she said. Pete went to speak but she put a finger to his lips. "You got a problem with that?"

Pete thought about saying something more but decided a simple shake of the head was sufficient. She kissed him again and started the engine.

Janine had been trying to speak to Pete all day. She'd called Kathy Blake's house repeatedly, and was just about to lose her temper when on the tenth attempt Kathy picked up the phone.

"Hey Janine, how are you? Ah yeah, sorry about that. We've been out getting Pete some new clothes. Then we went to see Surinam Chandra up in Saratoga Canyon and we've just got back. Do you want to speak to him?"

Pete took the receiver from her. "Hey Janine what's happening?"

"Pete, you have to keep in touch. I'm in Manny's office and things are happening here that we need to speak to you about."

"Listen, Janine," he said interrupting her flow. "Kathy has asked me to accompany her to the Oscars. How cool is that!"

"Hang on a sec," Janine turned to Manny covering the mouthpiece with her hand. "What date is the Oscars, Manny? Kathy wants Pete to go with her, can we fit that in with the Johnny Carlton Show?"

Manny looked up from his desk. "Damn right we can! Tell him to accept, and we'll speak with our guy and get him to make sure the dates work."

Janine spoke to Pete again. "Pete, listen, it's cool for you to go to the Oscars, and we've got you a Johnny Carlton Show in New York to promote the tour which we'll arrange at the same time. Manny wants you to ask Kathy if she'll come on it with you as well; it'll be great publicity. See what you can do. I'm sure you can use your immense powers of persuasion."

He laughed and was about put the phone down when he remembered about Mandy. "Hey Janine, don't hang up! I've just remembered something. When I was at this *Gathering* I recognised one of the women on the stage with this Surinam character. It was Mandy, Manny's secretary."

"Are you sure?"

"Yeah, positive. You wouldn't forget her in a hurry. Strange though. Wonder what she was doing there."

"Very strange, considering she's just left Manny's office supposedly because of something to do with her ex-husband." Janine said.

"Look I've got to go, I'm needed," Pete said as Kathy appeared at the bottom of the stairs naked apart from a pair of sunglasses.

CHAPTER TWENTY-TWO

Ray and Don met up at Whitland Studios, and over coffee talked about old times. Ray had been amazed at how many gunfights Don had been involved in. He imagined what would happen back in the UK if the police were ever armed and shuddered at the thought. He made a mental note to call Matt to find out the verdict on the case with Bobby McGregor. He was sure a guilty verdict must have been passed. But strange things happened, and he'd learned never to take anything for granted.

Don had phoned Manny's office earlier, after hearing about Mandy leaving.

"There's something strange about that woman," he said to Ray. "Don't get me wrong, she was a good secretary but her husband, the guitarist, I never liked him. I always got the impression he was bad. I drove his band around for one tour when they signed to Westoria. He was a good musician, but he always seemed more interested in guns and violence. I was surprised when Mandy married him. He seemed dangerous, d'you know what I mean?"

"What's he doing now?" Ray asked.

"See that's just it. The band split and the next thing you know, him and Mandy are separated and according to Manny he moved down to Miami. She never talked about him after that, so I don't know."

"But according to Janine, Manny told her she'd left because of trouble with her ex. All sounds a bit strange to me. Anyway, you never said how you got on with that very attractive young actress I saw you with yesterday."

Don smiled. "Yes, well all I'm prepared to say is she had more sex aids in her bedroom than I've seen in a porn warehouse!"

Ray laughed. "I thought you looked a bit tired. So are you going back for more later?"

Don raised his eyebrows. "I'm thinking it would be rude to refuse. And considering we're gonna be hitting the road again soon, I may as well make the most of what I can get."

After her day with Manny, Janine called Ray and they decided to go for something to eat at Barney's Beanery in West Hollywood; the famous restaurant where Janis Joplin was rumoured to have eaten her last meal a few years earlier. They settled down in one of the booths and ordered two burgers, a beer for Ray and a Cosmopolitan for Janine. Ray was starting to tell Janine about his meeting with Don, and how they'd heard about Mandy leaving, when she told him what Pete had said earlier. Ray's ex-cop radar began to work again and he suddenly became very interested. "Maybe I should check out this Surinam Chandra and his Supreme Enlightenment," he said as their drinks arrived. "I'll give Pete a call and get some more information."

Janine laughed. "I think you'd best leave it until tomorrow. I got the impression he's going to be kept pretty busy for the time being."

They finished their burgers and Ray called Don from the call box in the foyer. Ray thought he might have been in the middle of something, but carried on regardless. "Hey Don, sorry to interrupt, but listen, something really important has just come up."

"Two minutes later and I'd have been in the same position," Don replied with a laugh. "What can I do for you, Ray?"

"What do you know about this guy Surinam Chandra and his Supreme Enlightenment Gatherings?"

"Surinam Chandra," Don repeated. "I know that when I was on the force he was a bit of a con artist, always being brought in but nothing would ever stick. Why?"

"Janine spoke to Pete earlier. Kathy Blake took him to one of his *Gatherings*, and who should he see there but Mandy, Manny's ex-secretary. According to Pete she was on stage with him along with a load of other women." Ray replied.

"Interesting. Best I can do is give my old boss a call first thing tomorrow and see if he knows anything. In the meantime I have a special friend here who is desperate for my attention. Y'understand?"

Ray ended the call and he and Janine left the restaurant hailing a passing cab. He was thoughtful as they drove past the clubs and bars on the way home. Something had piqued his interest and he was desperate to find out more about this Chandra character.

In the hills above Malibu, Surinam Chandra relaxed in his sumptuously furnished lounge, safe in the confines of the private piece of land deep in the Saratoga Hills; surrounded by a high wall which kept unwanted visitors out, accessed by only one entrance constantly patrolled by an armed guard. He loved to sit and admire his collection of elegantly framed *Masters* hanging on the walls, as he drank a large crystal balloon of Rémy Martin cognac after another successful *Gathering*. He'd just finished counting the envelopes of cash donated by his followers, and was considering which one of his female entourage was going to share his bed later, when the phone rang. He stood up taking the piles of cash and his cognac with him, and answered the call in his private office.

"Benny, how are you?... Yes, excellent, a hundred thousand again today. That's nearly half a million already... When's he coming?... OK, I will arrange it... Yes, we can start as soon as he arrives."

Surinam replaced the receiver. He picked up the two-way radio on his desk and called his head of security. Moments later there was a knock on the door and Miguel Lopes his trusted right-hand man entered.

Surinam looked up. "Ah Miguel. In two days time José Valasquez is arriving at LAX from Miami. You will arrange for him to be picked up and brought back here. He can stay in one of the guest rooms. with Mandy. He has the final plans and we will start preparations immediately. Make sure all the men are ready. Ask Mandy Valasquez to come in."

Miguel nodded and left the room. Surinam walked over to the large Monet painting on the wall and swung it towards him, revealing a wall safe. He dialled the combination and opened it, putting the pile of cash inside. He closed the door and reset the combination, swinging the picture back in place. There was a quiet knock on the door and Mandy walked in.

Surinam gave her a kiss on the cheek. "Good news. In two days time José will be here to organise the operation. I've arranged a room for you and him. I hope that's to your liking."

Mandy felt less than enthusiastic about meeting her ex-husband again, but knew to keep her emotions under control. "That will be fine," she said and left the room. Surinam watched her leave. He reflected that she didn't seem as happy as he'd expected, but he had more pressing things on his mind. Soon the plan to commit one of the biggest bank robberies in LA would start in earnest, with the arrival of Benny Mulligan's representative José Valasquez. He would be in charge of training the group of men hand-picked especially for the job.

Miguel Lopes went himself to meet José Valasquez at the airport, and spotted him immediately he walked into the Arrivals hall. His long black hair tied in a ponytail, the gold earring and aviator sunglasses gave him the appearance of a rock star, and he took off his black leather jacket to reveal a typical Miami-style shirt, while scanning the crowd waiting at the barrier. Miguel lifted his hand to attract his attention. After a brief greeting they made their way to the car park where Surinam's red Ferrari was parked, and were soon on their way back to the house in the Saratoga Hills. Miguel had made a couple of attempts to engage José in conversation, but on both occasions a one-word answer convinced him that José would prefer to keep his own counsel. To his relief they finally reached the house, where he was thankful to park up the car while Surinam welcomed his guest. Mandy had been summoned to meet him, and after a frosty greeting she showed him to their room.

"Hey baby, why the long face?" José asked as he threw his bag on the bed. "Aren't you glad to see me again?"

Mandy kept her distance, avoiding his attempt to kiss her. "What happened between us finished when you left. You're here to do a job. So as long as you do that everyone will be happy, including me and Benny. Understand!"

José stepped back with his arms open wide. "Baby, that's no way to greet your ex-hubby. Think of all the good times we had."

"Fuck you, José!" She walked out of the room slamming the door behind her.

Miguel had been passing by and inadvertently caught the conversation. He ducked into the next room as Mandy stormed out. He would be interested in Surianam's reaction when he reported what he'd heard.

Mandy was already in conversation with Surinam when Miguel found him, which meant he would have to bide his time before reporting the argument. Full of bravado, José followed him into the room as if nothing had happened, and ordered Surinam to gather his troops together for a briefing.

"OK, so we've got ten days until Oscars Night." José addressed the room full of Surinam's guards. "Which means we don't have much time. Benny Mulligan doesn't like mistakes, and neither do I. So if you all listen carefully and do as you're told we're gonna get on fine. Understood?"

Some of the guards nodded. José slammed his fist down on the table in front of him, making some of them jump. "Understood?" This time he yelled.

"Yes sir!" All the guards shouted in unison.

"That's better." He turned to a large board which had been set up behind him. "This is a map of the area of LA where we'll be operating. He picked up a long stick and began pointing at various places that had been highlighted. "This is the Dorothy Chandler Pavilion where the Oscars ceremony will take place, here is City Hall, this is Union Station and here is the Bank of America. Now listen carefully. This is how we're gonna pull it off."

Ray had been about to call Don when the phone rang, and expecting it to be the ex-cop he was surprised to hear the voice of DCI Matt Burgess calling from the UK. "Hey Matt, how's things? Any news?" Ray asked.

The line was a bit crackly but he could just about hear him. "The case ended yesterday. Bobby McGregor was found guilty of Involuntary Manslaughter and sentenced to five years. Wendy Garner is appealing but James Muirhead is confident she's wasting her time."

"Great news, you must be happy."

"Of course, it's always good to put another one away as you well know."

The line was really bad and started going on and off.

"Oh and there's…else you…"

"Matt the line's really bad," Ray said. "Can you say that again."

There was a slight delay before Matt continued. "We…to the Lexx…weekend. Your friend Judy…looked…She's…" Beeeeeeeeeeeep.

"Hello Matt. Matt? Matt? Shit!" Ray put the receiver down.

"Who was that?" Janine had just come out of the bathroom with her red hair wrapped in a towel.

"Matt Burgess. Bobby McGregor got five years for Involuntary Manslaughter."

Janine looked down sadly. "Oh!"

"Look you can't feel like that," Ray said. "Remember what you heard Gerry and him saying. I never mentioned that, I should have, but I didn't. Justice has been done, so let's draw a line under it and move on. OK?"

Janine came over and he put his arms around her. She looked into his eyes. "Yeah, let's do that."

"Oh and he said something about Judy, but the line was bad and I couldn't hear what he was saying."

"Maybe I'll give her a call," Janine said. "It's a while since we spoke."

He suddenly remembered he was about to phone Don when Matt had called. He dialled his number while Janine went into the bedroom and started to get ready.

"Hey Don, how you doin'? Did you manage to find anything on Surinam Chandra?"

"Yeah listen man, you and I need to meet up at police headquarters. I spoke to my ex-boss and he said there's a whole file of stuff on him and thinks we should come down and check it out. He said we'll be interested in what he's got."

"That's great," Ray replied. "How about midday? Where is it?"

Don told him the address and rang off.

Don's ex-boss, Captain Lewis, a veteran cop in his late fifties, broke into a beaming smile when Don and Ray walked into his office. His desk was piled high with files, and the room was thick with cigar smoke as he jumped up to embrace his former Sergeant. Don introduced Ray and he shook his hand with a vice-like grip. They sat down and he poured out two mugs of coffee, before reaching behind him and passing them a thick folder.

"That's everything we've got on Surinam Chandra. Started off as a street hustler working Venice Beach and Santa Monica, small-time stuff mainly, ripping off punters with stolen merchandise, nothing too serious. Then he went upmarket with drugs, supposedly he got involved with some cartel down in Miami though we…"

Ray interrupted him. "Hang on, Miami, you don't mean Rota Bocan do you?"

"Well it was only a rumour. We could never make anything stick. Why? Do you know that lot?"

Ray looked at Don. "This gets more and more interesting by the day." He turned to the Captain. "I think we're gonna need more coffee."

Four cups later and Ray was starting to feel wired. They'd gone through all of the notes relating to Surinam Chandra but that was all they were, just notes. Reports made by officers who knew he was guilty of most of the petty crimes he'd been arrested for, but always there was never enough evidence and he walked free. It only started to get curious when he got involved with the drugs trade. He seemed to be using his Supreme Enlightenment as cover for something more serious. He'd built up a large following of rich, high-profile people, the most noticeable being Kathy Blake, the Oscar-nominated actress who was dating Pete Peterson, and both had been recorded as visiting his latest event a few days previous. What had got Ray interested was the appearance of Manny Oberstein's secretary who Pete had spotted on the stage, even though she was making an effort to disguise herself. There were too many coincidences for his liking and Don agreed. What they had to try and do was link them together in a way that made some sense.

They wrote down each incident on a noticeboard to be able to see them more clearly.

Don approached by two men in San Fransisco.

Two men attack gig in San Fransisco.

Bill Graham mentioned trouble with Miami-based Rota Bocan trying to muscle in on drugs trade.

Message left addressed to Janine - only Mandy knew they were going to the gig.

According to Janine, Mandy lay down on the floor when the gunmen struck.

Janine and Mandy followed by two men after visiting the restaurant.

Mandy handed in resignation at Westoria, and appears with Surinam Chandra.

Kathy Blake and Pete attend Gathering in Saratoga Hills

Mandy's ex-husband seen arriving LAX - met by a member Surinam Chandra's security team.

His interests - guns and violent films.

Don was due to see Pete in a couple of days for rehearsals, but Ray thought it would be a good idea to talk to him sooner, to ask him more about his visit to Surinam's house. His first call to Pete's Venice Beach apartment went unanswered, so he tried Kathy Blake's private number he'd got from Janine. She answered it on the second ring sounding slightly out of breath. Ray explained who he was and that it was important he spoke to Pete and she passed him the phone.

"Hey Ray, how's it going? What can I do for you?" Pete sounded out of breath too.

"Look man, I'm sorry if I've disturbed you, but something really important has come up and Don and I need to speak to you pretty urgently." Ray guessed he'd caught them mid-sex, but this was serious.

"Well yeah, I guess if it's important. Where do you want to meet?" Pete asked.

Ray could hear Kathy asking questions in the background but he ignored it and carried on. "Look Pete we're in Downtown at the police headquarters. Can you get here now?"

"Yeah man, I'm on my way. Is it cool if Kathy brings me?" he asked.

"If she's OK with that, even better. She might be able to help us too."

Ray gave him the address and hung up.

An hour later the rumpus outside the police headquarters announced their arrival. Since it had become public news that Kathy was dating an English rock musician, they were constantly hounded by a pack of reporters and photographers. Although annoying at times it was doing a great job at raising Pete's profile, as well as keeping Kathy's face in the papers, despite her not working on a film for over a year.

They finally burst through into the foyer amidst the sound of clicking cameras and shouting journalists. Don was already there waiting, and brought them up to the Captain's office, which was becoming more crowded and claustrophobic by the minute. The Captain vacated his chair and left them to it, which enabled Ray to open the window for some blessed fresh air.

Pete and Kathy were studying the notes they'd made on the noticeboard, when she pointed to her name. "Hey! I didn't know I was being watched," she said.

"You weren't," the Captain's voice came from the doorway. "We've had Surinam Chandra under surveillance for quite a while, and we keep a list of all the visitors to his house up in the hills. It just so happened your name popped up on it."

"So how can we help?" Pete asked.

"Try and remember everything you saw when you were there," Ray said. "Anything that struck you as unusual."

Pete thought for a moment. "Well I commented to Kathy afterwards how many armed guards there were, considering it was supposed to be all about peace and expanding your mind. There must have been at least twenty all with machine guns plus the one at the gate."

"What about you, Miss Blake; was there anything that you thought strange?" Don asked.

"Please, call me Kathy," she said. "Well not really, but I did find it odd that Surinam made a big fuss of talking to me at the end."

"Yeah I noticed that," Pete said. "I just thought it was to do with who you were."

"Well he already knew who I was, but that's the first time he's actually spoken to me."

"What did he say?" Ray asked.

"It was weird. He was asking me lots of questions about the Oscars ceremony; like what time did it start, how long did it go on for, was there lots of security? Not the usual stuff I get asked, like how does it feel to be nominated?"

"How long have you been going to these *Gatherings*?" Ray was writing notes down as she spoke.

"It's my third time," she said. "It was fun at the beginning, but I must admit he was a bit over the top about asking for money this time."

Pete agreed. "Yeah I noticed that. Considering you said he would blow my mind, all he did was bang on about how important your donations were."

Ray finished writing. "Thanks guys, that's really helpful. There's definitely something fishy going on. I'm not sure exactly what, but I'm going to have to dig a bit deeper and see what I can find." He turned to the Captain. "Can I take this file with me?"

"Be my guest. I'll be the first to buy you a drink if you can finally pin something on him. We sure as hell've been trying long enough!"

Kathy offered Ray a lift back with her and Pete, but as they reached the front doors, the pandemonium of reporters and photographers started again. Then when he saw her pink Mini and the thought of having to squeeze into the back, he graciously declined her offer and hailed a cab parked across the road. As they drove off he saw Pete and Kathy posing for photos on the steps outside the police headquarters, she with her arms around his waist looking the perfect couple. 'If nothing else,' he thought, 'it's great publicity for Pete. I just hope he knows what he's doing.'

Janine had arrived home minutes before Ray and was already sitting out on the balcony sipping a glass of champagne.

"Hey babe, how did it go with Don?" she asked. "Can I get you a cold beer?"

Ray took off his linen jacket and tossed it on a chair as he went over to give her a kiss.

"I would love one," he said. "It was so hot in the police headquarters it's a wonder they don't melt never mind solve any crimes, and the smoke in Don's ex-Captain's office was killing me."

She turned towards him and suddenly pulled a face.

"Uugh! You stink of smoke. Why don't you go get a shower and freshen up."

As he put the folder with all the files on Surinam Chandra down on the table it burst open, and a few photographs spilled out.

He was walking towards the bathroom when Janine, who had picked one of them up called after him.

"Hey who's this?" She waved the print at him.

Ray came back to look. "It's this character Surinam Chandra that Pete went to see with Kathy Blake. The one who he saw Mandy with. Why?"

She was thoughtful holding the photo. "I've seen him somewhere before. I never forget a face. I just can't place him at the moment."

Ray went off to the bathroom leaving her studying the photo as she walked back out on the balcony.

Five minutes later as he came out of the bathroom wrapped in a towel, Janine suddenly shouted. "I've got him, now I remember where I've met him," she said excitedly. Ray came out with a bottle of beer and sat down next to her.

"He lit my cigarette for me in a club in Santa Monica. The first night I met Mandy. It's definitely him. Good looking guy, really distinctive aftershave." She paused. "But hang on, it was when Mandy kissed me. She completely ignored him and he just left us alone. She certainly didn't seem to know him the way she pushed in between us."

"Are you sure it's him?" Ray asked.

"Positive. No way I'd forget a good-looking guy like that!"

Ray took a thoughtful pull on his beer. "This is getting weirder and weirder by the minute. So let me get this straight. Surinam Chandra sits next to you in a bar, lights your cigarette and hits on you. Then Mandy appears, blows him out and takes over." Janine was nodding. "Then at her suggestion you drive up to San Fransisco, where two possible Rota Bocan members attempt to attack the gig and you receive a threatening letter delivered to the box office. She then resigns from Manny's office saying she was having trouble with her ex-husband, and turns up at one of Surinam Chandra's *Gatherings* where Pete recognises her. Surinam quizzes Kathy Blake about the Oscars, and then the next day Mandy's ex turns up from of all places Miami and is met by one of Surinam's security guards."

He picked up the phone. "I'm gonna have to call Don again."

CHAPTER TWENTY-THREE

Judy Watson's mother had passed away peacefully. Now she was busy trying to organise her funeral, book the next month's bands for The Lexxicon, finalise a tour of clubs for one of the new bands she'd recently signed to FAM, and fit in her monthly hospital appointment. It had been a stressful few weeks and although saddened by the loss, she was relieved her mother was finally out of her pain. Thankfully her own doctor at the hospital was happy, so it was one less thing to worry about. She'd been keeping an eye on how Pete's career was progressing in the States, and had tentatively pencilled in a date later in the year for him to appear at the club when he was on the European leg of his tour. She'd have to speak to Janine and make sure the figures balanced, but she was sure she could pull it off.

'What a gig that would be!' she thought to herself sitting in her office. If only she could get the timing right! She wasn't too pleased when she'd read the news in all the gossip columns about his relationship with the Hollywood actress Kathy Blake, but on reflection that was so Pete Peterson.

She knew she'd promised to call Janine to give her an update on how things were, but she was sure it wasn't top of her priorities, so a letter with the latest accounts would probably satisfy her for now. She had given George, her new assistant the responsibility to handle all the correspondence. He was desperate to become more involved, and it would be the ideal opportunity for her to see how he was shaping up. She heaved herself out of her leather office chair and walked across to Lexx 1, where they were setting up the sound for the opening night of a week of shows by soul stars, *The Four Tops*, as part of their UK tour. She'd been lucky to get them, along with Liverpool band *The Chants* were also on the bill, and she wanted to make sure everything was running to schedule. She marvelled at how the style of music changed from one week to the next, yet they had full houses most nights. Gerry Fortuna certainly was a genius when it came to setting up successful clubs, and she was happy she was upholding his legacy.

She felt a twinge and made her way back to her office where George, who was on the phone noticed she looked a little pale.

"I'm fine really, George," she said sitting down as he ended his call and came over, looking concerned.

"You know what the doctor said," he fussed. "All this worry about your Mum and now this month's shows, never mind that bloody stupid tour. You should take some time off and put your feet up."

"You know damn well I can't do that," she replied a little harshly. "Once my Mum is at rest I'll be OK, but thanks for your concern. I really do appreciate it. Now there's a few things I need you to do that can't wait, so fetch your notepad and let's get started."

José Valasquez had been working day and night for a week with Surinam's men, and finally they were beginning to act like a cohesive group. The plan to rob the Bank of America was a bold one, and required split-second timing along with complete co-ordination. They would set off four small explosions simultaneously which would act as diversions; one inside a trash can outside the Dorothy Parker Pavilion where the Oscars ceremony was taking place, one similarly placed outside City Hall, one in the concourse of Union Station and one outside the front entrance of the Bank of America. The devices consisted mainly of smoke canisters, activated by small explosive charges guaranteed to cause more confusion than major damage. José would be directing operations from a command centre set up in the back of a dummy LAPD truck parked outside the bank, and would intercept the emergency calls; making sure half of his team dressed as police officers attended the bank sealing off the surrounding area. At the same time he would ensure the rest of the LAPD would be investigating the three other incidents. The other half of his men dressed as security guards, would access the bank itself aided by one of Surinam's *Gathering* members, a bank guard called Raul. He would be working inside the building at the time of the robbery and let them in, having first disabled the remote alarm connected to the police headquarters as well as all the cameras. Once inside they had a ten-minute window to open the safe, remove the contents, and take them out, via the rear loading bay, to their waiting truck. Once the ten minutes were up, the alarm system and the cameras would reset and be reactivated. Hopefully if all went to plan, the police would be kept so busy no one would notice the disruption to the signal until it was too late. By which time they would be on their way back to the Saratoga Hills before the LAPD had the chance to set up any roadblocks.

Another one of Surinam's followers worked in the clothing trade, and had been coerced into supplying the police and security guard uniforms, under the impression they were to be used in a film. Most of LA at one time or other was used as the backdrop for movie productions, so convincing him his outfits would be featured in the next big blockbuster had been easy, and he had no hesitation in waiving any costs as a special favour to Surinam.

The Oscars was fast approaching, and with the delivery of the outfits along with the dummy LAPD van which was parked undercover around the back of Surinam's house, José was confident the plan would work.

Benny Mulligan was lounging in a teak steamer chair smoking a Montecristo cigar, on the balcony of his ten-bedroomed 1920s Mediterranean-style villa. It was situated in the exclusive Coconut Grove estate, overlooking the calm waters of Biscayne Bay in Miami. He liked living there because he could maintain his anonymity behind the large electronic gates he'd had installed. His neighbours seemed to have the same way of thinking. In fact he had no idea who lived next door and he didn't really care.

He'd been following José's progress in the Saratoga Hills closely, and was loathe to admit he was relying on this heist being a success. His once feared Rota Bocan cartel had suffered heavy losses recently, and his attempts at setting up his drugs business in cities across the United States, as well as in the UK, had been failures. As a result his finances had dipped alarmingly. There was also the added annoyance of the woman called Janine Fortuna and her boyfriend Ray Law, whose names had been linked to the disastrous Birmingham endeavour, and who were both now in Los Angeles. He didn't like people interfering in his business, and the two of them were becoming tiresome. The ex-wife of his right-hand man José had already failed in her mission to deal with Ms. Fortuna which was irritating. Now her ex-cop boyfriend was starting to poke his nose in. But one thing at a time. Surinam Chandra, previously a small-time hustler had come to him with a clever plan, which if it succeeded would put him back on top again. According to his information, the Bank of America branch would be holding around five million dollars of used notes which were due to be replaced by newly minted ones. The old, unmarked notes were waiting to be taken to an incineration plant to be destroyed. All they had to do was get in and out before the alarm went off alerting the authorities something was wrong. According to José everything was running according to plan, so with any luck in a few day's time he could relax. Five million dollars, minus a few expenses would go a long way to solving his cashflow problem, and at the same time get his South American suppliers off his back.

He was thinking what he might buy with the money when Shanice, his pretty Filipino maid brought him his daily five o'clock Bloody Mary. As she bent down to put the drink on the side table, he reached out and caressed her tanned buttocks under her French Maid outfit. She knew what he wanted, and although she despised everything about him, she needed a roof over her head for her and her son. Soon the day would come when she'd be able to walk away, and with that thought firmly in her mind she knelt down and unzipped his shorts. His manhood was pathetic compared to some she had experienced but there was a difference, it being his paid the bills, and she went about her business closing her ears to his whimpering groans. As usual it only took a few moments and she looked back at the feared cartel boss with contempt as she left the room. 'If only his enemies could see him now,' she thought wiping her mouth on the white lace-trimmed pinny he insisted she wear.

Since José Valasquez had joined the organisation, he'd rapidly become a valuable right-hand man to Benny Mulligan. He was ruthless when necessary, extremely loyal and his knowledge of firearms was second to none. His attempt at becoming a rock star had been short lived, and after he decided to quit the music business and move to Miami, he came to the notice of Benny Mulligan. He proved his worth when he masterminded a robbery in Lake Worth's sea-front casino, removing the week's takings without a single shot being fired, while at the same time leaving with a hoard of fine jewellery from the ultra-rich clientele. It made all the headlines as the State Governor and his wife were there attending a dinner in aid of Homeless Charities, and a masked José was heard to shout "Viva Rota Bocan" as he left the room.

With Benny's authority to take control of the operation, he'd been excited to learn his ex-wife Mandy had joined Surinam's *Gathering*. With a possible reconciliation in mind, he had arrived at the house in the Saratoga Hills looking forward to seeing her again. However, it hadn't gone as smoothly as he'd hoped, and Mandy had been less than enthusiastic to see him; but it was a minor setback and he had much more important things on his plate. So he'd gone about the task of shaping a group of gun toting amateurs into a professional unit, capable of pulling off the job which would net his boss five million dollars.

He'd noticed in the list of Oscar nominees the actress Kathy Blake. She was currently dating the English rock star Pete Peterson, who had signed to Manny Oberstein at Westoria, his old boss. He'd listened to Benny Mulligan talking about the problems he'd had in the UK. How his plans to move into Birmingham were thwarted by a club boss called Gerry Fortuna who he'd eventually had murdered. So what a coincidence that Pete Peterson's manager was Janine Fortuna, Gerry's millionairess wido. Surely there was an angle there that he could use to his advantage. Despite her coldness towards him, he would speak to Mandy to find out more.

CHAPTER TWENTY-FOUR

Pete and Kathy Blake were becoming the new darlings of the press in LA. Their faces were rarely off the front pages of the showbiz papers, and the gossip columns were awash with talk of a possible engagement, although this was news to Pete. When Marshall Thomas his drummer, had jokingly waved the article at him as they were setting up at Whitland Studios for rehearsals, he had called Kathy. "Hey babe, what's all this in the press about you and me getting engaged?" he asked, trying not to sound too alarmed.

"Oh don't worry about that," she said nonchalantly. "That's just my PR company drumming up a bit of excitement before the Oscars next week. Don't forget you've got a fitting for your suit tomorrow."

"Yeah, that's all cool. I'm just not used to all this bullshit that goes on," he said feeling relieved.

"My publicist wants to know is the Johnny Carlton Show still happening. They're going to book us in the Waldorf Astoria for a couple of nights. That will be so amazing; it's one of my favourite hotels in New York."

"It is as far as I know, but Don's on his way here so I'll ask him. Are we still getting together later?"

Don walked into the reception area as he was speaking.

"Yeah, can't wait," she replied.

Pete motioned to Don. "Listen babe I gotta go, I'll catch you later."

"OK. Love you!" she said as she rang off.

Pete suddenly felt his stomach flip. Did Kathy Blake, the Kathy Blake just say she loved him! Shit!

Don noticed the look on Pete's face as he came over. "You look like you've just had a shock, Pete. You OK?"

"Er yeah, I'm cool, I think," Pete said still trying to take in what just happened.

As soon as they entered the rehearsal room, Don announced they would be playing a live spot on the Johnny Carlton Show in a weeks' time in New York. It coincided with the start of the Northeastern leg of their tour which would take in some great cities including Chicago, Philadelphia, Minneapolis, Boston and New York's famous Bottom Line.

Things were really starting to happen. The album was selling and climbing the charts, and for them to get such a prestigious show as Johnny Carlton was guaranteed to boost sales both for the record and the upcoming gigs. The band would be travelling over to New York separately, while Pete accompanied Kathy Blake to the Oscars. Pete was well aware of the guys possibly being jealous about what he was doing, but the one thing they were was professional. There were a couple of funny remarks, but other than that they just got on with what they did best, playing amazing music.

Pete was so proud of this band and for a brief moment thought back to his old lineup and what they would have made of the situation. He remembered the last night in the dressing room at the Lexxicon and immediately dismissed it from his mind. 'That was then, but this is now!'

He'd met Kathy at the little deli in Santa Monica where she'd taken him the first time. It was becoming their favourite place to hide away for a quiet meal instead of being in the spotlight. The press had started camping outside both of their places, so they would be followed wherever they went. The waiter, who was the son of the Italian family who owned it knew them by name, and had their favourite bottle of Rosé already chilled. They sat in the corner under a lemon tree hanging with fruit.

Kathy was excited when he told her the Johnny Carlton Show was confirmed. "Oh my God that is incredible," she cooed. "I've been trying to get on that show for ages."

"Well you're gonna be on it with me," Pete said proudly, for once he was feeling like the important one.

"We'll fly over the day after the Oscars," she said. "You'll love the hotel, and we'll have dinner in Bamonte's. It's my favourite Italian in New York. Maybe we could get my PR to arrange for us to go up the Empire

State at dusk, it's so romantic. Then you could get down on one knee and propose."

Pete nearly choked on his glass of wine.

"Oh, don't be stupid, I'm only joking," she said laughing, and putting her hand behind his neck she pulled him towards her and kissed him.

"Seriously though, we need to go through what we're going to say in the interviews we've got coming up. The reporters at the Oscars are going to be quizzing us about our relationship, and Johnny Carlton is a shrewd old dog. He knows how to get the best quotes from his guests, so we'll need to be on our A-game for that one." She realised she was running away with herself. "Anyway, how's the band sounding? Are you looking forward to the next bunch of shows?"

"Yeah we sounded great in rehearsal today. The guys are just so amazing. I've never worked with musicians like them before in my life. And according to Don the album is doing really well."

He seemed pensive for a moment. "You know, at times I find all this hard to come to terms with. Not that long ago I was working in a clothing shop in Birmingham selling shirts and ties. Now here I am sitting in Los Angeles with the most beautiful film star in the world."

Kathy held his hand and looked in his eyes. "You're the most incredible musician I've ever heard. You're talented, amazing looking and I'm in love with you. There I've said it! I love you Pete."

This time Pete was completely dumbfounded, and for once in his life lost for words. "I, I er, I love you too Kathy," he found himself saying.

"So how about we go back to my place and prove to each other what we've just admitted," she said standing and leading him by the hand to her Mini parked outside. There was one lone photographer passing by, who happened to get a great photograph of them standing in the street kissing passionately. His image made all the next morning's front pages with the headline *KATHY BLAKE AND HER ROCK STAR GET SERIOUS*.

Ray was still puzzling over the files on Surinam Chandra. He'd written out the list of suspicious events from the police headquarters so he could compare the notes he was making, but he was still struggling to make the pieces of the jigsaw fit. His policeman's intuition told him something was wrong, but what? Why did Surinam have so many armed security guards? What was one of the main men in Rota Bocan doing in LA? Could it be to organise something on a large scale? And was there a connection to the Oscars? What would be the point of attacking the ceremony at the Dorothy Chandler Pavilion? Granted there would be plenty of expensive jewellery being worn, but it would be *hot* once it was stolen and difficult to turn into cash. Could it possibly be something connected to the Oscars ceremony itself? Not forgetting Pete Peterson would be attending with Kathy Blake, and if anything happened to him it would be disastrous.

Janine had been out shopping, and returned to find him standing staring at the sheets of paper spread across the table and spilling onto the floor.

"Ray, give it a rest. You've been at this for days now and you're still no further forward." She gave him a kiss. "Come and sit out on the balcony."

He saw how fabulous she looked. Sometimes when he used to be involved in a case back in the UK he'd forget the time, and work through the night ignoring everything else. He had other priorities now, Janine being the main one, and he had to make sure he didn't slip back into his old ways.

"So how did the trip go? You seem to have been out for ages," he said putting his arms around her.

"Well I went into the bank to change some sterling into dollars and got talking to one of the tellers. He's a nice guy, and since he found out I was Pete Peterson's manager he's become my best friend. He's got the album and was at the Whisky gig."

She had a sip of her glass of champagne Ray had just poured her. "Anyway I'm not sure if he should, but he told me this long and involved story, of how it's becoming a real pain for him at the moment. Evidently there's a big changeover of bank notes from the old used ones to new ones, and because he's the branch representative he has to oversee the transfer of their old stock to the central storage. He was hoping to go to see the Oscars, but he can't because it's that day it all happens and he has to be on duty. Evidently all the banks in LA are doing the same thing so it's quite a big deal."

Ray was taking a mouthful of beer when he suddenly stopped mid-swallow almost choking. "Wait a minute. Did you say this big changeover of cash is on the same day as the Oscars?"

"That's what he told me."

He jumped up. "Did he say which bank it was where it was happening?"

"Well he works for the Bank of America, and he said it was not far from where the Oscars ceremony was taking place, which was why he was so annoyed."

She watched as Ray started flicking through the sheets of paper on the table. He found a map of Los Angeles and spread it out across the files.

"Look," he said stabbing his finger at it. "Here's the Dorothy Chandler Pavilion, and here's the Bank of America. It can't be a coincidence they're so close together." He thought again and suddenly slapped his hand on his head. "It's not the Oscars they're going to do, it's the bank. They're after the old notes. I need to speak to Don."

Surinam Chandra had been watching the last-minute preparations for the following day's audacious bank raid. José Valasquez certainly knew his stuff, and was still barking orders at the two teams of men making sure every one of them knew exactly what they had to do. He finally decided they'd done enough for the day, and allowed them all to go and get some rest. He then spent a couple of hours with Surinam drinking his fine brandy before making a call to Benny Mulligan in Miami, reassuring him everything was ready.

By now it was getting late and he decided to go to bed himself. As he made his way back to his room he shared with his ex-wife Mandy, he wondered what kind of mood she'd be in tonight. So far she had refused any advances he'd made, and it was winding him up; so much so that he decided he was going to take her tonight whether she wanted it or not. His adrenaline was flowing as he opened the door and saw her lying in the bed. She appeared to be asleep, although he knew at times previously she'd been pretending. He called her name but she didn't respond.

His pulse was racing as he undid his belt, stepping out of his combat trousers. As he walked over to the bed he slid his knife out of its sheath and called her name again. Still she didn't reply but José had made up his mind. Ripping the sheet covering Mandy off the bed, he straddled her naked body. Her eyes opened wide and she tried to scream, but José's hand was already covering her mouth. She began to struggle, but he was much stronger than she was, and when she felt the tip of his knife touch her neck she froze.

He leaned down with his mouth close to her ear and whispered. "That's better. I don't want to use this, but if I have to I will. So just relax and everything will be fine, just like it used to be."

She made another move to try and escape, but he pushed the knife a little harder this time. It nicked her skin causing a drop of blood to run down her neck.

"Now look what you've made me do," he said as he licked the blood from her throat. "You know what I want, so don't be stupid."

He dropped his knife and reaching down pulled her legs apart at the same time as he pushed himself towards her. She tried again to resist but he was too strong and he forced himself inside her. She arched her back trying to throw him off and bit his hand which was still covering her mouth, but by this time he was in control and pinning her down. She eventually accepted it was futile to try and fight him, so she stopped writhing and lay still until he finally came with a grunt.

"You see," he said rolling off her with a smile. "That wasn't so bad was it?"

She stood up and glared down at him as he lay on the bed.

"One day José I'm gonna kill you, and that's a promise!"

She picked up the sheet from the floor wrapping it around herself and walked out into the corridor.

CHAPTER TWENTY-FIVE

Pete was at Kathy's house in Malibu nervously pacing up and down in the lounge. He looked amazing in his tailor-made evening suit, white shirt and bow tie. He'd never worn a bow tie before and didn't have a clue how to tie one until Kathy came to the rescue, standing in front of him tying the perfect knot.

"You've done that before," he said as she disappeared upstairs to her bedroom to get ready. Ten long minutes later she came down wearing a cream silk Oscar de la Renta dress with high heeled shoes perfectly complemented by a diamond necklace and bracelet worth $200,000, lent to her by the world-famous jewellers, Van Cleef and Arpels. As she walked into the room Pete's heart missed a beat. He stood speechless as she came over to him. She looked so calm and collected while he was wound up like a spring.

"Baby, calm down," she said. "Just remember, it's all bullshit. There's no way I'm going to win, I'm too new. It's bound to be one of the old established lot. Probably Jane Fonda. But don't worry, my turn will come. Let's have fun, make sure we get in all the photo shoots, and remember what we rehearsed to say. You're going to be doing this a lot soon, so get used to it."

The tension was high at Surinam Chandra's compound as the two teams drove out of the gates. José was in the dummy LAPD van along with his team, with Miguel behind driving the truck containing the security guys. There was a team of four men already in LA dressed as street cleaners, planting the devices at the targets. Their identity cards were good forgeries, but José had been astonished at the lack of security when he'd done a recce. Something the LAPD would have to attend to in the future he thought, as they headed down the canyon towards their target. The helicopter which was high in the sky at a discrete distance behind them, radioed that the package was on it's way.

Back at police headquarters Ray and Don stood at the side of Captain Lewis listening to the messages describing the progress of the two vehicles. Don had called his ex-boss late the previous night and excitedly told him what Ray had worked out. At first the Captain was sceptical, but the more Don explained Ray's reasons the more he believed it and first thing that morning they had called the bank and put their plan together.

Although they weren't exactly sure where things would happen, Ray was positive there would be some kind of diversion to keep the police occupied, while they entered the bank. The Bank of America had confirmed the undercover team were in place in the vault of the branch close to the Dorothy Chandler Pavilion. The main worry to Captain Lewis was the sheer amount of manpower required to control the crowds at the Oscars, waiting to see the stars arrive and walk downn the red carpet. The proceedings were due to commence at four o'clock and the limousines bringing the stars had already started arriving. It was now coming up to three o'clock and the two suspect vehicles were about an hour away allowing for traffic, which meant they would get to the bank at the same time as the ceremony itself began.

Inside the limousine Pete's heart rate was through the roof, as they waited in line for the queue of luxury vehicles to disgorge their precious contents. It was difficult to see who was walking down the hallowed carpet due to the lights of the television cameras, but he was sure he saw Charles Morse with a beautiful young woman on his arm stop and pose for the photographers. Then suddenly it was their turn and Kathy was holding him tight as they stepped onto the crimson strip. The barrage of flashbulbs was blinding, and for a moment Pete couldn't see a thing, but Kathy was expertly guiding him along and making sure the photographers were getting the best shots. A voice called out from the scrum of press held back behind the ropes, which stretched to the front doors of the Pavilion, and they both turned as the reporter from America Today thrust his microphone towards them.

"What's the latest on the engagement, Kathy?" he asked as all the attention focussed on them.

Before Pete had chance to think she pulled him close, planted a kiss on his cheek and with a coquettish look straight into the camera lens said. "Well that would be telling, but we're both doing fine thanks."

The mob were yelling questions at them, as holding his hand tightly she strode off towards the entrance, pausing only for one last pose with Pete before disappearing inside.

"That should keep them guessing," she said scanning the foyer for her agent.

Pete was still dazed and coming to terms with what was happening, when a familiar voice made him turn around. Charles Morse had been standing talking to a group of people when he spotted Pete and broke away.

"Well! Fancy meeting you here dear chap," he said coming over and shaking his hand.

Kathy, who was still looking for her agent turned around to find them talking like old friends. "Aren't you going to introduce me?" she asked Pete.

"Kathy Blake, this is my friend from the UK, Charles Morse," Pete replied.

Charles with all his typical charm took her hand. "What a pleasure to meet you Miss Blake. I've been reading all about you two in the papers. I believe congratulations are in order."

Pete and Kathy looked at each other and burst out laughing. A waiter walked by with a tray of champagne, and they grabbed a glass each. They chinked them together and said "Cheers!" before heading off towards the auditorium, leaving Charles Morse with a bewildered look on his face.

The two vehicles arrived at the bank five minutes before the Oscars ceremony was due to begin. José in the LAPD van parked in the next street, while the truck drove round to the rear loading bay awaiting the signal to begin.

The helicopter reported their arrival to Ray, Don and Captain Lewis, who were waiting for them to make their moves. As it turned out they didn't have to wait long. At exactly four o'clock the first explosion happened outside City Hall. Followed moments later by the ones at Union Station, the Dorothy Chandler Pavilion and finally at the bank. José's plan to monitor the police calls would have been a good one, had

Ray not figured it out, and as a result the police had changed their emergency frequency. Captain Lewis had allocated three teams to attend the incidents, allowing José to think his plan to divert them away from the bank had worked. Minutes later after the explosions had gone off, the dummy van pulled up outside the bank, and Surinam's men dressed as police officers climbed out, setting up roadblocks to seal off the area. At the same time, the truck reversed up to the loading bay at the rear, and the fake security guards entered the bank through the door opened for them by Raul. He'd disabled the alarm linked to the police headquarters, and the countdown had started. They now only had nine and a half minutes to enter the vault and transfer the notes to the truck. Still comfortably enough time.

José was sitting in the van outside listening to Miguel giving a running commentary on their progress as they descended into the depths of the bank. Everything was going fine until they reached the last lock which opened the three-foot-thick door. Miguel typed in the access code Raul had given them but nothing happened. He checked the numbers and slowly typed them in again. Still nothing. José was now getting impatient up in the van, and started shouting down the walkie talkie. "Six minutes left, why aren't you in the vault?"

Miguel grabbed the handset. "They must have changed the access code, it doesn't work. We can't get in!"

José was screaming now. "What! Where's the guy who let you in? What the fuck is going on down there?"

Miguel looked around and noticed Raul was no longer with them. They'd been set up!

José estimated they had about four minutes before the alarm reset and told him to get out. They were making their way up to the back door when Miguel was met at the top of the stairs by four real LAPD officers. They had their guns pointing at him and his men.

"Face down on the floor, now!" the sergeant in charge shouted.

"You won't need that," he said as Miguel tried to switch the walkie talkie on.

Up in the van José was looking at the revolver belonging to another LAPD officer which was pointed straight at him.

"Looks like you guys have had a wasted trip." The cop laughed as the rest of José's team were corralled into another waiting police van. "Oh and by the way, the money's gone. It went at ten o'clock this morning."

He then made the mistake of glancing to see what was happening behind him, giving José the slightest of opportunities to leap out of the side door and run off down the street. By the time he realised what had happened, José had disappeared around the corner at the end. His expansive waistline, due to sitting in a squad car for hours and eating takeaway pizza, wasn't conducive to chasing runaway prisoners, and when he eventually reached the top of the street blowing hard, José had vanished.

The show had just started inside the Dorothy Chandler Pavilion when the faint sound of an explosion could be heard. Moments later they were informed by the show's host Jack Lemmon, that everything was under control; it was probably Walter Matthau crash landing nearby promoting Charlie Varrick, and after the laughter subsided things carried on as if nothing had happened. As expected, Kathy didn't win, the prize going to Jane Fonda as she'd correctly predicted and Pete was impressed with the way Kathy graciously accepted the fact that she hadn't won, going over to publicly congratulate the winner.

Later at the obligatory after-show party, he stood watching as Kathy expertly schmoozed the important guests, making sure she and Pete were in the photographs which would appear in all tomorrow's newspapers. He'd spotted Charles Morse again, who along with his glamorous female friend were looking a little worse for wear. As with most of the guests who hadn't won, they were determinedly drowning their sorrows with the never-ending champagne which was still flowing late into the night. It suddenly dawned on him that he had an important show coming up in New York in two days, which he'd completely forgotten about. The performing didn't bother him, in fact he was desperate to play again with the guys. It was the interview with Johnny Carlton and Kathy that worried him. She'd warned him about the famous chat show host's renowned ability to get things out of his guests that they may not want to talk about. He thought that although it had been dealt with at the time, his spell in the rehab clinic was a skeleton in his cupboard he wouldn't want revealing. When he'd told her about it, she had just shrugged and said everybody's been in rehab, don't worry about it.

In fact he hadn't mentioned it at the time, but he was getting concerned over her cocaine habit of late. She'd made a big deal about him stopping smoking, which he was doing his best to do, but he found it ironic that her growing addiction was conveniently being overlooked.

The first thing José did when he was back in the house in the Saratoga Hills, was call Benny Mulligan in Miami to tell him the news. He'd taken it really badly and was threatening to come over to LA and sort out Surinam and anyone connected to him as revenge. But José had convinced him to leave it for now and wait until he returned. He had a plan he wanted to discuss with Benny which he thought might solve a few of their problems. He also knew Surinam kept most of the donations he'd been given by his *Gathering* at the house. There should be about half a million dollars in the safe which he would take back with him.

Don, Ray and Captain Lewis were celebrating their victory at the police headquarters, although it had been tainted slightly by the fact that José had got away, and once again there was nothing they could pin on Surinam Chandra. The guards who they had arrested during the bank raid were small fry. Despite threats of long sentences, they were saying nothing, knowing full well they would be out on bail soon and could then quietly disappear. The officer who had allowed José to escape had been severely reprimanded by Captain Lewis, and an APB had been issued for José's arrest.

There was one thing José wanted to do before he left, and that was to find Raul from the bank who had obviously double-crossed them. Surinam had given José his last address, and borrowing the silver Porsche parked at the house, he had driven off on a mission of retribution. When he saw the look in José's eyes, Surinam thought he wouldn't like to be in Raul's shoes when he found him. The address he'd given José was in East Hollywood which was not the kind of area he would visit himself, but he knew José had no fear of things like that. In fact his main concern was that the Porsche was returned in one piece.

Just as José was driving towards the address in East Hollywood, Ray was leaving police headquarters in a taxi, and unknown to each other they sat on opposite sides of Santa Monica Boulevard at exactly the same time waiting for the traffic to move. Ray glanced out of the side window and spotted the silver Porsche, a car he'd always wished he could afford, as it moved off past him. José oblivious to anything around him was concentrating on finding the address on the piece of paper he'd been given by Surinam, and although he saw the taxi with Ray sitting in the back seat he was just another black guy in a cab. Ray had called Janine as he left, and she was on her way to meet him for a drink at the Beverly Hills Hotel.

Ten minutes later the silver Porsche pulled up outside a run-down block of condos. He found the address he was looking for on the first floor and banged on the door. It had peeling red paint, and the window at the side had a broken pane of glass which had been repaired with a sheet of old hardboard nailed to the frame. There was loud music coming from the apartment next door, and the smell from the rubbish piled up outside was unbearable.

José waited for a minute then banged again. A voice from inside told whoever it was banging on the door to "Fuck off," which made him repeat it again this time harder. There was cursing and rattling of bolts being pulled back. From the startled look on his face as he recognised who it was banging on the door, José knew he'd found Raul. He pushed him down the narrow hallway into a small lounge containing a threadbare sofa, a grubby armchair and a brand-new TV set. There were empty beer cans and the remains of a pizza on the floor. José pushed him again, and Raul stumbled backwards over a glass topped coffee table ending up on his backside. José stood over him and surveyed the scene. There was a large bag of white powder and the remains of a long white line across the glass.

"Well, well, well! Looks like we've been enjoying our ill-gotten gains," José said.

Raul looked up at him. "It's not what it seems," he pleaded. "I had a few friends round."

José picked up the bag. "With our compliments too by the look of it!" He slowly tipped the bag and emptied the contents on the table as Raul watched.

"It wasn't my fault." He was sweating. "They…they knew. They changed the codes, I swear."

Reaching behind him José pulled out a pistol and aimed it at the man's head. "Who knew?"

Raul was frantic, trying to scrabble across the floor. "The black guy from the UK. An ex-cop. He knew."

José stood for a moment and shook his head. "Well Mr. Mulligan sends his regards and hopes you enjoyed the party."

He pulled the trigger putting a bullet right between Raul's eyes, spraying blood and brain matter all over the wall. As Raul collapsed backwards on the floor, José licked his finger and dipped it into the pile of cocaine. He rubbed it on his top gum feeling the numbing sensation from the pure high-grade drug. He walked out of the apartment leaving the door wide open. There were two men trying to break into the Porsche down below. He looked down from the walkway pointing his gun at them and shouted.

"I don't think that would be a wise move guys, do you?" He pulled the hammer back and aimed, as they set off running away. With a laugh he slid the gun back into the waistband of his trousers and made his way down to the car. Fortunately for them there was no damage, and as he dropped it into first gear he thought about what Raul had said. 'The black ex-cop from the UK.' He'd need to let Benny Mulligan know about this. Then his mind switched back to his plan, which if successful would put a smile on the face of his boss, and at the same time give the cartel's bank balance a major boost.

Unfortunately, the first thing he had to do was talk to Mandy, which wasn't going to be easy after the last time they were together.

CHAPTER TWENTY-SIX

Janine was packed ready for the trip to New York. Pete and Kathy had arranged for her and Ray to join them in the private jet Kathy's agent had organised. Ray had been undecided whether he wanted to go, but Janine finally persuaded him with the promise of a trip to see the Statue of Liberty by helicopter, as well as two days luxury in the Waldorf Astoria courtesy of Kathy. She was watching with interest the growing intensity of Pete and Kathy's relationship. Having been told by both Manny and Don that Kathy was well-known for her habit of choosing good looking young guys to accompany her to public appearances then discarding them and moving on to the next suspect, so far there were no signs of it slowing down. The mysterious rumours of an engagement just added more fuel to the fire. It was great for raising Pete's profile, but was it great for Pete? She hadn't had a moment alone with him since their row at the TV station before the Whisky A Go-Go gig, which worried her slightly. As his personal manager she should be in regular contact with him, and she decided she would put that right.

They had all met up at LAX in the private VIP lounge, with Kathy sitting surrounded by a stack of designer luggage. Janine noticed Pete appeared nervous and not himself. She went over to sit with him for a chat and sensed something was wrong.

"Hey Pete, are you OK? You look strange, not your usual self."

"Yeah well it's a bit delicate," he replied not wanting to look her in the eyes.

"Come on, if you can't talk to me, who can you talk to?"

He took a deep breath. "Well I don't know how to put this any other way, but Kathy thinks I should get another manager. She's been talking to her representatives and they're interested in signing me."

Janine felt like she'd been punched in the stomach. She sat motionless for a few moments then stood up and walked over to where Kathy was standing next to Ray.

"I think you and I need to talk, NOW!"

Kathy looked at her and smiled. "Sure."

They walked over to the other side of the lounge and before they had chance to sit down Janine turned and stood inches away from her.

"What gives you the right to interfere with the business of my artist?"

"Pete and I have been talking, and I think it might be good for his career if he moved on to a bigger management," Kathy replied.

"Oh, you mean like your management who can't get you another film because no director will touch you and your coke habit? That management? What do you know about the music business? Only that it supplies you with gullible young guys to hang on your arm and take to awards ceremonies, none of which you win. Then when you've had enough you dump them and move on to the next one."

Kathy paled in the face of Janine's onslaught.

"So what's your next plan? Use Pete to get on the Johnny Carlton Show who weren't interested in you on your own, and pull some kind of stunt like getting engaged live on air just to keep your name in the press?"

Janine turned to Pete who looked shocked. "You didn't see that one coming did you!"

She walked over to Ray and picked up her bag but stopped and spun round, turning back to Kathy.

"And if you ever make a pass at my man again it'll be that last thing you do! Come on Ray I don't need to travel with that kind of trash."

Ray looked at her as they left the lounge. "So you knew after all."

"Of course I knew, and thankfully for you, you turned her down. If you'd have said anything else I'd have killed you."

He pulled her arm and stopped her. "You are one of a kind babe." He held her close and kissed her.

She kissed him back. "I know!"

"So what do you think Pete will do now?" he said.

She looked over his shoulder as Pete came out of the lounge heading towards them. "I think we're about to find out."

"Fuck me, Janine that was awesome," Pete was out of breath. "Talk about shooting from the hip!"

"So what now Pete?" she asked.

"I'm with you guys. After what you said about the engagement scam I challenged her, and she couldn't give me an answer. It was all bullshit. And that thing about Ray, was that true?" Ray nodded. "Shit! Well I don't think she'll be making an appearance on the Johnny Carlton Show tomorrow. The last I saw was her slamming her way out of the back door dragging those ridiculous designer cases behind her. Do you think it will make any difference?"

Janine thought for a moment. "Pete Peterson fresh from his breakup with Kathy Blake! Damn right it'll make a difference," she said excitedly looking for a phone box. "Ray, you go and book tickets on the next flight. I need to call Manny. This is one hell of a story."

She stopped and turned back to Pete. "Pete, I'm sorry I had to do that but you needed to know. Women like her are all over LA and you deserve better."

They hugged each other and he kissed her cheek. Then he smiled. "Rock and Roll!"

The breakup of Pete and Kathy was the best thing that could have happened. The press had already found out by the time they touched down at JFK, and there was a posse of reporters and photographers waiting as they entered the Arrivals Hall. Janine and Manny had concocted a story which had been leaked to all the major papers, and the heart-broken rock star was besieged as they waited for the limousine to take them to the Waldorf Astoria.

Janine had told Manny about the rooms at the hotel, and he'd said he would deal with it for them. As they settled into the huge car provided by the hotel, Pete leaned back and closed his eyes. 'What on earth can happen next?' he thought. As if dating a film star wasn't enough, he was now going to be on prime-time TV explaining the breakup of his relationship. He wondered if anyone back in the UK knew what was happening. He briefly thought about Judy in Birmingham and what she was doing right now. He was jolted out of his reverie as their driver slammed his brakes on, cursing a yellow cab for cutting them up. They were driving down Fifth Avenue passing the world-famous Tiffany's where Audrey Hepburn had gazed forlornly in the window, heading downtown towards Times Square, Madison Square Gardens and the Empire State Building. Pete's favourite was the art deco Chrysler Building, and he was going to make sure he visited the Cloud Club on the 66th floor. Even though it was private, he was sure someone connected to Johnny Carlton could get him an invitation, maybe even Johnny himself!

They checked into the Waldorf Astoria, and it appeared Manny back in LA had been so persuasive on the phone, they'd been given the Presidential Suite on the 35th floor. Janine and Ray were in the Royal Suite named after the Duke and Duchess of Windsor and Pete had the Cole Porter Suite, complete with its own kitchen and dining room.

However, as soon as the management had found out he was an English rock star appearing on the Johnny Carlton Show, they requested a meeting with him and Janine. They were informed the hotel's policy was that since The Who in 1968 when Keith Moon had blown the door off his room, all English musicians were banned from staying there. Thankfully Manny Oberstein himself had personally guaranteed their stay and was flying in tomorrow to see the show, which was news to both Janine and Pete. But who could argue when the head of Westoria Records himself had decided to join the party.

All of America was watching when the English rock star Pete Peterson sat down opposite Johnny Carlton the following night. Dressed in a sparkling white shirt and black leather trousers, the screams from the girls in the audience were deafening as he waited to talk to the host.

Johnny Carlton was all smiles as he allowed the noise to die down. "Welcome to the show, Pete Peterson. How do you like your time in the States so far?"

"It's amazing," Pete replied. "I'm having a ball. I've got the best band in the world and it's going great."

Johnny Carlton paused. "There's been a few hiccups on the way though wouldn't you say?"

Pete looked puzzled. "I'm sorry?"

Johnny Carlton carried on. "Well your recent failed relationship to actress Kathy Blake. Was that anything to do with your previous drug problems back in the UK?"

There was silence then a few boos from the audience.

Pete was stunned and looked around while he composed himself. Eventually he spoke. "With respect sir, we all have times in our life when we do something which we later regret. I'm sure if we looked close enough there's a few skeletons in your wardrobe. Thankfully that's in my past now and I'm here just to play my music." The audience roared their approval and stood up cheering.

Pete's answer had taken Johnny Carlton by surprise and he acknowledged his response. "Well that's great news, and we can't wait to hear you and your band play. What song are you going to sing for us?"

"It's the title song from the album *In Flames* and we'll be touring all along the East coast starting next week." Pete replied. "So we hope you'll come and see us."

Johnny Carlton leaned across his desk and shook Pete's hand. "Ladies and Gentlemen, the latest star from the UK, playing his song *In Flames*, Pete Peterson!" The screams were louder than ever as he made his way over to the band who started the intro.

Manny Oberstein who had been standing side stage with Janine and Ray touched her shoulder as they started to play and shouted in her ear.

"That bastard will pay for those remarks. That's the last Westoria artist he gets on his show until he personally apologises to Pete for what he said." Janine looked surprised. "But I tell you what, that was an unbelievable answer Pete gave him. I don't think I've ever seen an artist cut him down so eloquently."

The band were coming to the end of the song and the credits were rolling as Johnny Carlton stood up from behind his desk. As soon as they had finished he walked over to Pete and shook his hand again. "I'll give you one thing young man, you've got balls!"

Pete shook his hand back. "Well there's a favour I'd like to ask Mr.

Carlton."

"Go ahead."

"I would love to go to the Cloud Club in the Chrysler Building, could you get me an invitation?" Pete asked tentatively.

Johnny Carlton laughed. "The Cloud Club? Not a problem. In fact as I'm an honorary member I'll take you myself. Where's Manny, and your delightful manager. We'll all go together."

"Hang on a minute," Pete interrupted. "We can't leave out my band and Don my tour manager."

Johnny Carlton laughed. "I like your style son. Of course, they will all be welcome. Come on I've suddenly developed a very large thirst!"

Manny Oberstein came over to Pete standing on his own, taking in the incredible view across Manhattan from the Cloud Club on the 66th floor of the Chrysler Building. It was everything he imagined when he'd first read about it. The art deco interior was stunning and he couldn't believe he was actually there inside it.

"That was an amazing interview tonight Pete," he said slapping him on the shoulder. "It's the first time that bastard Johnny Carlton has met his match for a long time, and along with the performance it's the perfect launch for the next set of gigs. Carry on like this and we're gonna have a number one sooner than you think."

He walked over to join Johnny Carlton at the bar as Janine came up to Pete and put her arm around his waist.

"Just one question. Would you really have left me?"

He looked at her with a wry grin. "Just try and get rid of me!"

CHAPTER TWENTY-SEVEN

José Valasquez switched off the TV set in the huge lounge at Surinam Chandra's house as the credits for the Johnny Carlton Show finished. His ex-wife Mandy had sat and watched Pete Peterson not only hold his own, but come out on top as the host had tried to embarrass him. José had asked her to watch the show with him and Surinam, and against her better judgement she'd agreed. Now she was pleased she had. Pete had been brilliant and she had a twinge of regret that she'd walked out on Manny when she did, and wasn't part of his success anymore. She'd joined Surinam's *Gatherings* because he intrigued her with the way he spoke and his ideas. She had become one of Surinam's special female supporters, succumbing one night to his charms when he chose her as his *favourite*. It had been an experience, but somehow not quite as she'd expected. In fact it was all about pleasing him rather than her.

She had gone to his luxurious bedroom which was decorated with animal skins covering the walls and floor. Responding to his requests, she slowly stripped as he lay playing with himself on the huge waterbed. Then she knelt down and took his frantic thrusts from behind her. She found herself secretly wishing she was with Janine. Their lovemaking had been spectacular. Her only regret was that she hadn't been able to convince Janine to join her.

She was just recalling their night in San Fransisco when José began outlining his plan to kidnap Pete Peterson. She'd only been half listening to what he was saying when suddenly she was all ears.

"Wait a minute. Did you just say kidnap Pete Peterson?"

"Yeah, it's a great idea and really simple," he replied. "He's going to be touring on the Northeast coast starting next week, so we need a list of all the venues he's going to be playing, details about how they get the equipment in and out and where they park up the coach."

Mandy looked at him skeptically. "This is not gonna be another Bank of America screw-up is it?"

"No it fuckin' isn't!" he snapped back at her. "And let's get one thing straight, that plan would have worked except for that bastard Raul." He scowled at Surinam. "So this is how we do it."

The TV appearance on the Johnny Carlton Show had sent ticket sales through the roof for Pete's upcoming shows, with the queue for the gig at the Bottom Line stretching round the block. Don had taken delivery of their new bus which was pretty much a carbon copy of the one they'd left back on the West Coast. The band had enthusiastically claimed their bunks and installed their personal belongings while it was parked outside the club.

The audience in New York was a little more high-brow than they'd had before. They sat studiously through the first few numbers listening intently. But it didn't take long before Pete's personality and the sheer power of the band had them rocking, and demanding two encores at the end of the show. Pete and the band were relaxing in the dressing room when Manny burst through the door.

"Guys that was fuckin' awesome," he enthused. "And great news. After last night's TV show the album has just gone into the top ten and the single is number five with a bullet."

Janine had followed him in with a bottle of champagne and popped the cork pouring out glasses for everyone.

Pete stood up and made a toast. "To the best record company and the best manager in the world. After everything that's happened we're finally on our way. Nothing's gonna stop us now!"

They all drank and Pete clinked his glass with Janine and Manny.

"I really mean that," he said. "You guys are the best."

There was a knock on the door and Don Rosario walked in.

"Pete there are some very attractive young ladies out there waiting to talk to you."

He drained his glass. "Best not keep them waiting then," he said as he followed Don.

While the band set off on the next run of dates, Janine and Ray took the opportunity to do a bit of sightseeing around New York. The helicopter ride to the Statue of Liberty frightened her to death, even though it had been her idea. Then going to the top of the Empire State Building at dusk. The lights of Manhattan were twinkling and it was the most romantic setting as Ray held her in his arms and asked her to marry him. Her tears were of happiness, although with a slight tinge of sadness, as she remembered when Gerry had got down on one knee and asked her the same question in Georgie's. But she was laughing when she said yes, and they kissed as the fellow visitors who had heard Ray ask her all applauded.

It was a magical moment and one she knew she would always remember. They spent the night in their sumptuous hotel suite making love and drinking champagne, and the following morning as they were eating breakfast Ray had another question.

"This might be crazy, but what about getting married in Las Vegas?"

Janine stopped eating and looked at him.

"Are you serious? Las Vegas!"

"Never been more serious," he replied. "So what do you say?"

"I think you're crazy, but that's never bothered me before. So when?"

Ray was on a roll. "Actually I was talking to Manny the other night. If we get married in August, Elvis Presley is on at The Sands and he can arrange for tickets to the show."

Janine looked at him aghast. "You're kidding, Elvis!"

"That's what he said. So that gives us four months to get everything organised."

Janine jumped up from the table. "Oh my god! Four months, we'll never do it," she said starting to panic.

Ray was as calm as ever. "Take it easy, of course we can do it. First we need to make sure Pete isn't on the road somewhere because I'd quite like him to be my best man."

"Oh that's a wonderful idea," Janine said. "Who should I get for my bridesmaid? Maybe I could ask my sister again. Would that be bad luck though? And what about guests? Would your parents come over, and what about mine? Do you think we could try and find them again?"

"Calm down, one thing at a time. Firstly it won't be as grand this time. We'll be in a small chapel so there won't be room for loads of guests, but it will be just as meaningful. As for finding your parents I could try giving Matt Burgess a ring to see if he could help."

"What about yours?"

Ray thought a moment. "They haven't spoken to me since I went to see them before we left, so I doubt anything's changed. I can ask but don't hold your breath. To be honest I'd rather we had a quiet ceremony with a few close friends. It would make it much easier to manage and maybe we could have a big party over in the UK later."

"What a great idea. Manny's booking some British dates later in the year, and there's talk of Pete possibly playing a gig at The Lexxicon. We could combine the two."

Judy Watson had already been in touch with Manny Oberstein's office to suggest Pete's band play The Lexxicon, and it was looking good for the end of September, which if her calculations were correct might just be perfect timing. She knew there would be no problem in selling tickets for the show, as the last time he'd played his home town he'd sold out the Town Hall, and he was a much bigger star now. The only thing she was worried about was if he still remembered her.

Manny had had a meeting with Janine in New York before he left to fly back to LA, and they'd discussed the possibility of tagging The Lexxicon on at the end of the UK and European tour they were currently booking. Janine knew Pete would definitely want to do it, and had given Manny the go ahead to add the date to what was shaping up to be a great tour. Hopefully by the time they arrived in the UK he would have a number one album both sides of the Atlantic.

Pete and the band were on their way to Chicago having played to packed houses in Cleveland, Pittsburgh and Cincinnati. All the radio stations were playing the single and the album was still climbing the chart, so they were expecting another sold out gig at Park West that night. But the excitement wasn't so much about the gig, more to do with Chicago's infamous Cynthia *Plaster Caster* Albritton whose speciality was to make plaster moulds of rock stars' penises. The guys had been winding Pete up all the way to the gig, and he was understandably nervous when he found out Jimi Hendrix was one of her most famous conquests. All through sound check he was on edge expecting any moment to be accosted by Cynthia and her moulding gel. In the end he needn't have worried. She'd sent a message to Don apologising that she couldn't be at the gig due to illness. However, his relief was short lived when she finished by saying she would catch up with them later in the tour, as she hadn't got any English dicks in her collection yet.

The gig was one of their best yet, which the guys put down to Pete's manhood having survived to live another day. It did see some action back on the bus though, with a very attractive young blonde who had made a fuss about being a big fan. She left with one of Pete's signature neckerchiefs and once again Don cursed himself for not taking advantage of an obvious merchandising opportunity.

The next gig in Detroit was a let down. Being the Motor City and home to Tamla Motown, Pete was maybe expecting too much, but the venue was only half full. For once they were disappointed, especially as they heard from Manny back in LA signs were good for the album to go top five. The single had stalled at number three but was still selling well and when they set off on the eleven-hour trip to Boston they were once again in high spirits.

CHAPTER TWENTY-EIGHT

José, Mandy and Tino, one of the shooters from the Fillmore in San Fransisco, had arrived at Logan International airport in Boston on the Friday evening before the gig. They made their way to an empty hotel called the Province, situated on the south bank of the Charles River in a once fashionable area called Back Bay. It was boarded up waiting to be renovated, and José had easily managed to break in unnoticed, especially as the new factory units surrounding it were all deserted at the weekend.

It had obviously been a grand building in its heyday, with decorative mouldings now crumbling where elaborate chandeliers had once hung. The four floors of bedrooms, some still containing beds, were ideal for their purpose. The venue Pete's band was playing, *Benrotty's,* was minutes away from where they were in the Province. It was a typical rock club with the bar and stage on the first floor and stairs at the rear down to an alley which led to the car park where the bands loaded in and out. After dark they'd driven down to recce the place, and noticed the alley was badly lit with only one lamp above the exit, and then nothing until the car park which was about twenty yards away. Also there were two doorways one either side halfway down, where José and Tino could hide in the shadows. This would all weigh heavily in their favour, as after the band had finished playing and were taking the equipment out to the bus, they could wait for an opportune moment to grab Pete. Then they would bundle him into the back of the old delivery van José had bought earlier, which would be parked with the engine running at the side of the band's coach. Mandy would be driving, and once back at the hotel with Pete as their hostage, José would contact Janine Fortuna with his ransom demands and she would be forced to pay up. It was the perfect plan because of it's simplicity. What could possibly go wrong?

The evening of the gig José and Tino were both hyper, having snorted the best part of a bag of cocaine between them during the day. Mandy watched them strutting up and down aimlessly in the derelict foyer as it started to get dark. It would soon be time for them to leave, but there was a bad atmosphere as earlier Tino had angrily stormed off because

José had refused to let him have any more drugs. In his temper he had fired a couple of rounds at a rat in one of the bedrooms. He missed it by a mile, but the sound had echoed around the building.

Unknown to the three kidnappers, a security guard was across the road checking one of the factory sites on his round and heard the gunshots. He knew the old hotel was supposed to be empty as he'd only recently helped evict some squatters, and driving off in his van thought he would report the incident to the office when he finished his shift later that night.

The first problem the kidnappers encountered on leaving their hiding place was the van's reluctance to start. After a fraught ten minutes inspecting the distributor and ignition leads, the engine finally started and they made their way to the club. This put them behind schedule, and as they pulled into the car park at the back of *Benrotty's* their second problem became apparent. Since the increase in popularity of the band after their appearance on the Johnny Carlton Show, Don Rosario had become more security conscious. He had parked their bus across the end of the alley to stop any inquisitive female fans sneaking onto it after the show. Instead of leaving space for the band to get onto the bus at the front and load their equipment into the side, he'd only left a tiny gap at the end of the alley, meaning José and Tino had to squeeze through one at a time. This meant there was not enough space for them to easily get Pete back to where Mandy would be waiting in the van.

After a fruitless tour around the car park looking for an alternative, Mandy pulled up at the rear of the bus. As the two men climbed out, they noticed that the sound of music from the club had already stopped. Entering the narrow gap into the alley they could hear someone coming down the stairs which meant they had to move fast. They had just pulled on their black balaclavas when Pete came out of the doorway with his arm around a girl.

José, not even having had time to hide in either of the doorways as planned, pointed his gun at Pete. "Leave the girl and come with us," he shouted menacingly.

José grabbed Pete's arm forcing him down the alley. As they passed Tino he moved across to cover them. Everything was going fine until the girl started to scream.

Tino shouted at the girl to stop screaming, just as Don and Richard Kaye the keyboard player came out into the alley carrying a long flight case. Tino, brandishing his gun threateningly grabbed the girl. With his arm around her neck he started to drag her backwards down the alley, glancing over his shoulder to see where José was.

Don took the split second that Tino was distracted. He dropped his end of the flight case and slipped his Magnum 45 from the rear waistband of his trousers. As Tino spun back round he saw the pistol in the ex-cop's hand and panicked. He fired blindly in Don's direction, but made the fatal mistake of releasing his grip on the girl, who collapsed on the floor and Don calmly put a bullet through Tino's right eye killing him instantly.

As the dead kidnapper fell to the ground, there was the sound of an engine revving loudly at the back of the coach, but before Don had a chance to give chase Marshall the drummer shouted his name. He and Randy the bass player were standing over a body slumped on the floor at the side of the case he'd been carrying seconds earlier. It was Richard, but as Don instinctively felt for a pulse, the pool of blood under Richard's body told him there was no hope. The bullet from Tino's gun had missed him but had obviously hit Richard in the chest. He looked up slowly at the two stunned musicians, while noticing the girl who had been with Pete was still lying on the floor in shock. He told the guys to take her back in the club and call an ambulance, but before they could the sounds of sirens arriving in the car park filled the air.

Don took his jacket off and laid it across Richard's lifeless body. Then looking around suddenly realised Pete wasn't there. He remembered seeing him walking down the stairs with the girl as he and Richard were packing the flight case. In all the confusion he'd completely forgotten about him, and after a quick search of the bus he came to the conclusion that the vehicle he'd heard driving off in such a hurry had probably contained his most valuable asset, Pete Peterson.

The alley was rapidly filling with police and he calmly raised his hands in the air, before handing over his weapon to one of the officers.

CHAPTER TWENTY-NINE

Ray and Janine had decided to stop off in Las Vegas on their way home from New York to get the ball rolling with their wedding arrangements. They'd set the date in August and booked the famous White Chapel on the Strip, as well as making a reservation to stay at The Sands which was where Manny had said Elvis would be performing. They were both buzzing with excitement as they flopped down on the large king-sized bed in their hotel room that evening. Ray automatically switched on the TV, absentmindedly flicking through the channels. He eventually stopped on a news channel which had the headline *ROCK STAR MISSING AFTER TWO MEN SHOT DEAD IN ARMED KIDNAPPING* at the bottom of the screen. He turned up the volume just as a reporter appeared on camera standing in an alleyway. Before he'd even spoken a word Ray's blood ran cold, because he recognised the bus in the background.

The reporter looked up and started his piece to camera. "There was high drama tonight at Benrotty's rock club in Boston, with the sensational kidnapping of English rock star, Pete Peterson. He was abducted by persons unknown as one of his fellow musicians and one of the kidnappers were both shot dead in this alley behind the club. As yet there has been no word from the kidnappers."

Janine who was in the bathroom froze as she heard what the reporter had just said. Ray was trying to remain calm while he watched the images of Don in handcuffs, and Marshall and Randy standing looking shocked. A body bag was being wheeled out on a stretcher and Ray suddenly knew it must be Richard Kaye, the keyboard player. The reporter had said one of the dead was a musician from Pete's band and the other two guys were there in the background.

Janine rushed out into the room. "Ray! We need to get there. Now!"

José had handcuffed Pete and put a bag over his head as soon as he was in the back of the van, telling him to lie down and keep quiet. Being threatened with a gun was not something Pete had experienced before, and he did as he was told.

At the sound of gunshots José screamed at Mandy to drive.

Now after a short journey Pete felt them come to a stop, and he was dragged from the van. Even though he still had the hood on he could tell they were entering an old building of some kind, because it had a damp, musty smell and there were the remains of carpet on the floor which he could feel as he walked. They guided him up a flight of stairs and he could hear them opening and closing doors as he was led down a long corridor.

Finally they must have found what they were looking for and he was pushed inside a room. His handcuffs were removed and his hood pulled off as they left, locking the door behind them. It was dark inside, but he could just see thin slivers of light coming through the gaps in the wooden boards that had been used to block up the window, which meant there must be streetlights outside. There was no noise inside the building but as he listened he could hear the sound of running water close by, which he thought could possibly be a large river. There was also the distant sound of traffic, so he decided he was still somewhere in Boston.

He fumbled his way around the room and found a light switch, but it didn't work. As well as a bed, there was a wardrobe and a sink which could mean he was in some sort of hotel considering the number of rooms they'd tried when they brought him in. He sat down on the bed and thought back to what had just happened. He remembered he had been on his way out to the bus with a young girl who'd made it obvious why she wanted to go there with him. Then there was a man in the alley wearing a balaclava with holes cut out for his eyes, who had pointed a gun at him and forced him to get into a van. He'd had an accomplice but from the sound of gunshots he'd heard, something must have happened, because there only seemed like there were two of them now, and one was the driver who had been waiting in the van. He was suddenly overcome by tiredness now that the initial burst of adrenaline from the attack had dissipated, and laid down on the bed to try and sleep. Just as he closed his eyes the door was unlocked again and his two kidnappers came into the room shining a bright torch in his face. They were still wearing their balaclavas and the taller one of the two who was holding the torch spoke.

"If you do as we say you won't be hurt."

Pete was holding his hand in front of his eyes shielding them from the bright light.

The man continued. "My partner here is going to take your photograph, so move your hand away from your face and look at the camera."

The smaller one pressed the button on the Polaroid camera and seconds later a print appeared.

"Not one of your best poses for your fans, but it will do," the man said and they both started to walk out of the room.

"Why are you doing this?" Pete shouted and the man stopped and turned around.

"For money, what else?" he said, and closed the door locking it again.

Under her breath so José didn't hear as he walked away down the corridor, Mandy whispered. "And revenge!"

But Pete heard, and now knew one of his kidnappers was a woman. And although it was muffled he thought he recognised her voice although he couldn't place it.

Janine and Ray landed at Logan International Airport early the next morning on their way to a hurriedly arranged meeting with Don Rosario and the Chief of Police at the Boston police headquarters.

At the same time an envelope was delivered to the local television news station addressed *For the attention of Janine Fortuna, manager of Pete Peterson*. The reporter who had made the broadcast from outside the club had immediately called the police and arranged for it to be sent over to them. In it was a Polaroid photograph of a tired and unsmiling Pete and a ransom letter demanding five million dollars for the safe release of her artist Pete Peterson. At the bottom were the details of an account registered in an offshore bank in the Bahamas where the money was to be deposited within 24 hours. Failure to do so would result in her artist being returned to her in a box.

Janine had called Manny Oberstein back in LA for his advice, and while they were talking, Don and Ray had sat down with the Chief of Police to discuss the situation. The kidnapping was now headlining news right across the country with reporters from every major news channel descending on Boston, which was bothering the chief.

"We need to keep this under control otherwise it'll turn into one of those media circuses," he said. "There's already calls coming in from people reporting sightings of a van being driven away from the club after the gunshots."

Don who had been briefly arrested for shooting the kidnapper but later released pending an investigation, explained his and Ray's history as ex-cops. He asked that they be given 24 hours to carry out their own investigation. This was personal to them and although the chief was initially sceptical he agreed. After that he would take over.

"It's a bit like looking for the proverbial needle in a haystack," Ray said as he and Don began sifting through the information they had so far. "We could do with a lucky break."

While they were going through the calls already recorded, an officer brought in a message from a security guard who had been watching the morning news. He reported he'd heard gunshots fired last night in a deserted hotel in Back Bay, opposite one of the sites he patrolled.

Ray was immediately on high alert. "Maybe we just got it."

The security guard, Sol Adams, had left a phone number and Ray and Don arranged to meet him just down the road from the old hotel.

He was already waiting when they arrived in an unmarked police car which they'd managed to borrow, and explained he was an ex-Boston cop now working for a company called Securex.

From a distance everything looked quiet. The old hotel was situated on the bank of the Charles River about a thousand yards from the main Longfellow Road Bridge. By the look of it, in it's heyday the hotel would have been a popular destination for tourists, but was now boarded up and surrounded by new factory units.

Ray and Don told Sol what they wanted him to do, and then waited while he drove up to the factory unit across from the Province and carried out his usual inspection. He'd then carried on to the end of the road to turn round and check out the back of the hotel. It was well hidden, but he'd spotted the van and driven back to Ray and Don to report what he'd seen.

Mandy hadn't slept a wink all night. She'd kept a watchful eye on José who had been in a foul mood when Tino hadn't returned. He'd paced up and down snorting more cocaine, threatening to just shoot Pete and forget the ransom. It had taken Mandy all of her persuasive powers to stop him, and finally he'd agreed to carry out the next part of the plan and he'd left earlier to deliver the envelope containing the photo and ransom letter, to the local TV station.

Pete had woken up and remembered the events of last night. Although it was daytime there wasn't much light because of the window being blocked. He tried the light switch again, but then saw there wasn't a bulb, and looking at the state of the place he doubted there was any electricity either. He needed to go for a pee and banged on the door, but no one seemed to hear him.

Mandy had heard Pete knocking on the door, but without a gun she wasn't going to risk opening it until José got back.

When he eventually returned with some supplies of coffee and doughnuts, José told her about Tino after seeing the headlines in the newspaper. He'd also called Benny Mulligan, who had not been happy seeing the reports on TV about the two dead bodies. Benny had warned him if this heist didn't come off not to bother returning to Miami, which had made José's bad mood even worse.

By now Pete's need to relieve himself was becoming desperate and his knocking louder. Making sure they both had their balaclavas on, José unlocked his door and took him at gunpoint to one of the bathrooms along the corridor where he stood watching as Pete emptied his bladder.

Any attempt at conversation was ignored and he was returned to the same room with the door locked again.

Sitting on his bed Pete was now sure he knew the identity of one of his captors. And after hearing her voice last night and seeing her today, he finally remembered where he'd seen that walk before.

José had stormed off after taking Pete to the bathroom, and leaving him to cool down, Mandy had taken a walk up to the top floor where some of the windows hadn't been boarded up. She was casually looking out across the surrounding factories and the river when she noticed a security guard in his van drive up to the unit across the road and check all round the perimeter. That in itself wasn't unusual on a weekend when everywhere around was closed, but what she didn't understand was why he slowly drove down to the end of the road behind the hotel before turning round, driving back and then pulling up at the side of a large car parked further down. It was just far enough away for her not to be able to make out who was in the car, but she had the feeling that something was wrong and ran down the stairs to find Jose.

Sol Adams had driven back with the news he'd spotted the van, and now they knew there was a strong chance this was where Pete was being held. So far they were hoping they had surprise on their side, although parked facing the hotel Don could have sworn he saw a face at one of the top floor windows. If so they would have to use some old-fashioned fieldcraft which was where Sol came into play. He had told them how, in his younger days before he joined the Boston PD, he had been a Special Forces guerilla warfare expert having served during the Cuban Missile Crisis. Although now working in security, he was still pretty active, and he had a plan. Ray and Don were all ears.

Evidently when he'd helped evict the squatters from the hotel, they'd found an old coal delivery hatch at the rear that was no longer used, and he was sure he would be able to get inside without the kidnappers knowing. The main problem would be finding where they had Pete and ensuring his safety. Ray and Don were aware the clock was ticking on the ransom demand, and they had to decide what would be their next move.

Suddenly the sound of glass shattering as a bullet pierced the windscreen of Sol's van made the decision for them, and Don slammed his foot down reversing out of range. Fortunately Sol had been sitting in the back of their car at the time.

"Shit! That's really screwed us," Ray exclaimed as they parked up around the corner.

"Well it means they know we're here for sure," Sol replied.

Don turned around in his seat and spoke to Sol. "Are you carrying?"

"Of course, wouldn't go anywhere without it," he answered, proudly showing him his .45 ACP Colt.

"Nice!" Don nodded appreciatively as Ray watched on enviously. Don saw his expression and opening the glove compartment handed him a 9mm Beretta. "Don't want you to feel left out," he said as Ray took it from him. "You sure you'll be OK?"

"Don't worry about me," Ray said. "We might not carry them in the UK, but I was champion shot three years on the run in our gun club."

"Yeah well we're not dealing with paper targets this time, so just be careful." Don replied.

Mandy had found José and the pair of them ran back up to the top floor with the combat rifle he'd brought just in case of trouble. He was an expert shot, and considering the distance had easily taken out the windscreen of the Securex van. They both watched as the car alongside reversed backwards at high speed before disappearing around the next corner.

José looked pleased with himself but Mandy wasn't so sure. "OK. So what are we going to do now?"

"I don't know, but we need to get out of here," he replied.

"But where will we go?"

José was getting flustered by her questions. "I don't fucking know!" he shouted. "Go and get the van ready."

Mandy laughed. "You're not seriously thinking we can outrun anything in that pile of shit are you?"

José spun round and glared at her. "Just do it!"

"What about our guest downstairs?"

"I'm working on it." José was thinking.

"Give me your pistol," Mandy said holding out her hand as she turned to leave.

He handed her the pistol stuck in the back of his jeans, and checking it was loaded she flicked the safety catch off as she went downstairs.

Sol had given Don directions which took them via a service road round to the back of the hotel. Leaving them in the car, he slipped through some rusty metal fencing and cautiously made his way to the secret entrance. He carefully lifted up the old wooden hatch and slid down the chute into the basement, landing on a pile of soil and coal dust that had accumulated over the years.

Brushing himself down he manoeuvred his way through the now derelict kitchen and quietly slipped through the service door into what was once the restaurant. From there he crept up to the reception area, just as Mandy came down the stairs on her way to the van parked out the back. He ducked into a doorway and watched as she opened the door José had first used to gain entry, then stopped dead in her tracks. Hurriedly pulling the door closed, she ran through reception and back up the stairs.

The moment Sol had disappeared inside the hotel, Don had radioed back to police headquarters updating the chief with what had happened. He had immediately sent the armed response unit to the hotel, while another team sprang into action sealing off all the escape routes in the vicinity.

Ray and Don had been spotted by Mandy as she was about to leave by the back door. As she pulled the door closed they jumped out of the car and ran over, cautiously entering the building.

As Mandy ran past him, Sol slipped out from his hiding place and silently followed her, pausing at the first floor as she carried on upwards. Even though it was daytime it was dark inside because of the boarding on the windows, and he could just make out there were two corridors off the landing. Something told him Pete was close by. He listened carefully and thought he heard knocking coming from one of the rooms off to his right. Knowing he had to act quickly he set off down the corridor checking each room, until he reached the last one where there was definitely someone inside. The door was locked but trying to be as quiet as he could he tapped on the door and called Pete's name.

The knocking stopped and a voice replied. "Help me! Get me out."

Sol stepped back and listened again for any noise coming from upstairs but it still appeared to be quiet. He tried the door with his shoulder but to no avail. There was no other choice.

"Stand back," he said and lifting his leg kicked the door just above the lock splintering the wood, causing the door to swing open with a loud crash.

Not exactly the result he was after, but there was no time to think about that now. He could make out Pete in the semi-darkness and started to lead him out of the room.

At the same time, José and Mandy came running down the stairs to investigate the noise they'd heard.

José saw Sol a split second before Sol saw him, and fired his gun. He caught Sol in the shoulder spinning him off balance as he attempted to fire back, while at the same time pushing Pete back into the room again. José laughed as Sol's bullet missed its target, and started to walk down the corridor. But he wasn't expecting the ex-special forces man to be able to gather himself so quickly and fire again. This time he hit José in the stomach.

Downstairs in the foyer, Ray and Don just had time to get their bearings when they heard the loud crash from upstairs, followed seconds later by two gunshots. Without a moment's hesitation Ray had set off up the staircase followed closely by Don. As they reached the first landing another shot rang out, causing them to dive for cover. Peering through the top of the bannister, Ray could just see Sol sitting on the floor at the end of the corridor, and Mandy dragging her wounded accomplice into the bedroom. As she did so she kept her pistol pointed at Sol to dissuade him from firing again. Once inside she tried to push the door closed but it was hanging off its hinges after Sol's kick. There was a noise from behind her, and turning round she remembered that in the corner was their valuable hostage, and suddenly things weren't so bad. She went back to the doorway and peeped out, just as Sol reached the landing where Ray and Don were helping him to safety.

Mandy shouted down the corridor to them. "This changes nothing. We still have your precious Pete Peterson."

Pete had fallen back into the room when Sol had pushed him as José opened fire, and he'd ended up on his back between the wall and the end of the bed.

He sat up. "Why are you doing this Mandy? I mean, what's the point?"

She looked round at him. "You'll never understand, so just keep your mouth shut for once," she snarled.

José groaned and tried to sit up but he was in too much pain and losing a lot of blood.

"He needs a doctor, even I can see that," Pete said standing up and looking at him.

Mandy pointed her gun at him. "I said shut up. Sit down on the bed and keep quiet."

She went back to the doorway. "I want to speak to Janine Fortuna. Fetch her here now or her boy dies."

Ray who was at the end of the corridor helping Sol heard her.

"That will take a while, she's back at police headquarters in Boston."

"I don't give a shit where she is. I said I want to speak to her or Pete Peterson gets a bullet," Mandy replied.

Ray ran down the stairs and went out to their car to use the radio. He contacted the chief who fetched Janine to the microphone. As quickly as he could Ray explained what had happened, and how Mandy was holding Pete hostage in a room along with her ex-husband who had been shot. Janine passed the mic back to the chief who agreed to organise a car to bring her to the hotel. He also explained to Ray that because it had become a hostage situation, he was considering sending the armed response team in, but was worried as it could easily become a blood bath with Pete caught up in the middle.

Ray agreed and ran back upstairs to speak to Don, before letting Mandy know Janine was on her way.

Sol's wound wasn't as bad as they first thought. The bullet had gone straight through, and between them Don and Sol had managed to stem the bleeding and fashion a crude sling from a piece of sheet they'd found in one of the rooms. As Ray was explaining what the chief had said and that Janine was on her way, he decided it was up to him to take charge of the situation. He'd had hostage negotiation training back in the UK, and apart from the one occasion with Frank Kelly when he'd rammed his car into a concrete block, there had never been the opportunity to use it. Now was the time!

Janine arrived ten minutes later, and he met her at the door where he quickly explained the current situation. She was wearing a Boston PD jacket over her top which Ray thought a bit unusual; maybe she was cold, but he ignored it as they made their way through the foyer, and up the stairs to the landing where Don gave her a reassuring hug.

"Don't worry, everything's gonna be fine," he said. "Keep calm and do what Ray says. We'll be right behind you."

She looked him in the eyes. "And when it is, your arse is mine for losing him in the first place," she said. "Come on Ray let's do this!"

Ray looked at Don and raised his eyebrows. He walked to the end of the corridor and called out to Mandy.

"I have Janine Fortuna here with me now."

There was a pause then Mandy's head appeared around the door frame.

"Tell her to come down here slowly, on her own, with her hands out in front of her where I can see them. No funny business or your boy gets it."

Ray looked worried but Janine seemed calm. "Let me do it," she said. "I can talk to her." Without giving Ray chance to answer, she set off down the corridor with her hands spread wide in front of her and stopped at the doorway.

It was dark inside, but she could make out Mandy standing pointing a pistol at her, with Pete sitting on the bed. A man was on the floor slumped against the wall. He was covered in blood, looking in a bad way.

Mandy smiled at her. "Janine! Come on in and join the party. I'm sorry there's no champagne."

Janine slowly entered the room as Ray and Don silently crept down the corridor staying close to the wall. There was the slightest creak of a floorboard and Mandy looked beyond Janine and shouted. "And unless your friends stay on the landing, I'll shoot him now. You hear me!"

Ray and Don froze and slowly made their way back to where they had started.

Janine looked around the room and back at Mandy.

"Why Mandy? Why are you doing this? You had everything going for you at Westoria. So what made you change?"

Mandy let the hand holding the gun drop to her side.

"Excitement. I needed some excitement. You think it was all hunky dory at Westoria? Manny was a bastard to work for, and I was going through the motions. Then you came along. You were a breath of fresh air. I really thought we could have had something. But no. You had your man, so I went back to Surinam."

"You knew he would be there that night when we met at that bar didn't you?" Janine interrupted her.

"Yeah, he insisted on coming to check you out. He wanted to get you involved in his *Gatherings*. He thought because you were rich you'd be an easy target, but I made sure he knew you were mine that night."

"So why did you get involved with him?" Janine asked.

"He was rich and treated me well, and there were loads of good-looking women who were game for anything. It was going great until this piece of shit turned up again." She pointed her pistol at José who looked up at her and groaned.

"He needs a doctor, Mandy," Janine said.

Mandy swung back round at Janine with hate in her eyes.

"A doctor! Do you know what that bastard did to me? Do you? He raped me with the point of his knife at my throat. He thought he was so big and powerful. Fucking me while I lay there helpless." She turned back to José and pointed the gun at his head. "Well you're not so big and powerful now are you?"

She fired the pistol and the explosion in the small room was deafening, as pieces of José's brain were splattered on the wall behind him.

Ignoring her threat, Ray and Don ran down the corridor and got to the doorway as Mandy grabbed hold of Pete pulling him in front of her and pressing the gun to his head. They watched powerless as she screamed at Janine.

"I LOVED YOU! I FUCKING LOVED YOU AND AFTER ALL WE DID YOU THOUGHT WE COULD JUST BE FRIENDS. FUCK YOU JANINE FORTUNA!"

Before either Ray or Don could move she shot Janine in the chest and then put the gun in her mouth and pulled the trigger.

"NOOOO!" Ray shouted as Janine fell backwards and landed on the floor in front of him. Almost in slow motion he had watched his future wife gunned down by a crazed woman, who had then put the pistol in her mouth and blown the back of her head off. He knelt down in shock and cradled Janine's head in his arms as his tears began to fall on her face. It seemed like he held her for ages, when suddenly she opened her eyes and looked up at him.

"Jesus, Ray; stop blubbing and help me up will ya."

Ray was speechless as she stood up and pulled off the jacket she'd been given by the Chief before she left headquarters, which was covering the Kevlar vest he'd insisted she wear.

Ray choked back a sob as he grabbed her in his arms and kissed her but she pushed him away. "Owww, that's really sore! I'm gonna have a feckin' bruise there tomorrow!"

Don had watched from the doorway, amazed at Janine's recovery. He looked over at Pete who had been sitting quietly on the bed. "Hey man, I think it's time we got out of here," he said.

Pete slowly got off the bed and looked around the room, before following him out into the corridor.

"What happen to Richard?" he asked as they walked down the stairs.

The media circus was waiting outside as they emerged. They'd been kept well back by the police, but now as they saw Pete, the clamour for interviews and photographs was frantic and they surged forward. Janine was acutely aware of the traumatic experience that Pete had just been through, and was doing her best to keep him away from the barrage of questions, but he asked her to allow him to speak to the gathered throng and a hastily assembled press conference was set up right outside, with the hotel as a dramatic backdrop.

He'd taken a few minutes to compose himself, before finally walking up to the array of microphones and beginning to speak.

"What happened to me over the past few hours has been a nightmare. I've just learned that my keyboard player, Richard Kaye, tragically died after being shot in the alley outside the club. He was a wonderful guy; an amazing musician and my thoughts are with his family and friends. I would like to thank Sol Adams who until today I had never met, my incredible tour manager Don Rosario and my good friend Ray Law for their unceasing support and bravery, and finally to my manager and personal friend Janine Fortuna, without whose tenacity and devotion I wouldn't be here today. I have one final thing to say to whoever was responsible for this atrocity. This will not stop me and I will come back stronger than ever. Thank you."

Pete turned and walked away with the shouted questions from the journalists ringing in his ears.

Janine had stood at the side watching him, and embraced him with tears in her eyes as they walked over to the waiting car. He smiled and gave her a sly wink as they climbed into the back.

"I'm getting good at this don't you think?" he said.

She gave him an inquisitive look. "You're not telling me you didn't mean what you've just said?"

"Of course not," he answered. "But it'll certainly sell a few more albums and tickets to the gigs!"

She rolled her eyes. "Oh my God Pete Peterson, you are incorrigible!"

"Yeah but you wouldn't have me any other way," he replied. "Now I could murder a drink!"

CHAPTER THIRTY

Pete, Janine and Ray had flown back to LA the following morning and gone straight to Manny's office. There was a huge crowd of journalists at the airport, but they'd managed to slip out of a side exit, jumping into a cab instead of the limousine parked out front. Manny was waiting in his office when they arrived and welcomed Pete with a huge bear hug.

"That was one of the greatest press conferences I've ever witnessed," he gushed. "You know it's been shown worldwide. It's sent your album and single straight to number one. Genius, sheer genius!" He popped the cork on a bottle of champagne and poured them all a glass. "Bollinger, your favourite, Janine."

"So what's the next step?" she asked as they sat down.

"We get Pete on a few chat shows, and he relives his darkest moments. They're queuing up for him, including Johnny Carlton." He laughed. "Oh and we've already been offered the rights for a film script. It's all gone crazy. But first things first, how are you Pete? What are your thoughts?"

Pete sat quietly for a few moments. "I need to talk to the band and Don. I love those guys and what happened can't affect us. Also I have an idea. Janine, you remember I always rated the keyboard player back in the UK. The guy who joined The Flames on the last tour? Dave Sanchez. He's a great player and I always said we'd work together again. We can fly him over to start rehearsing straight away. With the tour of Europe and the UK coming up it's the perfect time to get him in. What do you say?"

"He certainly was a great player," she replied. "What do you think Manny?"

"Well he's gonna have to be some player to replace Richard, but if Pete rates him I'm happy to go along with it."

"Great, I'll call him later. I've still got his number. He'll be perfect," Pete said. "Look guys I really need to get back to my place and chill out, so if you don't mind can we catch up again tomorrow?"

"Sure," Manny said. "How about down at Whitland Studios with the rest of the guys? I'll get Don to arrange for them to be there at midday."

Manny took Janine to one side as Pete was leaving. "I think we need to talk about this situation with Rota Bocan don't you?" he said seriously. "I spoke to Don and he told me about the episode up in 'Frisco. You didn't think it was worth mentioning it to me?"

Janine had to think carefully. She knew she had to tell him the truth but at the same time how would it impact on their situation?

"Look Manny, as you know, when Gerry was murdered there was a rumour that it was linked to the Rota Bocan, although there was never any concrete proof. Ray was in charge of the case and got absolutely nowhere. Then when the stuff happened up in San Fransisco I assumed it was a coincidence, because the promoter told Don about the drugs feud. But when Ray came back he became suspicious. I mean I'd never have dreamed Mandy was involved, but after yesterday and what she said, who can you trust? I just can't believe she's dead."

"Benny Mulligan has the reputation as an evil gangster, and the last thing you and Pete need now, is for him to start a vendetta against you," Manny said. "I suggest you and Ray go and speak to Don and his exboss before this escalates out of hand. Let's hope this latest episode was just that jerk José trying to make a name for himself; don't think for a minute Benny Mulligan will give up that easily."

In his luxury villa in Miami, Benny Mulligan had just watched a re-run of Pete's press conference from outside the Province hotel and was livid. He'd lost the chance of ten million dollars in the space of two weeks. It was lucky for José he was dead, because Benny would have shot him himself. First the bank and now the kidnapping, it was making him look a fool, and nobody made Benny Mulligan look a fool, and lived!

He'd been on the phone for ages to Surinam Chandra in LA, shouting at him.

Shanice, his Filipino maid had sensed he was in a bad mood, and was doing her best to keep out of his way in one of the bedrooms upstairs. He finally slammed the phone down and shouted her name. She came downstairs and entered the lounge where he was sitting smoking one of his Cuban cigars which she hated. He beckoned her over and unzipped his shorts. "Don't just stand there," he said blowing out a cloud of smoke. "You know what to do, don't you?"

She approached him trying to hide her distaste as she knelt down and took his pathetic manhood in her hand.

"Go on, suck it bitch," he sneered as he lay back in his leather armchair while she worked on getting him hard.

He grabbed her hair and pushed her face down to his crotch as he arched his back forcing himself in her mouth. She gagged as he pushed her head down harder, then suddenly pulled her away. He lifted her up so her legs straddled him and lowered her down onto him. It wasn't as if he were of any size to get her excited and she hated him doing this to her, but she went through the motions to make him think he was satisfying her. She climbed off him and walked away wiping herself with her duster. Going into the bathroom she threw it into the bin as she vomited.

Janine and Ray had done as Manny suggested, and were sitting in Captain Lewis' cramped office at LAPD headquarters with Don Rosario. Coupled with the fog of the captain's cheap cigar smoke, the heat was stifling, and Janine was dying to get some fresh air. She was amazed the others didn't seem to notice as they discussed the situation regarding Benny Mulligan.

"This last couple of weeks must have hit him hard," Captain Lewis pointed out. "If you take into account what he would have made from the bank robbery and then the ransom for Pete. You're looking at ten million dollars.'

"Yeah and also his failed attempts at taking over the drugs supply in San Fransisco and a few other cities. He must be seriously running low on funds right now," Don said.

"So what do you think his next move will be?" Ray asked.

Captain Lewis stood up and blew more of the acrid smoke into the already thick atmosphere.

"It's hard to tell, because the way he works is so random. But I've a feeling he'll be looking for revenge, and you two guys will be high up on his list of names."

Janine had been sitting listening. "So what are we supposed to do, hide away? Because you can forget that! Who the hell does this Benny Mulligan think he is?"

"Well he's one mean motherfucker," Don replied. "There were stories of him having people murdered just for trying to skim a little off the top in deals. And look at what happened in Birmingham with you guys."

"We could never prove any connection, but when he came out with that statement it was pretty blatant." Ray said.

"Well I for one am not gonna be constantly looking over my shoulder." Janine said. "So can we get out of this feckin' oven before I die of heat stroke. C'mon Ray, we've a wedding to plan."

"Congratulations!" Captain Lewis said as they got up to leave. "But be careful. Don't underestimate Benny Mulligan."

Don followed them out. "So what are your plans then guys, are you still going ahead with Vegas?"

"Damn right we are," Janine said. "We've booked the chapel, got a suite at The Sands and Manny's got us tickets for Elvis. Pete's gonna be Ray's witness, and I'm flying my sister out to be mine. We were both hoping you'll be there too? It's not going to be a huge affair, just close friends. Maybe you could bring that nice actress you were getting friendly with at Kathy Blake's party. Ray said you'd been seeing a lot of her recently."

Don gave an embarrassed laugh. "Well since Pete's rather public split with Kathy that relationship has gone rather quiet. But hey, I'd be honoured to be there either way."

Since the press conference outside the hotel in Boston, Pete had been busy doing interviews, talking about his harrowing ordeal at the hands of drug-crazed kidnappers. Manny's press office at Westoria Records had excelled themselves, and there wasn't a TV channel, newspaper or magazine that hadn't run a feature on the English rock star. He'd even flown over to New York specially to appear on Johnny Carlton's show.

This time Johnny had been the complete opposite of their last interview, and treated Pete with the utmost respect. He'd even arranged for him to go to The Cloud Club afterwards, remembering it was Pete's favourite place to visit in New York.

At the same time, he'd been fitting in rehearsals with his new keyboard player Dave Sanchez, who had flown over to LA in preparation for the upcoming European and UK tour. He had settled in straight away, and although the guys were still saddened by the death of Richard Kaye, they had quickly accepted Dave as one of the family. It also helped that he was an amazing musician and had played on all the tracks on *In Flames* that were in Pete's show. Exciting information had come through from the agent booking the tour that since the news stories of Pete's kidnapping, every date in the UK had sold out and the album had rocketed to number one all over Europe.

Whilst Pete had been attracting all the headlines, Janine and Ray had been discreetly organising their wedding, and as the weeks went by suddenly the big day was upon them.

Janine's sister Jackie had flown in with her husband and were enjoying a couple of days at The Sands where Janine and Ray had joined them. Much to Ray's surprise, his parents had been delighted to accept their invitation arriving on the same flight as Janine's sister, and were already the best of friends. Pete was flying in on the day by private jet, along with Don and his actress friend, Manny and his wife and the guys from the band with their girlfriends. Sadly the situation with Janine's parents was still the same and they remained somewhere in hiding in the Republic of Ireland.

Although it was a much lower profile affair than her last wedding day at Birmingham Cathedral, Janine was just as wound up. Ray constantly assured her there was nothing to worry about, that everything was under control and she could just relax and enjoy becoming Mrs. Janine Law and after the wedding they had a private room booked for the reception where Pete had organised some equipment for him and the band to jam, and where everyone could let their hair down.

The actual service was over in a flash. With the marriage certificate signed, Mr. and Mrs. Ray Law were now legally married and they all headed back to the hotel.

Janine couldn't help notice that Manny had been busy on the phone since he'd arrived, and was looking pleased with himself as he joined the party. There were a couple of special guests who had been sent invitations who surprised everyone by showing up including Vince Boyd with his personal assistant, and the biggest surprise of all when Charles Morse walked through the door along with his PA who it seemed had recently become more than just his PA. He'd been in Las Vegas filming a commercial and was thrilled to have been invited.

They'd all had a delicious meal and as Ray's best man, Pete had made a speech followed by a toast to the bride and groom, and now he and the band were getting ready to play a few songs. It had turned out to be a wonderful day, and because the service had been in the morning it was still early afternoon. Everybody was chatting and not really paying attention as the band started to play the intro to *Can't Help Falling In Love*. Janine and Ray stood up and began to dance to the applause of the guests as Pete started to sing the first verse but suddenly a different voice took over.

Janine and Ray dancing hadn't noticed the change and as they approached the small stage they glanced up to see the person singing to them was...the King himself; Elvis Presley.

The room by now was totally stunned as he stepped off the stage and carried on singing to them. He finished the song to rapturous applause and gave Janine a hug and a kiss and shook Ray's hand. Janine looked across to where Manny was standing with a beaming smile on his face, and now understood what he'd been doing all the time he was on the phone since he arrived. It was the most incredible wedding present she could have wished for, and he'd organised it along with the band, without her having an inkling.

Elvis couldn't stay as he had a show that night, but before he left he made sure he had photographs taken with everyone, and in particular Pete Peterson the English rock star everybody was talking about. And then he'd left, shaking hands with Vince Boyd, Charles Morse and finally Manny as he went. Later that night as they were lying in their king-size bed looking out across Las Vegas, they recalled their amazing afternoon when the *King of Rock and Roll* had personally sung to them, and even Charles Morse and Vince Boyd had queued to shake his hand. Janine had watched how Elvis had talked to Pete and given him respect. There was something special coming, and she finally knew she was ready to handle it, whatever or whoever tried to stand in her way.

CHAPTER THIRTY-ONE

Pete's album had reached number one, and his European tour dates of five Capitol cities Paris, Stockholm, Madrid, Amsterdam and Brussels were a sellout. As they headed to the UK the buzz for Peterson was at fever pitch. He remembered the time when The Flames had their first hit, and played the charity gig at the Town Hall. That was the time he'd gone back to The Hideout and met Janine. He smiled to himself as he recalled their visits to the Metropole Hotel. 'How times have changed' he mused.

He thought back to the last Flames tour that ended so badly, and it was all his fault. Well it would never happen again. This was going to be his biggest tour ever. Manny and his agent had put together a great schedule, and he couldn't wait to get started. The band was better than ever, and with the addition of Dave Sanchez they were unstoppable.

The first date was in Manchester at the Apollo and then heading up North via Leeds and Newcastle to Scotland where they were playing two gigs. The Edinburgh Playhouse and the Glasgow Apollo, before heading back down to Liverpool, Sheffield, Cardiff at the Sophia Gardens, where the venue was in the middle of a park, then on to the Rainbow in London; finally to his home town of Birmingham for a very special gig at the club with so many memories for everyone associated with Pete and his phenomenal success. The Lexxicon was now the most successful club in the city, and even though he could have filled the Town Hall ten times over, both he and Janine had agreed it was the only venue he should play. Tickets had sold out on the day it was announced he would finish his tour there, and they were like gold dust. He'd asked Janine to make sure Tony and Billy, the twins and Jess Peters his original band all had VIP tickets. He was desperate to see them again and hoped they felt the same, although he knew Tony might still resent him, especially after the last night they had all been together there.

Janine and Ray had arranged to fly over for the last two gigs in London and Birmingham, and as it was the final gig of the tour, Janine organised a party for friends and family who didn't get to go to their wedding in Las Vegas.

By the time they reached Cardiff Don had noticed how many of the same fans were turning up at other gigs on the tour. There seemed to be a group of about a hundred female fans who wherever the tour visited, were already there waiting for them to arrive. It had a more tribal feel to it, and Pete's tribe were very loyal. He also noticed neckerchiefs appearing worn by his faithful followers, and decided there and then to make sure on his return to LA to introduce a new line of merchandise.

It was a wet and windy night in Wales, and for once there was a noticeable tension in the dressing room before they went on. There had been a problem with the catering only supplying cold food, and then due to it being a Sunday and the venue in Wales, there was no alcohol allowed for the rider in the dressing room. On top of which the lighting engineer had arrived still drunk from the previous night's after show party in Sheffield, and had fallen from the lighting truss resulting in a trip to hospital. Fortunately he hadn't broken anything, but the incident had meant the show was late starting.

The local promoters at each venue supplied the support band, whose job it was to go on before Peterson and warm the crowd up. That night's band weren't up to the usual standard, and by the time Pete went on stage the packed audience were beginning to get restless. Undaunted they launched into their opening number, and by the third song the fans were happily singing along. Suddenly there was a loud crunching sound from above the ceiling halfway down the hall, and a large section of roof was torn away by a strong gust of wind. Water was pouring down onto the crowd, and Pete and the band could only stand and watch as the large mass of people surged towards the exits. There were screams as some fell, and were trampled on in the resulting panic. It took an hour for the emergency services to restore some kind of order, having swiftly arrived at the muddy park which had rapidly turned into a quagmire due to the heavy rain.

Mercifully there were no major casualties, just a few cuts and bruises, but the concert hall was declared a disaster area. Some time later Pete and the band were finally allowed to leave. They were staying a few miles down the road at a motel which had frankly seen better days. Each member of the band had his own room in a separate block reached by an open corridor along the outside. Reception was back in the main building where there were food and drink dispensers along with a bookcase of paperback books for guests to read. The rule of no alcohol also applied to the motel, and the bar was closed with a shutter pulled down and locked by the porter who had left for the night. Not to be beaten and with Don keeping watch, Randy had used one of his never-ending talents to pick the lock with a tool he kept in his guitar case and the party had begun.

The following morning as they assembled in reception ready for the trip to London, Don noticed two members of staff removing the books from the bookcase and throwing them in a cardboard box. He overheard one say that they had to be dumped as someone had pissed all over them during the night! He couldn't help smiling to himself and watching Pete as he casually strolled by with an innocent look on his face.

Janine had been waiting in the dressing room when they arrived at the Rainbow. She had flown in from LA with Ray and had been concerned when she'd read about the events at the Cardiff gig. Although according to the reports, Pete and the guys had helped in making sure everyone was safe, signing autographs for both fans and police officers alike. There was a great photograph on the front of one national paper of Pete and a policewoman helping a young fan. Annoyingly some of the music press had made reference to the last time Pete had played in London and his mysterious illness which had been blamed on exhaustion, although thankfully the majority were focussing on the success of the tour and his number one album *In Flames*.

She'd been trying to contact Judy Watson to discuss the gig at The Lexxicon, but had only managed to speak to her assistant George Waters. It was strange she wasn't answering her calls, but George assured her everything was under control and that Judy would definitely be there tomorrow.

The Rainbow gig was fantastic, and afterwards in the bar as Pete was about to head to their hotel a familiar cultured voice called his name. He turned round and recognised the attractive blonde who had been the receptionist at the Metropole, Suzy. She looked amazing, and ignoring Janine's raised eyebrows he went over to give her a kiss. He took her hand and led her out of the room. There wouldn't be a threesome tonight. In fact Pete had something much more interesting in mind. Ironically the band were staying in the Metropole, although he didn't have the Penthouse suite this time and she no longer worked there. She explained on the way that she'd only taken the job as receptionist for some pocket money; her parents were extremely wealthy and lived in a three-storey town house in Cadogan Gardens. Once they were in his room they took no time stripping their clothes off. She still had the slim athletic body he remembered from last time, and climbing onto Pete used it to bring him to a shuddering climax.

She climbed off him and walked over to the bathroom. "Wait right there honey, I haven't finished yet," she said over her shoulder.

Pete picked up the bedside phone and dialled as she closed the door. A voice answered and he whispered, "My room, now."

He was chopping out a couple of lines of cocaine as she climbed back on the bed, when there was a soft knocking on the door. Pete stood up naked and opened the door to Don and the other two members of the band Randy and Marshall. They came in carrying bottles of beer and a bag of coke which they added to Pete's stash on the glass topped bedside table.

"Suzy, meet the guys, Don, Randy and Marshall. I thought you'd like a bit of fun," Pete said climbing off the bed and snorting a line as he sat down in the armchair in the corner.

"Well hello guys," Suzy said kneeling up on the bed as Don and Randy took off their trousers and shorts. "I haven't done this for a while, but hey, any friends of Pete's are friends of mine."

Within moments they were a trio of writhing sex. When the guys were spent she turned to Marshall who'd been watching from the side. "And what about you? You're not shy are you?"

The guys laughed as Marshall stepped out of his shorts. "Release the beast," they all chanted as Marshall revealed his manhood.

Suzy sat up and blinked at the sight in front of her. "Oh my God," she exclaimed as she leaned over and snorted another line of coke and took a huge swig of beer. "Let's take this slow, big boy," she said lying back as Marshall climbed on the bed. "Fuck! That thing should be in a cage!"

She buried her head in a pillow to stifle her ecstatic scream as they finally came together and Marshall rolled over leaving her lying on the bed. She sat up and looking around spotted Pete's neckerchief lying on the floor.

"D'you mind if I use this?" she said picking it up and wiping herself.

"It's kind of cool."

Pete looked at Don and they burst out laughing.

After the others had gone down to the bar to get a nightcap Pete and Suzy were alone.

"I feel like I've had all the fun" she said playing with him. "Let me just taste you before I have to go."

Pete lay back on the bed as she teased him, holding him tight and driving him crazy with her lips until he exploded.

"There that's better don't you think?" she said leaving him gasping for breath.

"Hey, What happened to the cute keyboard player?" she asked as they were getting dressed.

"Oh Dave? He prefers the guys more than the girls. He pulled some young thing earlier after sound check. He said they were going to the club downstairs."

They caught the lift down to reception and were walking through to call her a cab, when they saw the others talking to Dave. He looked to be in some distress as Pete and Suzy joined them. It appeared that his young companion hadn't been dressed appropriately to be allowed in the club, so Dave had taken him up to his room and lent him the brand-new leather jacket and trousers he'd bought that afternoon from Kensington Market. They went back downstairs, and after a few drinks his friend made the excuse of visiting the gent's toilet which was situated by an emergency exit. After waiting for ages for him to return Dave went to investigate. The exit was wide open with no sign of his young friend, his new leather jacket or his trousers.

CHAPTER THIRTY-TWO

Birmingham was buzzing with the return of Pete Peterson.

Tickets for the gig at The Lexxicon had been changing hands for astronomical prices, and as they drove into the city Pete could almost feel the excitement. It was just ten months since he, Janine and Ray had left, and what an incredible journey it had been. Now he was back where it had all started. Gerry Fortuna's dream had come true. The club was regarded as the best in the city if not the whole of the Midlands, and what a thrill it was to be playing there again.

Janine had arranged a string of interviews with the local press, who had kept him busy since he arrived. He'd had to laugh as he read the pile of messages from people he hardly remembered, who were suddenly his best friends. Strangely they were all looking for tickets. There were a few genuine ones, and he was thrilled to see Johnny Rhodes had been in touch, who despite not being in the best of health would definitely be coming. It would be great to see his old band leader again. Judy had been noticeable by her absence, but her assistant George had said she would be in later, and as Pete walked out onto the stage to do the sound check, memories of that opening night came flooding back. He vividly recalled standing on Gerry's left as he introduced him and Janine. He got a shiver down his spine as he stood in the same spot. The band had self-destructed that night as certain members showed their true colours, but that was all in the past. He had the best musicians possible now, and tonight he was going to show Birmingham just how good he was.

The support band, *Dark Sky* had been on and finished their set. Hand picked by Judy they were one of the new up and coming acts she'd signed to FAM and Janine and Pete were impressed. The thing was, where was she? Suddenly there was a commotion outside the dressing room door and Judy came bustling in carrying a baby's carrycot. She looked flustered and apologised for being late due to sleep time. Janine watched as she turned to Pete, picking a small baby from the cot.

"Pete, I know this might be a shock but I'd like you to meet Richard William Peterson, your son."

The dressing room was silent as Pete stood speechless. He didn't know what to do or say. He took the small bundle from Judy and looked at the tiny person. His son. HIS son. There were thoughts spinning through his mind as he stood there.

Janine's voice snapped him back. "Judy this is incredible and I think we need to talk about it later, but right now Pete you have a show to do."

She took his arm and guided him into the other dressing room which was empty. "Whatever has just happened you need to put to the back of your mind and focus on this gig."

He nodded as she held his arms "Are you OK? Pete, look at me."

He gave her a look full of determination. "Of course I am babe. I ain't gonna let you down. Johnny Rhodes is out there and I've got a point to prove. Just watch this."

He gave her a hug and kiss on the cheek and walking back in the dressing room picked up his guitar. He strode out on stage to one of the loudest cheers he'd ever had. As the band started the intro to the first song he stood taking in the incredible scene of the sea of faces screaming his name. The club was packed to bursting point, everywhere he looked were people and they were all there to see him! He strutted up to the microphone and shouted. "Hello Birmingham, remember me? I'm Pete Peterson and I'M BACK!"

As Pete started his set Judy had taken the baby into her office followed by Janine. She had put him down and turned expecting a smiling face, but she was mistaken as Janine slammed the door behind her.

"And exactly what did you think you were going to achieve by pulling that stunt? I always had you down as an intelligent lady but honestly Judy, that takes the biscuit! What even makes you think it's Pete's? He's been in the States for god knows how long, fucking everything that moves."

"I know it's his because I planned it, "Judy replied calmly. "Right down to the night before he left. We had sex in his apartment and I made sure I was ready, and I was. Nine months exactly. Oh and I haven't been with anyone else since, so unless three wise men are going to appear in the foyer I'm pretty damn sure it's his. And you don't have to worry that I'm going to make a fuss. I told him as he left I'd always have a part of him, and now I have. We're fine and well taken care of. Mother left me enough for us to be happy, so Pete can carry on just as before with whoever he wants. I just wanted him to know."

"So what do you want him to do?" Janine demanded.

Judy was close to tears. "I don't want him to do anything! It would be disastrous for it to be known that Pete Peterson had a child in the UK. Don't you think I know that! He'd lose half of his female fans overnight. So it won't be me who goes to the press. I just want him to know we'll always be here waiting. Now go and do your job. Make him the biggest star he deserves to be. And remember I'm on your side. Now go."

Judy wrapped the baby up in his blanket and called to Janine as she walked away back to the stage. "Tell him I'll always love him."

She turned and left through the back door just as the baby started to cry.

The roar from the crowd was deafening, and louder even after their third encore. Pete Peterson was definitely back, there was no doubt about it, and as the band came bouncing off stage into the dressing room they were jubilant. They were met by a stoney faced Janine who was waiting on her own with her back to the door.

"Guys, before I unlock this door to let all your friends and fans in, there's one thing I want to say." The room went quiet. "What you heard in this dressing room before the show must not be repeated. No one and I mean NO ONE must say a word to anyone. And if I hear anybody has talked to the press I'll find out who it was and you'll be sacked. Do you all hear me?"

They silently nodded. She let the silence hang for a couple of beats then laughed. "Right, now we've got that out of the way, that was the best feckin' show I've ever seen," she yelled. "You guys are incredible! LET'S CELEBRATE!"

They all roared and she hugged each member as the door burst open, and Don came in followed by the three members of The Flames. Jess, Billy and at the back Tony who came straight over and hugged Pete lifting him off the floor. Pete was so glad they were there and was struggling to hold back the tears when Johnny Rhodes came in walking with the aid of a stick, and suddenly they were all crying tears of joy. It was an amazing sight. Don and Janine stood together in the doorway watching and smiling, as the man on the verge of becoming a global rock star sat laughing and reminiscing with his friends.

The celebrations went on long into the night, and by the time Janine and Ray got to bed at the Holiday Inn it was four o'clock in the morning. Thankfully there were no interviews or appointments the next day, apart from the private party Janine had arranged for a few friends and family who hadn't been at the wedding in Las Vegas. She'd managed to book a small suite at the hotel, and the proceedings were planned to start at eight that night. It wasn't a formal affair and Ray was glad he didn't have to wear a suit for once. Janine had insisted on buying a new outfit especially for the night though, and he had to admit she looked stunning in the little black dress that hugged her amazing figure in all the right places. She had also been to the hair salon in the hotel, where they had fashioned her striking red hair in a plait down her back. When Ray accompanied his wife into the room that night he couldn't help but notice the looks she received. Every woman wished she could be her and every man secretly wished he could be with her. It was a strange experience.

There was an interesting array of guests when they walked around the room greeting them all individually. Don and the guys in the band had arrived looking a little worse for wear after the previous night's antics. Pete had turned up suitably late, and brought along his acoustic guitar promising them he would do something special. Ray's friend DCI Matt Burgess and some of his old colleagues including George Williams, the retired Chief Constable and his wife were also there. Janine's sister Jackie and her family along with a table of aunts and uncles who'd flown over from Ireland were sitting in the corner enjoying themselves, and Ray's parents had made the trip down from Liverpool.

Things had been going along nicely with polite conversation for an hour or so when Pete decided they needed some entertainment, and taking his guitar he jumped up on the small stage in the corner and started to play. It was the same set up as Kathy Blake's party when he, Randy and Marshall had performed acoustic versions of some of the songs on his album. This time though he decided instead of playing his own songs, he'd sing some old favourites and started off with a couple of Beatles tunes, a cheeky version of *How Can I Be Sure* dedicated to Janine, *Light My Fire, Wichita Lineman* and they were about to take a break when Ray appeared at the front of the stage and asked Pete if he knew *Stand By Me* by Ben E King.

"Course I do man," he said about to start when Ray stopped him.

"Actually I was wondering if I could sing it."

Pete looked surprised. "Yeah man no problem, any idea what key?"

"Think it's in B, same as the record." Randy looked at Pete and raised his eyebrows.

Marshall tapped out four beats and Pete started the riff. Nobody was taking much notice until Ray started to sing.

Suddenly the room was quiet and the guests including Janine, and Pete, were hanging on his every word. His voice was like Marvin Gaye one moment, then Sam Cooke, Otis Redding in fact it was a fantastic blend of all the great soul singers rolled into one. As he finished the whole room jumped up and cheered. He stood for a moment shocked by the reaction, but Pete leaned over and said for him to do another and started the intro to 'Get Ready' by The Temptations which he felt sure Ray would know.

Without a moment'ss hesitation he launched straight into it with Pete and Randy coming in right behind him with the *alrights*.

The place was rocking and shouting for more and Pete convinced him to sing another, this time a version of The Isley Brothers 'This Old Heart of Mine' which Pete and Randy sang with him.

At the end he was mobbed by everyone telling him how amazing he was, what an incredible voice he had and how he should be on stage. He stood embarrassed to be the centre of attraction. After a couple of large brandies that Don had bought him, he had just felt like he wanted to sing, not to have this happen. He looked around and saw Janine talking with Pete and Don and the three of them laughing. He felt terrible and knew he had made a fool of himself and was about to apologise, when they saw him looking and waved for him to join them.

"Why the hell didn't you say you could sing like that?" Janine said. "Babe that was unbelievable. We have to talk to Manny. You need to get in the studio. Pete wants to work with you, he's just been saying he's got some new songs he's been writing with Dave that are perfect for you, really soulful."

Ray stood back holding his hands out. "Whoa, hang on a minute. I just wanted to sing like I used to do when I was a kid in Liverpool. It wasn't meant to be serious, just a bit of fun."

Pete stopped him. "Listen man you've got a fucking great voice and we can't let you waste it. Janine's right, I've got some stuff I've been doing with Dave that's not right for me but perfect for you. Wait until Manny hears you; he'll flip man."

Ray still wasn't convinced, but Don said, "Listen Ray why don't you come down to the studios when we get back and see how it goes. If it works great, if not then there's nothing lost. But I gotta tell you man, that's one hell of a cool voice you got there, it'd be a shame to let it go to waste."

So somewhat reluctantly, Ray agreed to wait until they got back to LA and go down to Whitland Studios with Pete and see what happened.

They were making their way back to their room at the end of the night when Ray thought he smelled a perfume he recognised. As the lift doors opened he was aware of a couple waiting behind them. He followed Janine in and pressed the button for their floor as the man and woman entered, and he turned to find himself face to face with Julia Davies. She smiled politely as the man she was with possessively pulled her to him trying to kiss her, but she held him away and pressed her floor button as the lift doors closed. He was obviously drunk and tried to maul her again, but this time she firmly pushed him away, smiling but embarrassed with his behaviour. Fortunately for Ray their room was on the second floor, and it only took seconds before they left her to fend her companion off again as the doors closed.

Janine walked down the corridor and said to Ray over her shoulder, "Some men are pricks!" Ray decided it was best not to comment and opened the door. She stepped out of her dress on the way in and pulled him to her kissing him lustfully.

"Anyone who can sing like that has got to make love to me, right here, right now." And she undid his trousers pulling him down on the bed as she kissed him again and lay back while he slipped off her black silk underwear and did exactly as she wished, slowly and sensually.

She was lying with her head on his chest later. "Did you know that woman in the lift? I'm positive I've seen her before, and you know me I never forget a face."

'Oh I've definitely seen her before,' he thought. 'Why is it every time I think she's gone from my life she has to rear her - it has to be said, attractive - head again?' "I don't think so," he replied.

"Well she certainly gave you the once over," she said. "I was starting to get a bit jealous."

'I should have punched that idiot's lights out,' he thought. "I like it when you get all possessive," he replied stroking her hair.

"Show me how much," she said, running her fingers down across his stomach and watching his excitement grow.

CHAPTER THIRTY-THREE

Pete, Don and the band had returned home the next day, but not before Pete had spent most of the morning trying to locate Judy and the baby she'd presented to him at the Lexxicon. He'd gone to the club and spoken to George her assistant who swore he didn't know where she was, and with time running out before he had to leave, he wrote her a note saying how he still constantly thought about her and that one day soon he'd return. He'd left it with George who he made promise to make sure she received it.

Janine had wanted to have an extra day to relax and visit places she remembered and missed. They'd gone to see where Rudi's used to be, which was now a brand-new block of offices, and then to The Hideout which was still there but looking tired and run down, and it was as they were returning to the hotel that she remembered. "I've got her," she exclaimed almost causing Ray to swerve the hire-car. "That woman in the lift, she was Gerry's solicitor when the police questioned him about Alex Mitchell. Surely you remember her."

"I don't think I did that interview; I think it was Matt," he lied looking straight ahead concentrating on the road.

"Well she certainly is a very good looking woman, even if her choice of partner leaves a lot to be desired."

To his relief before he had the chance to comment, they arrived back at the hotel's underground car park, and as they passed through reception a male voice called Janine's name. It was Judy's assistant George who came striding across to meet them.

"I'm glad I've caught you," he said. "Judy asked me to speak to you before you left. She was going to come herself but she's had to take the baby to hospital. I don't think it's too serious, but she has to be careful. Anyway she said she'll speak to you once you get back and not to worry, she won't say anything. Oh, and she asked if you could give this to Pete when you see him." He passed an envelope to Janine and left without saying another word.

By the time they checked into the First-Class lounge at Heathrow the next day they were both ready to get back home to LA. Thankfully this time it was a less eventful flight without any stars on board. Ray slept most of the way, while Janine dozed, although she made sure she drank her share of free champagne. They hadn't mentioned Ray's singing again, and he was half hoping it would slip by once they got back into the swing of things. Pete had another tour coming up, this time down South, and they'd had some exciting news that the Super Bowl wanted Peterson as the main act at the half time interval. It was difficult for someone from the UK to understand the significance of appearing at America's biggest sporting event, but once the viewing figures were taken into consideration alongside his tour dates, it was frightening how many people would be watching him. Needless to say Manny and the team at Westoria were over the moon with the news. Alongside the sales figures for Pete's album that since the kidnapping had already earned Platinum sales, *In Flames* was already the biggest selling debut album in the States.

Don had organised a rehearsal for the band at Whitland Studios to get them ready for their upcoming tour. While they were there, he'd called Ray and suggested it would be a good time for him to get together with Pete and Dave to see if the songs they'd mentioned would work. No pressure, just the three of them at first, and then if they felt good the others would get involved.

From the off it was a perfect combination, with Ray's voice adding a soulful edge to the piano and guitar. Marshall and Randy had been sitting listening in the other room and waited until they took a break before wandering in. They'd played the tunes at a couple of sound checks on the last run of gigs so they already knew them, and immediately started to lay down an amazing groove. Ray was relaxed and smiling as they started the first tune. Unknown to him, Don had called Manny earlier and asked him to come down and listen to a couple of Pete's new songs, without telling him who would be singing. They were in the control room for the recording studio in a different part of the building, and Manny was unaware that what he was hearing was any different until suddenly Ray's soulful vocals filled the room. Don was doing his best not to react as Manny's mouth dropped open and he looked at Don with a puzzled expression.

"OK so you told me I was going to hear some new material written by

Pete and Dave, but that's not Pete singing and it's completely different." He listened a bit longer. "But I gotta say he's got a great voice."

He listened again as they hit the chorus and Pete, Randy and Dave added some killer harmonies to the hook.

"He's got a fuckin' great voice. Man that's a hit song. Who is he? I want to meet him. He sounds like Marvin and all the others all rolled into one."

The song finished and before they could start the next tune Manny jumped up and strode down the corridor to the studio. He pushed the door open and walked in and stopped dead in his tracks. The man standing behind the microphone was Janine Fortuna's husband Ray. Ex-policeman Ray! He was lost for words.

"What the…!" He looked around at the guys who were all laughing.

"OK joke's over!" He turned to Ray. "You don't seriously expect me to believe that was you singing just then?"

Pete started the intro riff and Ray sang the verse accompanied by just guitar until they got to the chorus when they all joined in. Manny waved his arms above his head and stopped them.

"You mean to tell me you can sing like this and nobody knew?"

"We only found out at the party back in Birmingham when he got up and sang," Pete said. "Pretty cool huh?"

Manny was shaking his head. "Pretty cool!! Pretty fuckin' awesome you mean. You and I gotta talk Ray. I know just the man who's gonna flip his lid when he hears you. You got any more songs Pete?"

Pete nodded to Dave. "Yeah man, here's the second one we were working on."

Marshall counted the band in and they set up a slow groove to a soulful ballad which Ray sang as if he'd known it all his life. Manny couldn't contain his excitement.

"I need tapes of both those songs by tonight. Don, make sure they get to my office." He started to leave and stopped. "Ray, I need to speak to you and Janine first thing in the morning."

Don watched him leave and then turned back to Ray and the guys. "Did you get the impression he likes it?"

They all laughed and Ray followed him out as he left the studio. Don couldn't help noticing the strong smell of alcohol on Ray's breath when he stood next to him and thought that it had been the same in Birmingham. In fact he remembered he'd bought Ray a couple of large brandies just before he'd got up to sing. Well whatever, he certainly had a great voice, and judging from Manny's reaction Janine could soon be busier than ever.

Manny had invited Curtis Jackson, his young head of A&R from the soul and R'n'B department to meet Ray and Janine the next morning, and they were in Manny's office listening to the two songs from yesterday's session. Curtis was a slim six-foot tall, African American dressed in a baby pink double-breasted suit with a black silk shirt and gold cufflinks, sporting the biggest afro Ray had ever seen. His father, Otis Jackson had been a famous jazz pianist and an old friend of Manny and his son was one of the new breed of soul and R'n'B musicians employed by Westoria to run the black music department. He was sitting smiling and tapping his foot to the first tune and when the chorus came in he turned to Manny.

"Manny, that's a great hook."

He listened to the second song, the soulful ballad and looked at Ray. "Great voice man. There's shades of Marvin, David Ruffin, Sam Cooke. And you're English?"

"Yes I am, from Liverpool and proud of it!" Ray replied slightly insulted.

"Hey man don't get me wrong, it's just you sound so American when you sing, but nothing like it when you speak," Curtis replied.

Janine who had sat quietly up to this point spoke. "The sign of a great singer I'm sure you'll agree. So Manny what's the next move?"

"The sooner we get Ray in the studio the better." Manny replied. "But hey, what do you think Ray? You need to be comfortable with what's happening."

Ray was quiet for a moment. "When I was a kid back in Liverpool I used to sing with a bunch of guys and dreamt of one day having a record deal. I always thought I could have made it, but my dad was insistent I went to college and then University. So I gave it all up even though I didn't become the lawyer he wanted me to be. Now, in a way I've got a chance of realising that dream I had all those years ago, and as long as I've got Janine and Pete around me I'll be happy."

"Well Pete Peterson writing and producing you would be pretty interesting," Curtis said. "But I'm not sure how the soul scene would react to an out and out white rock star being involved. The two songs are great, don't get me wrong, but I've got some fantastic writers and a new hip producer who's just had three top ten records, who everybody wants to work with them. I think he'd be perfect for Ray, and he owes me a couple of favours."

Ray was looking confused and glanced at Janine who waved her hand for him to relax.

"I think there's a few things we need to get straight Mr. Jackson." Ray noticed how she always became formal when she was about to argue, and she was bristling as she stood up and started to talk. "Firstly we didn't have to come here today, we were invited by your boss. Secondly my husband, or let's refer to him as the artist, has just said he would be happy so long as both myself and Pete Peterson, right now Westoria's biggest selling artist were involved, and bearing in mind the two songs you've just heard and liked were both written by Pete. I also believe he would be up for working with Ray."

Curtis listened to what she said. "Hey let's be cool, and I prefer Curtis."

Janine didn't want to be cool. "I only address people by their first name if I like them, and I'm not sure if I like you yet," she replied causing Manny to choke on his coffee. "Just what did you mean by the soul scene reacting to a white rock star being involved?' If the music's good enough what difference does it make?"

Curtis looked at Manny before answering. "I'm sorry Mrs. Law, but you're in America now, and the whole soul and R'n'B scene is dominated by black people. If we want to break Ray we have to follow the rules. Once he's established further down the line he can do as he chooses, but right now we need everything on our side. You gotta trust me on this. Look why don't you have a talk with Manny. I'll get some songs together I think will suit Ray and send them over to you, then we'll speak again?"

"That sounds like a good idea. Thanks Curtis, let's speak later," Manny said as Curtis stood up and shook Ray's hand and tentatively offered his hand to Janine who shook it firmly.

Manny turned to Janine as the door closed. "He knows what he's talking about; he wouldn't be here otherwise. And what he says about the black music scene is true. Why don't you, Ray and Pete have a talk about it? To be honest I don't think Pete will have a problem, mainly because he's got another big run of gigs coming up and the Super Bowl show, and as Curtis said, further down the line once Ray's established there'll be no problem."

In the taxi on the way home Ray sensed Janine was still wound up about the meeting with Curtis, and suggested they stop off at their favourite restaurant in Hermosa Beach, where she could have a bowl of spicy shrimps, he could get a New York Strip, and they could relax. Pete was back at his apartment in Venice Beach but wasn't answering his phone, so it would have to be tomorrow when they got together.

In fact Pete was in a bar just off the strip, watching a new band playing some psychedelic rock accompanied by a light show complete with an oil lamp and bubbles, which was giving him ideas. He'd speak to Don at the rehearsal, who'd promised to bring a load of samples for Pete to choose from for their neckerchief merchandise idea.

He loved the area where he lived because he could just walk into any bar or club and no-one bothered him. A far cry from the UK where he couldn't step outside the hotel without being photographed or chased for an autograph. He was just buying himself another beer when he noticed a familiar face further down the bar smiling at him. It was Maud, the lady from TWA and she was making her way towards him.

"Hey, Pete, what's happening? You're looking really cool."

He thought there was something different since the last time he'd seen her. She'd definitely changed and looked very sexy and a lot trimmer than before.

"Yeah, I'm good, babe. So do you, how's things?"

"Things are great. I've finally got into films, not the mainstream yet, you know like your friend Kathy Blake's kind of films I decided to take up an offer to do a few adult movies and they really liked me, so now I'm doing loads and making lots of money. What do you think of my new boobs? Aren't they great? Say what are you doing here, I heard you were a big rock star now. I saw you on TV talking about that kidnap thing. Man that must have been awful. Do you want to fuck me again, you know for old times sake? It would be really cool. I've learnt some new tricks you'd love."

Pete was watching her closely. She was obviously out of her brains on something and he decided he should make a tactical exit.

"Look I'm sorry babe, I'd really love to but I've got an early morning tomorrow in the studio. Maybe some other time. I've got your number; I'll give you a call."

He slid a ten dollar note across to the barman who was smiling knowingly. "Get her a drink on me," he said as he jumped off his stool and made his way to the door.

He was just leaving when he felt a tap on his arm and froze for a moment. Expecting he was going to turn to see the dreaded Nadja, he was pleasantly surprised when he came face to face with an attractive brunette.

"Hey, Pete Peterson, I thought it was you," she said as if she knew him personally. "Allow me to introduce myself, I'm Carly Jones, music journalist for the LA Times, and I've been following your career closely since you first arrived here in Venice Beach. I live just down the Strip and I've seen you about a lot, but I've never had the opportunity to speak to you."

"Well Carly, it's nice to meet you," Pete said glancing over his shoulder and noticing Maud was deep in conversation with a guy at the bar.

"Can I buy you a drink? Ah, but preferably not here though."

She laughed. "Yes, I couldn't help but notice your friend at the bar. I know a quiet little bar just on the next block if you fancy it?

"After you!" Pete extended his arm for her to lead the way. He noticed she was smoking as he followed her out, something he'd tried hard to quit since he was with Kathy Blake.

The place was tiny with only four tables and two stools at the bar both of which were occupied already, so they sat down in the corner. Pete ordered a beer from the barman and she said she'd have the same.

"So, Carly Jones, what would you like to talk about?" Pete asked sitting down with two glasses of beer.

"Well for a start I'm not the kind of journalist who wants to know what kind of strings you use on your guitar or what was the inspiration for such and such a song. I want to know about you, the person. What turns you on; who turns you on."

Pete raised his eyebrows "Well, I must admit that's an approach I haven't had before."

"So what say we finish our beer and I make you a proper drink at my place? It's right next door and I've got some Bourbon I think you'll like."

The look in her eyes was hard to resist as she crushed her cigarette out in the pot ashtray on the table.

Her apartment was on the top floor of the same block as the bar. Pete followed her up the three flights of stairs, and was pleasantly surprised when she opened the door and revealed a luxuriously furnished lounge with a polished wooden floor. She kicked off her shoes and went over to the bar in the corner. Pouring a large measure of Kentucky Gold into two cut glass tumblers she dropped a cube of ice into each one.

"Sit down, make yourself comfortable," she said as she sat and curled her legs under her on a long black leather sofa.

He sat next to her as she took out a cigarette. He lit it for her with the table lighter on the glass topped coffee table as she reached forward and stroked his hand seductively in exactly the same way Janine had done that night in The Hideout. She had the same electrifying effect on him.

Carly sucked on it then tilted her head back and slowly blew smoke up to the ceiling revealing her long exposed neck which Pete found irresistible and leaning forward gently kissed her throat. He took the cigarette from her hand and drew deeply on it tasting her lipstick on the filter tip and held the smoke in as he felt the nicotine hit. He slowly released it as she turned her head to kiss his mouth while at the same time pushing him back on the sofa. He lay back as she undid the buttons on his shirt and jerked as she bit his nipple. She looked up with a devilish expression and he thought to himself he was in for an interesting night as she took the cigarette back and stubbed it out in an ashtray on the floor. She stood up and took his hand leading him into the bedroom.

Making his way down the three flights of stairs the next morning he felt sure he'd given her enough material for the first instalment of an informative article about Pete Peterson *The lover*. He was already looking forward to part two.

Without Pete, Janine and Ray had discussed his situation over their meal, coming to the conclusion that they trusted Manny, and with the situation with Pete being so good it would hardly be in his interest to upset them. There was still the problem with Janine and Curtis Jackson, but she was prepared to see how things went if Ray was happy. She had a couple of other things on her mind at the present, and Ray's surprise musical career was a complication she didn't need right now.

The first was that the tenancy of the house in Hermosa Beach was up for renewal, and she couldn't make up her mind if she should extend it or look for a suitable property to buy. It was a great house, and the situation right on the Strand was fantastic, but the annual cost was high and for what she was paying they could afford to buy a reasonable condo in somewhere like West Hollywood; a great area close to all the nightlife and cool places they regularly frequented. Alternatively there was Santa Monica, where they would still be near the coast. She also had a funny feeling they might be needing some extra space soon.

Curtis Jackson had turned up at Manny's office dressed this time in a powder blue suit with a white shirt and black ruffled cravat, carrying a stack of tape cassettes for Ray and Janine to listen to. They sat as he played them the songs he had chosen, and had to agree he knew what he was talking about. The two tunes Pete had written were good and had quality, but what Curtis was playing had class and *hit record* written all over them. Plus as a collection of tunes they would make an amazing debut album. Even Janine had to admit there was something special possible, and as Curtis left Manny's office she shook his hand. "Thank you Curtis," she said with a smile.

Manny was pleased, and called his contract department to put together an agreement for Ray Law to record an album under the guidance of Curtis Jackson starting immediately.

"The sooner we get Ray Law, the soul singer out there the better," he said to Janine and Ray as they left his office.

They called Pete and arranged to have a meal with him the next night at the Beverly Hills Hotel to celebrate. When Janine had explained about their decision to work with Curtis, Pete was cool. He had enough happening due to his tour along with the planning for the Super Bowl appearance. He'd asked if it would be alright to bring his new friend Carly, which intrigued Janine.

They'd decided to dress up formally as the restaurant in the hotel was rather special, although it remained to be seen what Pete would decide to wear. In fact Pete had made an effort, wearing the suit he'd worn to the Oscars, and his friend Carly was wearing a long psychedelic print silk dress with her brown hair pinned up in curls. They were already in the bar as Janine and Ray walked in. Janine remembered the time she'd met Charles Morse there after Ray had left to go back to the UK, but hopefully this would be a different sort of occasion.

Pete introduced Carly, explaining how they'd met and that she was a music journalist, which was one of the reasons why he'd asked if she could come. It was always good to have a friendly journalist on your side, and he thought she would be interested in Ray's new record deal.

It was a fabulous meal. Janine had ordered a medium rare filet, the same as last time. The waiter had shown a flicker of recognition as he was taking their orders, but Janine had given him a look that made sure he knew not to say anything.

Afterwards they had gone back out to the bar for a nightcap before they left, and there was a lull in the conversation as they waited for their drinks to be served.

Janine took a deep breath and spoke. "Actually I have a little bit of news myself." The others all turned to her. "I had the results from my doctor today. I'm pregnant."

The silence was deafening. The colour drained from Ray's face and he stood up. "No! You can't be!"

Unfortunately it coincided with Pete jumping up and grabbing her saying "Fantastic! Congratulations."

There was another moment of silence as everyone looked at Ray who was livid. "You can't be," he was almost shouting.

Janine laughed embarrassed. "Well I am, babe."

"How could you be so stupid!" Ray replied.

"It takes two you know," Janine answered. "It happened the night in Vegas, I still remember it well."

"Well I think it's great news," Pete said trying to defuse the situation, but Ray was shaking his head.

Janine challenged him. "Hang on a minute. I don't remember you ever being too bothered about any kind of protection."

"That's not the point. How the hell do you think you're gonna manage? Not only do you have Pete to look after but now me. I can't believe it!" He stormed out of the bar.

For the first time since he'd known her, Pete saw Janine cry. He put his arm around her but she shrugged it off quickly wiping away her tears. "Just you watch me, you bastard," she said under her breath.

But Pete heard her, loud and clear.

There was an embarrassing scene as Pete and Carly left to catch a cab back to Venice Beach leaving her on her own, but by then she'd pulled herself together and promised to get in touch with Carly. She eventually found Ray in the car park and they sat in the taxi without speaking all the way back to Hermosa Beach. As she reached into her handbag for her purse she found the envelope addressed to Pete, that in all the confusion she'd completely forgotten to give him. Maybe it wouldn't have been a good idea considering he had Carly with him. There would be another time she was sure.

Curtis had called while they were out and left a message to say could Ray meet him and the producer he'd mentioned, at the office early the next morning. By the time Janine awoke he'd showered and left. She was still surprised at his reaction the previous evening, but decided she wasn't going to make an issue of it, and chose instead to call Carly the journalist. She was interested in how she could be of use to both Pete and Ray, and arranged to meet her for lunch in Venice Beach. They met up in a trendy new wholefood restaurant, and over bowls of grains and seeds, which Janine hated, washed down with a pot of herbal tea which she hated even more, they discussed how Carly could possibly become involved. Between them they worked out the basis of a plan; The LA Times would publish two stories written by Carly, one that would follow the launching of a new soul singer from the UK now living in the US. It would be syndicated across all the music press and she would have exclusive access to new releases and gigs. The other showing the real Pete Peterson, revealing his inner self. Janine knew she was going out on a limb, but she felt it was worth a try. Carly was a strong character and assured her she had friends in the black music scene who would love the story about Ray, and she had already written about Pete.

"This is separate to whatever happens with Pete and I," she was at pains to point out. "I know his history with women. I've watched from a distance his scenes with Kathy Blake, and the crazy Russian woman. I was at the Whisky gig you know, and the TV show. But this will be between you and I."

Janine got a good vibe from her, and shaking her hand knew it would work, especially with Pete. As for Ray, she would deal with him later.

CHAPTER THIRTY-FOUR

Pete had turned up at the studios the next morning ready to rehearse the show they were going to play at the Super Bowl, but sensed something was wrong as soon as he walked in. Marshall's kit wasn't set up, and Dave's keyboards were standing on their own in the middle of the studio. Don wasn't there either, so he went in search of the guys and found them sitting in the cafe arguing. The loudest voice seemed to be Randy the bass player. 'It's always the bass player,' he thought to himself as he approached them.

It turned out that Randy had been offered another job on more money, which had annoyed Marshall because Randy hadn't said anything about it to him. He thought they'd had an understanding and were a team.

Pete's arrival calmed the situation down a little, but Randy still seemed adamant that he wanted to hand in his notice. Pete had always played fair when it came to money and made sure everyone was treated equal. He explained to Randy that as much as he wanted him to stay, there was no way he was prepared to pay him more than the others.

He motioned to Don to follow him and went out to the reception area.

"So how much more has he been offered?"

"Twenty dollars a gig," he replied.

Pete looked shocked. "Twenty dollars is that all! Leave this to me." He went over to where the others were still sitting.

"Okay here's the deal. Randy's been offered more money, so I'll match it, and you all get the same. How does that sound?"

Randy was taken aback by Pete's reaction. The others looked at him for a response.

"Well if you put it like that how can I refuse," he said.

"Great, that's settled then," Pete said. "Now get in the studio and set up, we've got work to do!"

They all stood up and left Pete and Don on their own.

"That was a bold move," Don said. "I honestly didn't expect you to do that."

"It's a great band, and having to start looking for a new bass player would be a real pain. Maybe after the next set of shows I'll think differently, but for now they're all happy. Do me a favour though, keep your ear to the ground just in case. It always pays to be prepared." He winked at Don as he opened the studio door.

Ray had been shocked when Janine had announced her news at the party and knew he'd overreacted, but he couldn't believe she'd said it like she did. Why couldn't she have saved it and told him on their own? Now everybody knew and thought he was a shit for acting like he did. He shouldn't have stormed off; it was a mess and most of it was his fault. The trouble was he hadn't had the opportunity to sort it out with Janine.

Curtis Jackson and his producer had booked Valerian studios in Van Nuys which were renowned for soul and R'n'B, and Ray was spending all his time there. Because of the distance it was from Hermosa Beach, most nights he was getting in late and leaving early the next morning, on the odd occasion staying over in the accommodation attached to the studio complex. Janine hadn't had chance to speak to him about it either, but when she asked Manny the reason why they were recording there and not at Whitland Studios where Pete was based, he said it was all down to the guys in charge. They were getting cut rates on studio time; also Whitland was regarded as a rock studio. But as long as the end product was great he was happy. They were certainly using some top musicians, and from what he'd heard it was sounding amazing.

Curtis had spent the first week recording the music tracks, and Ray couldn't wait to start singing. What he'd give to get his old school pals back in Liverpool all together and record something. Perhaps if he ever did a tour back home he could do that. But that was wishful thinking, and right now the main priority was the album.

Curtis and his producer finally decided they were happy with the rhythm beds the musicians had laid down, and it was Ray's turn to start recording guide vocals, so the backing singers had something to work to. The next day while he was in the studio singing, the singers had arrived. Curtis hadn't told him they were female backing singers. In a break he came into the control room to hear a playback, and Curtis introduced him. Two were already in the room listening and shook his hand complimenting him on his voice, then the third girl who'd been in the bathroom walked in, and Ray's stomach did a flip. She was the sexiest black girl he'd ever seen, with a soft wavy afro, the biggest dark brown eyes, and a mouth that was asking to be kissed. She was wearing a tight black leather jacket, a black mini skirt and long black leather boots. Her name was Josie Thomas, and Ray didn't care whether she could sing or not. He wanted her right there and then. It was like the first time he saw Janine with George Williams He'd known then that one day he would have her, and it was the same with Josie Thomas. He hadn't realised he'd been holding her hand for so long, until Curtis broke the spell by saying his name and asking if he was ready to carry on. Slightly embarrassed he went back into the studio to continue singing, but noticed that Josie's eyes followed him and smiled as he caught her watching him.

The session went well and Curtis called it a day at around eight o'clock. Ray was tired after singing, and decided to stay over instead of having to travel all the way back home and return early the next morning. Curtis agreed because he knew it would take Ray ages to warm up before they could start to record again. There was a bar next door called the *Lone Star* decorated in the style of an old cowboy western, and they all went for a drink to wind down.

Ray cleverly arranged for himself to be standing next to Josie and asked her what she'd like to drink. Without hesitation, she replied looking him straight in the eyes. "You!"

Momentarily lost for words he looked around to see if anyone else had heard what she'd said, but everyone seemed to be chatting and not taking any notice. He took her hand and pulled her out of the side door which swung to and closed behind them. They were in an alley running along the side of the bar with only one dim light high up on the wall, casting them deep in the shadow. He pushed her against the wall and her mouth found his. Her hands were down between his legs pulling his trousers open and he lifted her up with his hands under her bottom as she wrapped her legs around his waist, leaning back as she freed his erection. He drove himself deep into her as she gripped him harder with her legs controlling his rhythm. They were gasping with pleasure when she finally climaxed and he let her slide down onto her feet again.

She kissed him and whispered in his ear. "But I said I wanted to drink you."

She slowly sank to her knees taking his full size in her mouth and pleasuring him until he shuddered and almost collapsed as he exploded. She looked up at him and smiled. "Now that's what I call a cocktail!"

They walked back into the bar moments later as if nothing had happened, and Ray breathed a sigh of relief that nobody seemed to have noticed they'd been gone.

In the next few days the scene between Ray and Josie Thomas rapidly became intense. Curtis had noticed the symmetry between them straight away, and at first decided to turn a blind eye expecting it to blow over, but it was starting to have an effect on the album. Ray wasn't singing the songs the way the producer and Curtis asked and was becoming lazy, more interested in what time they were finishing so he could meet up with Josie again.

Finally Curtis' patience ran out and he asked Ray to meet him urgently. It transpired that one night when Ray had thought everyone had gone home, he and Josie had crept back and made love rather loudly in the studio. Unknown to them their whole performance had been recorded in glorious stereo, a copy of which Curtis was holding as Ray walked in to meet him.

"I don't usually interfere with an artist's private life," he said. "What you do in your own time is none of my business, unless it starts to have an affect on the product."

Ray sat listening although not really taking notice of what he was being told.

Curtis carried on. "Josie Thomas is a good singer and a smart lady. She's worked on a lot of sessions for me and will always be a good backing vocalist, although never quite good enough to stand that extra twenty feet up front. But she's a user Ray. I've seen her do exactly the same thing to so many new hopefuls, and the minute the next one comes along she'll be there and you'll be history. You need to wise up man!" He dropped the cassette tape in front of Ray. "And you gotta hope a copy of this doesn't end up on Manny's desk and get back to your wife."

Ray suddenly started paying attention.

"Oh and as far as the amount of brandy you're consuming. As long as your vocals cut it you can drink as much as you like, but don't for a minute think you're hiding it. I'll see you back in the studio." Curtis stood up and walked out of the office.

Ray knew what he was doing was wrong on every level. Wrong because his wife was at home expecting their baby. Wrong because he was committing the cardinal sin of becoming involved with another member of his team. And finally wrong because he was thinking more about the next time he could be with Josie and not about his songs.

But she was like a drug, and he couldn't get enough.

CHAPTER THIRTY-FIVE

Pete and the band had been working hard since leaving LA, flying down to link up with Don and the bus, then travelling to Atlanta, Memphis, Randy's home town of Nashville, Austin and finally Dallas before heading to New Orleans.

Janine had decided, even though she was pregnant, she would make the trip down to see Pete play at the Super Bowl. She'd hired a private jet to take her to watch the gig and fly back immediately afterwards. She'd called Ray at the studio to ask if he would come with her, but he'd said it didn't look like he would be able to make it. He would be recording vocals all that weekend and couldn't get away. Unperturbed she'd invited Carly, who had leaped at the invitation. How could she resist. Her usual class of flying was in coach, so a trip in a luxury Learjet was a rare treat.

On the morning of the big game Carly had driven over to meet Janine, and they had travelled together to Van Nuys airport to board their jet. Ironically at exactly the same time as Janine and Carly were taking off, just a mile way, Ray and Josie were in a hotel room having sex, oblivious to the sounds of overhead aircraft.

Making a hard turn the Learjet headed southeast down to New Orleans International Airport with a scheduled flight time of four hours. Carly settled back into the comfortable leather armchair, as the smartly dressed steward opened the bottle of Bollinger and filled two cut glass flutes with one of Janine's favourite champagnes.

Janine liked Carly, and the idea of the articles about Ray and Pete seemed to be working, with the LA Times already featuring a double page spread about Pete playing at the Super Bowl. A story which Carly would be following up once she was there. She had also been up to Valerian Studios with a photographer on a couple of occasions, working on the story about Ray's debut album. When Janine had quizzed her about the trips she'd said it was just like any other studio she'd ever been in, and Ray and the musicians were working hard on the new material which was sounding great. Out of respect, she hadn't mentioned the smell of alcohol on his breath or the ever-present glass of brandy.

Carly had given her some helpful tips about Super Bowl etiquette before they left. Such as making sure she didn't wear something that was either blue or turquoise which would favour one or other of the teams; the Cowboys played in white and blue and the Dolphins in aqua blue. Also if she spoke to the owners, she should ensure she spent an equal amount of time with each to avoid being accused of favouritism. Janine thought it was crazy, but then again the FA Cup Final back home in the UK was just the same. Anyway she'd decided to wear a loose fitting canary yellow cotton dress with matching sandals and a yellow leather tote bag, which hopefully wouldn't offend either side.

The Learjet had landed exactly on time in New Orleans and Janine and Carly were sitting in the back of the limousine taking them on the thirty-minute drive to the Tulane Stadium. They could feel the excitement building as they passed the hordes of supporters for both teams, and although she wasn't a fan, Janine found herself getting caught up in the atmosphere. Their car arrived at the stadium and pulled up to the VIP entrance where Don was waiting. He escorted them through the labyrinthine corridors to the dressing rooms set aside for the half time entertainment, where Pete and the guys were already waiting. Janine noticed straight away that Pete wasn't his usual relaxed self before a gig and took him to one side.

"Is everything OK? You look a bit tense."

"Tense! Do you know how many people are watching this? And it's going out live. Jesus Janine, I'm shitting myself!" She'd never seen him like this before.

Carly came over and his demeanour changed as she gave him a kiss and a hug. "You're going to blow them away Pete, I know it."

"Yeah well, I hope so. Hey Janine, where's Ray? I thought he'd be here." He knew from the look on her face it was the wrong thing to say.

She turned away and quickly composed herself. "He's tied up in the studio doing vocals but sends his best and said he'd try and watch it."

"Vocals? Yeah well I know what that's like. But I'm sure it's going great. Have you heard anything yet?" he asked trying to change the subject.

"I have. Just a few bits of songs," Carly said taking the hint from Pete. "I was up there last week and they sounded fantastic. We got some cool photos too for the article."

Suddenly a huge roar went up in the stadium above them, and Don explained it was the teams taking to the pitch which meant that the game would be starting soon. There would be two quarters before the half time interval, each lasting fifteen minutes plus stoppages and timeouts, but he thought they should start getting ready after the first quarter. As soon as the second quarter finished the stage would be erected and then they would be on. Janine and Carly wished them luck before making their way up to the VIP area to watch the game. Janine said that Carly would have to explain what the hell was going on as she didn't have a clue, which made them both laugh as they sat down.

Sitting two rows behind them, a man wearing a chauffeur's outfit and sunglasses was watching as they took their seats.

From the kick-off the game was a one-sided affair with the Cowboys leading 10-3 at half time, and Janine still as confused as she was before it started. She couldn't understand why they had to keep stopping all the time, unlike rugby which she'd seen a few times back home, where they played non-stop. It was just another part of American culture she was discovering; like why in baseball did they call it the World Series when the only teams who took part were from America?

Her attention was drawn back to the present as Pete and the band were led out on to the pitch. Pete stopped to take in the size of the stadium and the thousands of people all waiting for them to start. There was no time to be nervous anymore. They got a huge reception as they walked on stage, and from the first chord the crowd were with them singing along to every song. There was also a surprising number of girls wearing *In Flames* t-shirts as opposed to Cowboys or Dolphins merchandise.

Janine and Carly watched from their seats and were given a deafening round of applause when Pete introduced them and pointed them out to the crowd. Yet again Pete had come good when he needed to, and they were all in great spirits when Janine and Carly went back down to the dressing room afterwards to congratulate them. Pete had asked Carly to stay on for a couple of days as the band were staying over-night in New Orleans before carrying on to Houston which would take a couple of days. He thought it would be a great opportunity to experience what it was like on the road for her article.

Carly was worried about Janine going back on her own, but she'd said she didn't mind as she was going to get the limo to take her straight back to the airport, and hopefully she'd be in bed before midnight back in LA.

The man in the dark glasses had watched them leave their seats, and when they didn't return for the beginning of the third quarter he quickly left. After briefly climbing in the back of a large black limousine he'd got into the driving seat and parked by the VIP entrance with the engine running. Moments later Don appeared with Janine and he pulled up to them. Don leaned in the driver's window. "New Orleans airport for the lady."

The driver nodded and Janine sat down in the back.

"I've taken the liberty of already opening a bottle of champagne madam," he said as they pulled away.

'Nice touch' Janine thought and poured herself a glass. For a moment she thought she recognised his voice, but sat back and swallowed the chilled contents, and as she did so a familiar aftershave wafted into the back of the car. A fragrance so unique she couldn't forget it. Her eyelids were suddenly starting to feel heavy as she thought back to where she'd smelled it before. Then it came to her, the bar in Santa Monica with Mandy. The well-dressed Middle Eastern guy, what was his name? Her eyes were closing and her head nodded forward as she remembered before sliding sideways, unconscious.

Surinam Chandra removed his sunglasses and watched in the rearview mirror as the drug he'd put in the bottle of champagne took effect. Satisfied, he accelerated towards the private jet waiting at the airport. Twenty minutes later he pulled onto the tarmac and the pilot came down the steps to help him with his passenger who was still slumped in the back seat. He'd calculated she should sleep comfortably during the two-hour flight and still be out by the time they reached her host's villa.

'Yes,' he thought. 'Mr. Mulligan will be pleased to see you Mrs. Law.'

The first anyone became aware something was wrong was when the limousine company that had been booked to pick Janine up and take her back to the airport called the VIP office, checking if she was ready.

It was getting late and the Learjet pilot had booked a flight plan which was about to overrun. The call had been forwarded to Don at the hotel where they were staying for the night. He'd alerted Pete and they were understandably worried. Don had called Ray in Hermosa Beach but there was no reply, and when he'd called the studio the person who answered said they weren't recording that weekend because it was closed for Super Bowl but Don knew that wasn't what Ray had told Janine.

His next call was to Curtis Jackson to find out if he knew where Ray was. He initially said he had no idea, but when Don explained the situation he'd suggested they call a hotel in Van Nuys. Finally after Don had threatened the hotel manager, he was put through to Ray's room. The phone rang and a female voice answered.

Don said. "My name is Don Rosario and I need to speak to Ray Law urgently. I know he's there so get him to the phone now!"

There was a pause with a few mumbled voices in the background before Ray came on the line. "Don, what's up?"

"What's up? You're what's up Ray, but right now I don't give a shit what you're doing. Janine, your wife, is missing, I put her in a limo to take her to the airport and she never got there."

Ray was silent for a moment. "So what do you want me to do Don?"

"What I want you to do Ray is put your dick away and start thinking about your pregnant wife. How does that sound?"

Don slammed the phone down and looked at Pete. "He should be thankful he's not standing here right now."

He stomped off pondering his next move.

When he was in the LAPD he'd been sent down to the New Orleans Police Department on a secondment for six months, and he'd met a few good guys while he was there. Maybe now might be the time to rekindle a few friendships. Two phone calls later, and one of his old friends said he had a brother who worked at the airport and that he would give him a call. In a matter of minutes he called back to say his brother had found out an unscheduled private jet had landed earlier that day from Miami, and took off thirty minutes after the time Don had put Janine in the limo on the return trip. It didn't take him more than a moment to put two and two together. Miami, Rota Bocan, Benny Mulligan.

CHAPTER THIRTY-SIX

Ray had put the phone down in the hotel room and looked across at Josie. She was lying on their king-sized bed with her long shapely legs crossed at the ankles, naked apart from the black velvet choker Ray had bought for her. She looked at him confused. She wanted him again; he was an incredible lover and so big she ached after they made love, but she reached out and pulled him down to her. She started to kiss him and stroke him but he pulled away.

"I'm sorry babe but I can't do this right now," he said. "I have to go. Something bad has come up and I need to sort it out."

"It's your wife isn't it? I told you. She clicks her fingers and you go running back." Josie started to cry.

"It's not like that, she's in trouble."

Josie looked up at him with tears in her eyes. "Just one more time baby, before you go," she said lying back and opening her legs.

Ray looked at his watch for a moment, then climbed back on the bed.

It was late and Shanice was asleep in her room at Benny Mulligan's villa in Miami, when she was disturbed by the noise of someone arriving. She listened as Benny opened the door and started talking to the visitor. She heard them go outside still talking, and crept out of her room to the top of the stairs watching as they struggled carrying the limp body of a woman into the house. Shanice thought she looked like she was drugged as they passed below her.

They took her into Benny's private office and returned a couple of minutes later as he locked the door behind him. Shanice ducked back into the shadows and silently returned to her room before she was seen, then lay awake listening as Benny and his guest sat up until the early hours talking and drinking. Finally she heard the visitor leave.

Benny made his way upstairs and opened her door. She pretended she was asleep but he staggered over to her bed obviously drunk, and demanded she wake up and relieve him. She tried to push him away, but he held her hair as he pulled his trousers open forcing himself on her. Fearing he might get violent she did as he asked, and minutes later he left her room wobbling back to his bedroom past her sleeping son.

She lay in bed wondering what was going on, but decided to wait until the morning when she could investigate more whilst she was cleaning.

From New Orleans, Don had driven the band down to the next gig in Houston. They would then leave immediately after the show and travel to Miami where the tour was due to finish.

Carly had arranged to stay on with Pete. With the disappearance of Janine she was worried about her. But she was a journalist, and never one to miss a great story, she would be on hand to report anything that happened.

Don had eventually got hold of Ray again before they'd left Houston, and they'd agreed to meet up the next day in Fort Lauderdale which was thirty miles north of Miami. Their hastily put together plan was to arrive at the club as if everything was normal. Then later that night while Pete and the band were performing, Ray and Don would go down to Benny Mulligan's villa which was situated on Biscayne Bay, where Don was sure Janine was being held.

Janine woke with a thumping headache. She slowly opened her eyes to find herself still fully dressed, lying on a single bed. She was in a small room with no windows and a bare light bulb hanging in the middle of the ceiling. The only other thing in the room was a plastic bucket in the corner. She stood up unsteadily and made her way over to the door and tried the handle, but it was locked. She banged on the door and shouted, but there was no reply, so she sat back down on the bed still feeling slightly lightheaded. It was hot and stuffy in the confined space and she felt thirsty, which was when she noticed a bottle of water inside the bucket. She gulped a few mouthfuls, and after a few more gradually started to feel better.

She got up and went over to the door and started banging again, when suddenly she heard a voice from above her head.

"Welcome Mrs. Law, or may I call you Janine? It is a waste of your energy banging on the door. No one can hear you."

She stopped banging and looked around, spotting a tiny speaker in the ceiling over in the corner. "Who are you, and why have I been kidnapped?" she shouted.

"My name, Janine, I would have thought you might have guessed, is Benny Mulligan. And you are wrong my dear. You have not been kidnapped. I require no ransom." He paused. "You are here because of vanity. My vanity, and because I want to meet your husband face to face before I kill him. I might even kill you too depending on how I feel."

"Why are you doing this?" she shouted back.

"Why? You don't know?" he replied. "I thought I'd made it clear about interfering with things you don't understand when I had your last husband taken care of, but now your new beau has been responsible for losing me ten million dollars, and nobody does that to Benny Mulligan, and lives!"

"You're going to have to get him here first," she said. "He's not that stupid."

"Ah yes, the latest soul star recording his new album. Well now he's finished screwing his backing singer, I can assure you he's on his way as we speak, and will be shortly joining up with his old pal Mr. Rosario. Only this time they won't be so lucky, because they're dealing with me and not that pathetic fool José."

Janine hadn't fully understood what he'd said. "What did you say about his backing singer?"

"Oh did I say that? Forgive me for being so indiscreet, I'm sure he'll explain everything when you see him. But it won't matter because he's going to die anyway." The voice laughed. "You will notice a slot in the door. That's where your food will be delivered shortly. I apologise it's not up to your usual Beverly Hills Hotel standard." There was a loud click and the room fell silent.

Janine sat down on the bed again and fought back tears of frustration, as she went over in her head what Benny Mulligan had just said.

Shanice had started her cleaning early, and once she'd finished the lounge where Benny and his visitor had been drinking the previous night, she'd tried to open the door to Benny's office but found it locked. Carefully putting her ear to the door she could make out Benny's voice. He was talking to a woman who was shouting at him. The conversation went on for about a minute then stopped, and she heard a chair scrape on the floor. Assuming he had just stood up and was about to come out, Shanice backed away from the door switching on the vacuum cleaner, and was in the hallway by the time he opened the door. He locked it again behind him and told her he had to go out.

"I won't be long," he said as he went outside.

Shanice nodded like she always did, because she couldn't speak. She'd lost the ability to talk when she was young, due to the horrific experience of watching her parents murdered by rebel soldiers in the village where she lived. She'd managed to escape, but was so traumatised she'd never spoken since, and used a mixture of hand signals and grunts to communicate. Benny had employed her as a favour to an old friend who had smuggled her into the country.

She'd been working for him for six years. He gave her and her four-year-old son free board, although nobody knew who the son's father was, due to Benny and his friends using her for sex whenever they chose.

She watched from the window as he drove away through the electric gates which closed behind him. Switching off the vacuum she hurried back to Benny's office and using her master key she tried to open the door. It didn't work. He must have changed the lock recently because it had always worked before. But Shanice was streetwise and she'd picked up a few tricks in her youth. With the aid of a couple of hair grips she opened the door and entered the office. There was another door in the corner which was also locked but again she managed to open it using the same method. Sitting on a bed in the small room was the woman she'd seen carried in, still wearing the yellow dress from the night before.

Janine looked up shocked to see Shanice.

"Oh my god. Who are you? No never mind, can you get me out of here?" she pleaded.

Shanice wasn't sure what to do. She waved her hands at Janine shaking her head and then pointed at her mouth.

Janine was watching her and realised what she was telling her. "Are you saying you can't speak?"

Shanice nodded.

"OK, but you can hear me?"

Shanice nodded again.

"Where's Benny?"

Shanice made like she was driving with a steering wheel.

Janine understood. "He's gone out in his car."

Shanice nodded again.

Janine thought. "Do you know for how long?"

Shanice shook her head. Then she pointed at her wrist and made a sign with her finger and thumb with the gap between them getting smaller.

Janine watching knew what she meant. "Not for long?"

Shanice nodded.

"OK can you do something for me before he gets back? I need my handbag, it's yellow the same colour as my dress."

Shanice nodded again and went out of the room returning moments later with the handbag.

Janine was about to say something else when Shanice held her hand up. She'd heard Benny's car on the drive. She pointed to her mouth and then her wrist meaning they would speak later and left the room pulling the door closed behind her. She did the same coming out of Benny's office as she heard his key in the lock opening the front door, and just in time she was picking the vacuum up as he walked in.

Janine sat down on the bed and checked everything was still in her handbag, and was happy to see nothing had been taken. Her purse, cigarettes and steel tail comb were all still there. She felt like she could smoke a cigarette but decided against it. She was wondering what to do next when the slot on the door was opened and a pizza box was pushed through. It closed with a bang and then a voice above her said, "Bon Appetit!" and laughed.

Janine looked up at the ceiling where the speaker was. "Fuck you, ya Gobshite!"

It was the first time she'd had a pepperoni pizza for breakfast, but she was hungry and ate it with her fingers in the absence of a knife and fork. She was just thinking she was thirsty when the slot opened again and a bottle of orange juice dropped through. She hadn't really given it too much thought since her ill-timed announcement, but she knew she should be more aware of her pregnancy and take care of herself, which in her current situation was difficult. She wondered when she might have another opportunity to communicate with the girl who came in earlier. Then thinking back to what Benny Mulligan had said about Ray being on his way down. Did he know where she was, and would he be able to free her?

Benny Mulligan knew it was only a matter of time before Ray Law and Don Rosario would figure out where Janine was, and he had been working on the final part of his plan. He'd called on two members of Rota Bocan who had arrived in Miami that morning. Larry Carmichael and Alphonso Swann were the two suspects interviewed by Ray Law over their possible involvement in the bombing of Rudi's nightclub in Birmingham, and since their return had both been working for him up in Chicago. Benny knew they would be able to recognise Ray again, and planned for them to be waiting to discreetly follow him when he arrived at the airport. He was sure he would be meeting up with Don Rosario as Pete Peterson was due to play a gig in Miami that night, and he'd sent Surinam Chandra to watch the club just in case the other two missed him.

He sat back in the easy chair out on his balcony and called Shanice. He thought she'd seemed strange when he came back earlier or perhaps it was his imagination. There was no way she knew what was going on, he'd locked his office before he left, and kept it locked while he was inside talking to the woman. Maybe he'd upset her last night. Well screw her, that's what she was there for, and without him she'd be on the street back where she came from. Anyway he needed a drink to settle his nerves and maybe a little relief might help.

Shanice had been in the kitchen when he called. Since he returned he'd shown no signs of going out again, and she wondered if there would be another opportunity to get back in his office. She had no idea who the woman was, but she was expensively dressed so she must be someone important. Also she'd never seen her boss so agitated and on edge. She prepared him a large Gin and Tonic which he preferred during the day, and carried it out to him on a silver tray. She could tell straight away by the lecherous look on his face what he expected from her, and was just preparing herself for his demands when the phone rang. Relieved, she left him as he answered it, immediately shouting at whoever it was who had called him.

"What do you mean he's not arrived! You mean you've missed him you fucking pair of idiots. Get your big fat arses back here now."

In the city, Surinam Chandra had been hanging around the gig Pete was playing that night since early morning. He was beginning to get bored and hungry. Just as he was about to leave his surveillance position Pete's coach rolled into view, and he watched as the band went into the club followed by Don and finally Ray. 'Bingo!' he thought to himself and went to find the nearest phone box to call Benny with the news.

The phone rang again at Benny Mulligan's villa as he was pacing up and down wondering what had happened.

He answered it. "He's where? Well how the fuck did he get there?"

Surinam was holding the receiver away from his ear as Benny yelled down the phone. He waited for him to take a breath.

"If they thought you'd be waiting for him at the airport he could have flown to Fort Lauderdale and met them there instead. That would explain why Larry and Alphonso didn't see him arrive."

Benny was loathe to admit he was wrong. "Well you stay there and don't let the pair of them out of your sight. I want to know the minute they make a move."

He slammed the phone down and turned to the two men from Chicago who'd just arrived. "I need you patrolling the grounds. If those two are in town they're gonna come for her, and we gotta be ready."

He walked over to his office and unlocked the door. Shanice was back in the kitchen listening to what had been going on and pushed the door open slightly so she could see as he went into the room. This time he left the door open and she could hear what was said. Benny was talking to the woman.

"Well, well, well, Mrs. Law. As I suspected your gallant husband has rushed to your rescue. It shouldn't be long now before he walks into my trap."

She had to smile at the woman's feisty response.

"Fuck you, Benny Mulligan. If he's coming, you better be worried, you bastard!"

"We'll see about that, bitch!" Benny yelled back at her. He seemed rattled as he walked out and slammed the door behind him, but Shanice noticed this time he didn't lock it.

CHAPTER THIRTY-SEVEN

Back at the club Pete and the band had finished their sound check, and were in the dressing room when Don and Ray came in.

"Right guys, so here's the plan," Don said as they all sat and listened.

"We need to make this look as normal as possible, in case Benny's got anyone here watching us. The minute you go on stage, Ray and I are gonna slip out the back door and head down to his villa. I've managed to find a couple of guys from the club who from a distance look a bit like us and they're going to stand side-stage making sure they're seen. Hopefully it'll give us time to get over to Biscayne Bay. It's only a short distance so we should be there before we're missed. I called an old pal of mine who's a captain in Miami-Dade PD and he's going to get a couple of his men to cause a diversion for us so we can get into the property. After that we're on our own.

"How are you planning on getting out after?" Pete asked.

"Ah well that's where my pal has come in extra useful. He's got one of these high-powered cigarette boats which was recently confiscated from one of the local villains. Because he hates Benny Mulligan just as much as we do, he's going to take us down to Coconut Grove in it so we can enter the property from the water. Then he'll wait to get us out."

Pete had been nervous before they started, but as soon as the band played the intro to the opening number he relaxed and stood at the front of the stage surveying the audience. He thought he recognised the guy standing over to one side, then realised it was the man from the *Gathering*, Surinam Chandra. So, Don was right. Benny Mulligan was having him watched. He turned to look towards side stage and was amazed at the likeness of the two guys to Don and Ray. They were just far enough back in the shadows to make it difficult to know for sure if it was them or not, but if they fooled him they certainly would fool someone in the audience.

Don and Ray had met the Miami-Dade captain out the back of the club as soon as Pete had started. He took them to his boat which was moored in the Downtown Police Marina. Don had produced his Magnum as they were on the way, and given Ray a Smith & Wesson 59 19mm but warned him to be careful.

"You English guys don't get to use these things, so just watch how you go and only shoot if I do. You got that?"

Ray gave him a smile. "You won't let me forget that will you! Don't worry about me, I can handle one of these, no problem."

Once on board it was a short trip to Benny Mulligan's villa which was on the waterfront in the exclusive Coconut Grove estate on Biscayne Bay. The plan was for two local officers to drive up to the front of the villa and claim they had received a call about a disturbance at the property. While they were there creating the diversion, Don and Ray would enter through the boathouse and make their way up to the rear.

It was a calm night and the powerful cigarette boat moved easily through the water, before the captain throttled back and slowly pulled into the private waters of Coconut Grove, quietly mooring alongside the deserted boathouse. There was a full moon and Don and Ray could clearly see their way from the boat up to the back of the villa, but waited for the signal from the two patrolmen. They had radioed the captain earlier to say they had seen two armed men patrolling the front of the property when they had driven past. Now they were pulling up to the gates with siren blaring and lights flashing which was the signal. Hoping the two guards would be in the back of the squad car on their way to Police Headquarters, Don and Ray jumped off the boat onto the narrow dock and carefully climbed up the slippery wooden steps at the side of the boathouse which led to the garden. There were plenty of large shrubs for cover, and they made their way through the bushes up the manicured lawn towards the back door, which they could see opened into the kitchen.

They reached it without any problems.

Don whispered to Ray. "So far so good, that was almost too easy."

He quietly opened the door which was unlocked, and as they made their way inside. Shanice the maid surprised them by walking in. She just about managed to hold onto the tray she was carrying with the shock of seeing two armed men standing in the kitchen, and stared at them with wide eyes. Don put his finger to his lips telling her to keep quiet, and she nodded. Ray had gone over to the swing door which led through to the hallway. He was watching through the crack as Benny came out of his office holding a silver pistol to Janine's head, pushing her in front of him. Ray could see she was looking dishevelled and tired, but was doing her best to make a nuisance of herself by walking slowly. He noticed she was holding her yellow leather tote bag over her shoulder as they made their way into the lounge.

Benny called out to Shanice to bring some drinks.

"Oh and invite our guests to come and join us. I hate drinking on my own."

Don and Ray froze and looked at each other, shocked.

Benny spoke again this time louder and threatening.

"Gentlemen. Please, don't abuse my hospitality. Come and join us, before I get more annoyed than I already am!"

This time they did as he asked and slowly walked into the lounge.

"I have to congratulate you getting my two guards arrested like that. Very clever."

He was standing by a roaring log fire, holding Janine in front of him still with his pistol to her head. "I do so hate guns, don't you? Be good chaps and put yours on the coffee table where I can see them."

Don and Ray had no choice but to do as he said.

"Sit down, relax!" He waved his pistol at the large white leather sofa which was covered in colourful throws. They cautiously sat down. "That's better. Oh, and in case you're wondering, I have infra-red cameras in the garden and watched you all the way up from the boathouse. Nice boat by the way."

He pointed to the guns on the low wooden table.

"Oh my goodness that is a big one you have there Mr. Rosario!"

Don looked surprised as he said his name.

"What, you don't think I know who you are? Of course I know who you are. You're the one who shot Tino in Boston. He was a good man! Well, some say he was a good man. I just know he was one of my men and you killed him."

He still had a firm grip on Janine as he stood in front of them and suddenly turned the gun and fired at Don who slumped down on the sofa.

Janine screamed and Ray jumped up but Benny pointed the gun at him. "Sit down Mr. Law. He'll live! It's only a shoulder wound. Painful though I'm sure. You know something Ray? You don't mind me calling you Ray do you? Your wife wanted to know why I'd brought her here. It's not for money, although heaven knows I could do with some." He laughed. "No Ray it's because of you! You have lost me ten million dollars. TEN MILLION DOLLARS! I've been waiting for this moment when I could finally meet you face to face. The weird thing is, now I have, I'm finding it difficult to hate you. In fact, I admire you. There aren't many people alive who can say they got one over on Benny Mulligan. Sadly you're not going to be one either." He laughed again manically.

Shanice came back in the room with a tray containing a large bottle of Remy Martin and four glasses.

"Ah thank you Shanice," he said as she put it down on the table alongside the guns. Don moaned as he made an attempt to move, still holding his shoulder which was bleeding quite badly.

"Maybe Mr. Rosario there might like a drink to take his mind off the pain," Benny suggested to Shanice who obediently poured a glass and gave it to Don.

"Shame she can't speak," Benny said looking at Shanice. "But there again what she's seen and heard going on here it's probably a good job. Don't be rude Shanice, give my other guests a drink."

She filled the other glasses with brandy and stood to one side of the sofa putting the bottle back on the coffee table.

What Benny had failed to notice while he'd been talking, was Janine slip her hand into her tote bag. Ray saw her do it but she gave him a look that said ignore her.

Benny carried on. "So here we all are then. Nice and cosy. You must be wondering what's going to happen next. So let me explain. When I saw you two coming into the kitchen I set a timer back in my office. It will trigger a set of explosions around the house, by which time I will have dealt with you Ray, and your delightful wife along with your friend Mr. Rosario there. I shall then make my escape along with Shanice, leaving your charred bodies to eventually be found in the remains."

He looked at his watch which was on the same wrist as the hand he was holding the gun with. "Which leaves, let me see, two minutes to say goodbye."

Seizing the opportunity, Janine rammed Benny with her backside as hard as she could knocking him slightly off balance, while at the same time pulling her hand out of her bag holding her steel tail comb by the teeth. Swivelling around she plunged the long-pointed handle into his chest with a loud roar.

Taken completely by surprise, Benny fired the gun at Ray who had leaped up from the sofa, missing him and hitting the brandy bottle which exploded in a ball of spirit flame. Then with an expression of disbelief he looked down at the end of the comb sticking out of his body which had pierced his heart. He slowly collapsed on the floor, blood pulsing out of his mouth.

Janine stepped away from him and told Ray to take their guns and help Don, while turning back to look at Shanice who was standing staring at Benny in shock. "We have to go! Now!" she said pushing her forcefully towards the kitchen.

Shanice finally looked up from the body on the floor, and ran out of the lounge straight up the stairs to her room. Janine followed her shouting there was no time, but moments later she came running back holding the hand of a small boy who looked petrified. They made their way down the stairs as an explosion rocked the hallway.

"Get him down to the boat as fast as you can," Janine shouted as she hustled them through the kitchen and out of the back door, just as another detonation shook the villa. She could see Ray out in front of them desperately helping Don through the bushes as he struggled towards the boathouse.

It had taken Surinam Chandra until Pete's sixth song to figure out the two men at the side of the stage were not Don and Ray, and almost another song to push his way back through the crowd to the exit. He'd decided he didn't have time to phone Benny to warn him. Instead he ran to his car which was parked three blocks away. By the time he reached the villa he sensed there was something wrong. The gates were wide open and there were no guards in the front to stop him entering the property. He was sure Benny had told him the two men from Chicago would be there to do that, so he slowly drove up to the front of the house. He cautiously climbed out of his car and was approaching the entrance when he was knocked off his feet by an explosion which blew the shattered remains of the door across the driveway. This was followed by another similar eruption causing part of the front of the villa to collapse. Surinam picked himself up and ran around the back. The villa was rocked again as another charge went off.

He could just make out Ray helping Don towards the bottom of the garden, and behind them two women and a child struggling to keep up. He pulled out the gun that Benny had given him in case of trouble, and crouching down took aim and fired. The bullet hit the back of the boathouse to the left of Ray who stopped, turning to see who was firing at them.

Don was too weak by now to use his gun, but he handed it to Ray before slowly making his way down the steps to the jetty. Ray steadied himself holding the mighty Magnum with both hands and aimed at the figure who was now striding across the lawn towards them. The man fired again just as Shanice and her son were passing Ray with Janine right behind them. She turned to look back as the second shot slammed into the wooden boathouse wall. Ray remained standing, concentrating and pulled the trigger. The boom of the Magnum temporarily deafened him, so he didn't hear the scream from Janine as she lost her footing and tripped on the top step tumbling down all the way to the jetty, sliding off the edge and disappearing under the surface of the dark water. Oblivious to the drama down below, Ray saw his bullet blow a hole the size of a fist in the chest of Surinam Chandra lifting him off his feet, as he fell back dead on the grass.

The villa was now well ablaze with flames shooting up into the sky, and Ray turned to make his way down to the waiting boat. Both the captain and Don were frantically signalling for him to get down quickly, pointing in the water at the stern of the boat. He finally understood they were trying to tell him Janine had fallen in.

"I can't swim!" he screamed. "What can we do? Help me!"

Suddenly with an ear-piercing scream Shanice plunged into the water. Taking a huge breath she dived down out of sight. It seemed to take ages and Ray was starting to panic, when suddenly she re-emerged with a loud gasp holding Janine. Keeping her head above the water she brought her to the jetty. Ray and the captain managed to pull her out as Shanice climbed onto the wooden platform dripping wet. There didn't seem to be any sign of breathing, and Ray was becoming frantic when Shanice shouted, "Move out of the way." She pushed him and the captain aside, and knelt down beside Janine alternately pressing on her chest and then blowing into her mouth. After about a minute Janine suddenly coughed and brought up a large amount of water.

Shanice stood up and smiled at Ray and the captain. They were all starting to congratulate themselves when Janine let out a loud cry as she sat up and saw a pool of blood spreading on the jetty from between her legs. She collapsed backwards and her head hit the wooden planks with a loud bang. They carefully picked up Janine's limp body, gently putting her on board the boat, and the captain pushed the throttle powering them back to Miami while radioing ahead for emergency assistance.

It seemed only a matter of minutes before they were at the marina where Janine was hurriedly transferred into a waiting ambulance, along with Don who managed to climb unaided into the back.

The news of the incident in Coconut Grove reached Pete and Carly as he was about to play his encore. Details were sketchy at first, but Ray rang through to the club to tell them Janine had been rushed straight into the operating theatre and he was waiting to speak to a doctor. Don appeared wearing a sling as he was on the phone, bloodied but none the worse for wear. The bullet Benny had fired at him had gone straight through and luckily missed any bones.

A doctor dressed in green scrubs eventually emerged and told Ray that Janine was in a critical condition. They were extremely concerned about the amount of blood she had lost. It appeared she had been unconscious when she went into the water, but they were running tests and he would know more when he received the results. Don had pressed him for his opinion but he would only say that it was touch and go, and they were doing everything they could. "All we can do now is hope and pray," he suggested as he walked away.

Ray and Don were standing in shock as Pete and Carly ran in and joined them. They had left the club the moment Pete had finished his show, and he was still in his stage clothes. They all standing together trying desperately to take in what the doctor had just said when the regular beep coming from Janine's monitor changed to a continuous one, and the doctor and two nurses ran past them back into the room.

In the confusion Pete noticed a television set on the wall which was tuned to the local news channel with the sound muted. It was showing dramatic images of the fire at Coconut Grove. He couldn't help but think to himself how Janine would have smiled at the headline newsflash across the bottom of the screen.

FEARED ROTA BOCAN BOSS FOUND DEAD AS LUXURY VILLA IN FLAMES.

The third part of The Pete Peterson Tapes is ONE LAST ENCORE

ACKNOWLEDGMENTS

Once again I'd like to thank some special people who have helped me so much.

Andrew Sparke and his team at APS Books for their faith in my books.

Wendy Eckhardt for her advice on Police procedure and aspects of the law.

The wonderful team of readers whose feedback is invaluable: My daughter Beth and my friends Steve and Tracey.

And finally my best friend Cissy Stone, for her ceaseless encouragement and support.

Des Tong

For more information check out https://andrewsparke.com/des-tong/
I'm on Facebook www.Facebook.com/destong and Twitter @TongAuthor
And if you have time, go to my YouTube channel – www.youtube.com/destongtv where you will find promo music videos I have created, and everything else I'm involved in.

FICTION FROM APS BOOKS

(www.andrewsparke.com)

Davey J Ashfield: Footsteps On The Teign
Davey J Ashfield Contracting With The Devil
Davey J Ashfield: A Turkey And One More Easter Egg
Des Tong: Whatever It Takes Babe
Des Tong In Flames
Fenella Bass: Hornbeams
Fenella Bass:: Shadows
Fenella Bass: Darkness
HR Beasley: Nothing Left To Hide
Lee Benson: So You Want To Own An Art Gallery
Lee Benson: Where's Your Art gallery Now?
Lee Benson: Now You're The Artist…Deal With It
Lee Benson: No Naked Walls
TF Byrne Damage Limitation
Nargis Darby: A Different Shade Of Love
J.W.Darcy Looking For Luca
J.W.Darcy: Ladybird Ladybird
J.W.Darcy: Legacy Of Lies
J.W.Darcy: Love Lust & Needful Things
Paul Dickinson: Franzi The Hero
Jane Evans: The Third Bridge
Simon Falshaw: The Stone
Peter Georgiadis: Edilstein
Peter Georgiadis: Stoker Jolly
Peter Georgiadis: A Murderous Journey
Peter Georgiadis: Not Cast In Stone
Peter Georgiadis: The Mute Swan's Song
Milton Godfrey: The Danger Lies In Fear
Chris Grayling: A Week Is…A Long Time
Jean Harvey: Pandemic
Michel Henri: Mister Penny Whistle
Michel Henri: The Death Of The Duchess Of Grasmere
Michel Henri: Abducted By Faerie
Laurie Hornsby: Postcards From The Seaside
Hugh Lupus An Extra Knot (Parts I-VI)

Hugh Lupus: Mr. Donaldson's Company
Hugh Lupus: The Further Exploits Of Donaldson's Company
Lorna MacDonald-Bradley: Dealga
Alison Manning: World Without Endless Sheep
Colin Mardell: Keep Her Safe
Colin Mardell: Bring Them Home
Ian Meacheam: An Inspector Called
Ian Meacheam: Time And The Consequences
Ian Meacheam: Broad Lines Narrow Margins
Ian Meacheam & Mark Peckett: Seven Stages
Alex O'Connor: Time For The Polka Dot
Mark Peckett: Joffie's Mark
Peter Raposo: dUst
Peter Raposo: the illusion of movement
Peter Raposo: cast away your dreams of darkness
Peter Raposo: Second Life
Peter Raposo: Pussy Foot
Peter Raposo: This Is Not The End
Peter Raposo: Talk About Proust
Peter Raposo: All Women Are Mortal
Peter Raposo: The Sinking City
Tony Rowland: Traitor Lodger German Spy
Tony Saunders: Publish and Be Dead
Andrew Sparke: Abuse Cocaine & Soft Furnishings
Andrew Sparke: Copper Trance & Motorways
Phil Thompson: Momentary Lapses In Concentration
Paul C. Walsh: A Place Between The Mountains
Paul C. Walsh: Hallowed Turf
Rebecca Warren: The Art Of Loss
Martin White: Life Unfinished
AJ Woolfenden: Mystique: A Bitten Past
Various: Brumology
Various: Unshriven

Printed in Great Britain
by Amazon